BEDROOM EYES

BEDROOM EYES

stories of lesbians in the boudoir

edited by lesléa newman

alyson books
los angeles | new york

MANUFACTURED IN THE UNITED STATES OF AMERICA.

THIS TRADE PAPERBACK ORIGINAL IS PUBLISHED BY ALYSON PUBLICATIONS,
P.O. BOX 4371, LOS ANGELES, CALIFORNIA 90078-4371.
DISTRIBUTION IN THE UNITED KINGDOM BY TURNAROUND PUBLISHER SERVICES LTD.,
UNIT 3, OLYMPIA TRADING ESTATE, COBURG ROAD, WOOD GREEN,
LONDON N22 6TZ ENGLAND.

FIRST EDITION: NOVEMBER 2002

02 03 04 05 06 **a** 10 9 8 7 6 5 4 3 2 1

ISBN 1-55583-618-6

LIBRARY OF CONGRESS CATALOGING-IN-PUBLICATION DATA

BEDROOM EYES : STORIES OF LESBIANS IN THE BOUDOIR / EDITED BY LESLÉA NEWMAN.—1ST ED.
ISBN 1-55583-618-6
1. LESBIANS—FICTION. 2. EROTIC STORIES, AMERICAN. 3. LESBIANS' WRITINGS,
AMERICAN. I. NEWMAN, LESLÉA.
PS648.L47 B43 2002
813'.54—DC21   2002026055

CREDITS

• "PRIVATE LESSONS" ORIGINALLY PUBLISHED IN *SHE LOVES ME, SHE LOVES ME NOT.* © 2002 BY LESLÉA NEWMAN (ALYSON PUBLICATIONS).
• COVER PHOTOGRAPHY BY STONE.
• COVER DESIGN BY MATT SAMS.

for Angela

Contents

Introduction

You can look at the world in one of two ways: through your eyes or through your bedroom eyes. Through your eyes, the two old women lying on their backs on a beach blanket soaking up the sun in Adelina Anthony's "Missed Opportunities" are lifelong friends. Through your bedroom eyes, the same two women are so in love with each other, the sun is no match for the heat radiating from their sweaty, salty bodies. Through your eyes, the two young women sitting side by side in a classroom with their heads bent over the Bible in Raphaela Crown's "What I Learned in Yeshiva" appear to be studying their lessons. Through your bedroom eyes, you see they are really studying each other. The tattoo artist who perfects her art in Myriam Gurba's "First Rites," the police officer who goes cruising in Rosalind Christine Lloyd's "Cop Out," and Estela, the upstairs neighbor who knows how to cook in Lana Gail Taylor's "Heat Vents," will all make your bedroom eyes widen in surprise when you stop and take a good, long look.

These twenty-one stories were chosen from hundreds of manuscripts that were sent to me over a period of six months. I am very grateful to all the writers—those whose stories are between these covers and those who did not make the final cut—for giving me the privilege of reading their work. And of course, I am grateful to the "A" team at Alyson Publications for their support, encouragement, and enthusiasm.

As an editor, it's thrilling to open a manila envelope, pull out a sheaf of pages, and read a story by an exciting, emerging writer such as Yolanda Wallace or Alaina Zipp. It's equally thrilling, in a different way, to read a new, unpublished story by a beloved lesbian author such as Ruthann Robson or Jane Futcher. I am especially proud to present a roster of writers who range from women just starting their careers (writers to watch out for) to writers who have been sharing their work with us for many years.

I invite you to open your bedroom eyes wide and take in these stories. You won't be disappointed.

—Lesléa Newman

Missed Opportunities
Adelina Anthony

Missed opportunities—we are told that if we live a life without compunction, our golden years will not be trivialized by the remorse that accompanies musing over moments gone by, the ones we knew would change us forever. Am I right? Well, it's a bunch of crock! Retirement is just that. Self-bashing. Lying on the sands of Florida's South Beach, defiantly without suntan lotion because at age sixty-eight, skin cancer is the least of my worries, I watch my best friend resurface from a wave that has swallowed her and my grandson whole—to their ecstatic pleasure. I never made love to her. Now it would be almost ridiculous.

Yet we are shamefully sapphic in our affections. Even my grandson, Horatio, my gorgeous Haitian-German mixed doll, a blend of sky and earth, takes notice with every precocious year how I dote lovingly upon Analise. "Why don't you and Grandpa ever travel together?" he asks with an impish smile. He's grown up with two fathers and tanned all his life on the most liberal beaches, from Miami, where we now are, to my native California, and even the French Riviera, where bare-breasted mothers frolic among their naked children. It's a beautiful childhood, a privileged one my son's money affords him, and one I plan to perpetuate with an inheritance the day I die.

My silence never deters him. "Stop playing deaf, Grandma," he insists. "Well?"

I look at his glowing cherub face, the ebony skin salted with miniscule white crystals of sand, his sapphire-blue eyes varnished with playful impertinence, and a smile like a white shirt stretched arm's length on a clothesline, and answer, "Your grandpa's a bore and you know it."

"Yeah," he giggles, and then adds, "Besides, Tia Analise is the coolest. We check out chicks together."

As Analise and Horatio, the ebb and flow of my heart, approach me, I pretend to be highly engrossed in the real estate section of *The Miami Herald,* where the prices are a third of what they are in Southern California. "You don't sell houses anymore, Gretchen," says my best friend, yanking the paper out of my hand, as if I'm a child playing with a forbidden item. "This is a vacation."

Predictably, they gang up on me, and Horatio points out, "You haven't even gone in the water yet!" I defend myself with, "That's because I'm afraid my Depends will soak up the ocean, and then you'll be sore with me for taking your favorite part of Miami back home." The hyperbole throws him into a fit of laughter. Analise eases herself onto her Looney Tunes towel placed next to me.

"Hand me the lotion," she says in a mildly defeated tone. She rubs the coconut oil on her olive skin. Although she's seven years older, she looks ten years younger than me. According to Analise, it's all the extracurricular sex she has. Back home, she's a steadfast member of C.O.O.L., the Coalition of Older Lesbians. I argue with Analise that not many of the C.O.O.L. women are attractive—a remark I find myself making more often than not when my jealousy is aroused. This happens usually—always—when Analise opts for an outdoor excursion to Idylwild with "the girls" and leaves me alone with my "till death do we part" mate.

She'll tease me with rueful good humor. "Ah, *chula,* after all these years, don't you know you're my only true love? I'll come back," she assures me. "You know I don't want anything from those embittered old babes." And then with perfect comedic timing, just as she's about to drive off in her jam-packed Ford Ranger to forage for adventure and sex among pine trees and women who tote pill bottles, she quips, "It's their daughters who wet my panties!"

I'm shocked out of memory when Analise slaps a cold hand of lotion on my thigh. My skin jiggles. "C'mon, Horatio," she says, "let's rub your granny down before she turns into the Pink Panther."

"The who?"

"*Ay, mijo,* sometimes I forget the age difference between us," she says, her firm hand rubbing between my legs, around my thighs, and so close to that place she's never dared to touch since I married Ruben. Damn her scruples, and damn mine. Ludicrous! Ludicrous…at my *respectable* age…to let myself get hot and bothered with a fantasy I could have had during the heyday of feminism.

"Grandma, are you OK?" asks Horatio.

"Of course she is," answers Analise. "You know how she gets on the last day of vacations."

"How do I get?" I ask in a bothered voice, although I don't know why. Yes, I do.

"All pensive, *chula.* Nothing wrong with it. See, Horatio, your grandma's a thinker. She likes to analyze everything, before and after, make sure all the best possible choices have been made."

"Not like you," he teases. " 'Cause you're crazy!"

Analise pretends to make a wild leap for Horatio, who retreats behind a large sand mermaid they built earlier today. It is clearly the work of a heterosexual boy and an oversexed lesbian, because the mermaid's breasts are so enormous she would surely sink to the bottom of the sea if she were ever set afloat.

"I can be spontaneous," I mutter to Analise. She looks up at me with her mocha-colored eyes. The older she gets, the more Zen she embodies without even trying; nothing fazes her, not even my crabbiness. She responds, "I know," and gives my sunburned shoulder a quick kiss.

Behind us, a group of garrulous young women approaches. Analise's eyes sparkle with the mischief of those immersed in perennial adventure. Three nymphs, barely clad in rainbow bikinis and as anorexic as Guess? models, express boundless enthusiasm for the mermaid and our adorable Horatio. The boy radiates.

In an instant, Analise and Horatio are helping the would-be models with their disposable cameras as they clamber atop the beached siren and repose themselves along her side, by her curlicue tail, and, of course, between her breasts. During this impromptu photo shoot, I grab my watered-down pineapple juice and slip away as quickly as the last seconds of a sunset.

Back at the Holiday Inn, I enter the room while the cleaning lady is still changing the sheets on the two queen-size beds. She apologizes sweetly and explains that she's almost done. She's used an annoying lemon air freshener even after I've specially requested that no scents be used in our room because they aggravate my sinuses. But I won't complain.

The message light on the phone is flashing. While the young girl exits into the bathroom, I check my messages. I've missed a call from my son's husband, who wants to remind me they'll be picking us up tomorrow at checkout and that if I don't promise to stay with them on my next trip they'll both be personally offended; but then he thanks me for the much needed vacation.

And that's exactly the reason I prefer to stay at hotels. I know my son and his man are balancing stressful careers, along with the responsibilities of raising a child. I don't need them catering to me and Analise, something they would do without question. She's only missed one trip with me, and that was because her younger sister's health was failing.

Of course, the other seven messages are from Ruben. He's a good man with a penchant for women, one of the reasons he and

Analise get along, I suspect. My decision to have an open marriage in my late fifties opened the flood gates for him, as I assumed they would. It was the decadent '80s, a resurgence of the 1960s without the attempt of spirituality. In the '60s, I got pregnant with my son and was thankfully abandoned by his father, who eventually became a David Duke follower, as I later discovered to my horror and disgust.

Analise and I had the best time raising my son; he always boasts that he had two mothers before it was the '90s thing to do. After my son left to study business at the University of Miami, I frequented the bars with Analise. It was her way of getting me out of the house, of saving me from empty-nest syndrome. We rotated: One weekend it was a heterosexual club for me, and the following outing a lesbian bar for her.

But we never left with anyone except ourselves. We were too protective of each other, especially since a strange traffic of personalities always streamed by us while we danced. "He's got a belly bigger than yours when you were pregnant," she would warn. And I would oblige in my best friend duty with "She's lolling from so much vodka, you'll have to prop her up just to kiss her." It didn't really matter where we went; we usually spent the night dancing together, occasionally interrupted by strangers who departed when they sensed the current between us.

Yes, there was a current between us. It first came up in the '60s, when we were both undergraduates at UCLA. I was enthralled by Analise's passionate activism, which I first saw during a student rally against the Vietnam War. I listened to her arguments not only because I had a brother who was missing in action for two years but because there was a depth of empathy and charm in her arguments. It took me weeks to approach her, as she was always swarmed by other students involved in the same struggles.

One day on my way to chemistry class, I spotted her on a

bench, her head immersed in Marx. I think I said something ridiculous like "Nice dashiki." I didn't understand why I was so nervous around her. Yes, she was extremely pretty, but I admired who she was—someone already finding her way through life. I was fortunate if I found my classes.

We weren't supposed to be such fast friends, especially at the time. Not when I was a porcelain doll with Germanic roots from San Diego and consciousness was a seed waiting to be watered. And she did, with long speeches in which she deconstructed patriarchal capitalism, macho men, and the U.S. corporate world. She was frightening. Brilliant. And never once did she show off. I proved to be one of the "white people" who stood beside her in marches against the establishment. Color, language, culture, and class, all of those barriers, became our borrowed playgrounds, she in mine and vice versa. Sometimes we hurt ourselves on the monkey bars of friendship, but we were always there to tend to each other's scrapes.

I think it was respect. We've had that for each other since our friendship ignited. Maybe it was why the first time she kissed me— and I collapsed at her touch—that we both backed off. Respect for a friendship we knew would last a lifetime if we were careful. I let her go. I knew I wasn't ready for a lesbian affair, even if I cared for her immensely. At times, when I saw her hanging by a limb as she threw herself into a trapeze of romances, I wondered what it would be like if I could love her the way she wanted to love me.

I wanted her to find her equal, her soul mate, her life partner. It was a quest she pursued as fervently as any good cause. Funny how even today she has a zest for romances, while I still mitigate mine with work or family. Maybe that's why Ruben is also a special part of my journey. He was a former student of Analise's in the Chicana feminism course she taught at UCLA. He entered my life at a time when Analise and I were getting dangerously close again.

Twenty years after that college kiss, our bodies were pressing shamelessly against each other at dance clubs, straight and gay. This time around I was the one who edged up close to her while we danced, my nose traveling along her slender neckline, absorbing her scent of sandalwood, and my lips instinctually pressing softly against the vein that runs like blue yarn down her collarbone. I felt her chest rise, our breasts swell against each other.

But the following weekend she invited me to a dinner party she was throwing for her graduating seniors. They were a special group, she said, one that was sure to start up the revolution again. And there I met Ruben, an intoxicating young man who reminded me of Analise when she was in her twenties. For the first time in our friendship I was afraid to tell her about my attraction for Ruben. Were they feelings? Or a postmenopausal infatuation? But she knew me. She was the first to encourage my illicit affair. Analise thought it was wonderful: "Men give themselves permission to pick the fruit before it's ripe. You're a beautiful woman, Gretchen. If he loves you and you love him, be spontaneous!" I eloped with Ruben, and for two years I had the most incredible and athletic sex of my life. And then one day, as my lover was fidgeting with his shoelace, I realized I was raising another mother's son.

Her voice is barely audible. "Miss?" she repeats. I don't know how long she's been watching me stare out the window, my hand near my pubis. "Miss," she says again with urgency. I turn to the cleaning girl and realize I've lost my manners. "What's your name, darling?" I ask. She gives me a perplexed look and then answers, "Lupe."

"Um…I'm done with everything. I found something in the bathtub and just placed it on the counter. OK?"

"All right, dear." I grab a five from my purse and tip her. I don't understand why she's so bashful. After she leaves, I decide to take advantage of having the bathroom all to myself. I love traveling with Analise, but her morning showers last longer than rush hour traffic. I amble into the bathroom, humming my favorite song, "Strangers in the Night." Then I flush with embarrassment when I spot the Smurf-blue dildo on the counter. Analise. My forgetful urchin.

The relaxation I feel after taking my warm bubble bath is more soothing for my stiffening arthritis than my cetyl myristoleate capsules. As I lie down, the fumes of Noxzema rise from my pink shoulders and the hum of the air conditioner hypnotizes me to dreamland. But then I hear the door open. "There she is!" screams my grandson, as if he's spotted a ship about to land or the treasure at the bottom of the sea. He jumps onto the bed and kisses me wildly all over my face.

"Wait a minute!" scolds Analise. "Get in that shower before you leave a sand dune on your grandma's bed." Horatio's eyes widen, and he slaps his hands to his mouth, as if he were suppressing an "oops." In a flash he's off the bed and slamming the bathroom door behind him.

"Are you OK, chula?" she asks me timidly. I've missed them, but I want to know that they've missed me too. "I'm sorry we took so long. You didn't even tell us you were leaving."

"The cleaning girl found your toy," I scold her.

She repeats Horatio's clownish gesture, wide eyes and hands to the mouth. How I love her. I cannot feign anger toward my pretty girl. We hear the toilet flush and the shower comes on full blast, as if twenty typewriters were clicking away.

"I brought you something," she whispers in baby talk. It's the voice we adopt chiefly when we exchange secrets. She pulls something out of her rattan bag and lies next to me. The coconut scent on her skin sweeps up through my nostrils. My curiosity is piqued, she's holding her hand over her other as if she's captured a butterfly.

"This is part of the reason we took so long." She removes one hand and reveals a plastic hummingbird connected to a wire.

"What is that? A toy you bought for Horatio?"

"No." She shakes her head with mischief. "This is a toy for you. You wear it whenever you want. It's discreet. And you press this button here that's connected to the wire, which you can poke through a hole in your pocket," she explains.

"What does it do?"

"It hums." And then she chortles, the thin white braids of her hair swinging like wild jungle vines.

"I still don't understand."

"You wear it on your poochy," she continues. Our code name for "pussy."

"You took Horatio to a sex shop?" I ask, indignant. It's the lay Protestant in me.

"Of course not!" she answers offended. "I got to talking to one of the girls. Turns out she shoplifted quite a few of these hummers, and since I'm a veteran sister, she broke me a deal. Don't worry, Horatio was absorbed with the other two in a game of tag around our mermaid." She smirks with satisfaction.

"I'll pass. What if that thing shocks me? That's not how I want to go, with a plastic bird vibrating on my genitals."

"I'll just put it in your suitcase. I know you'll try it later," she says, calling my bluff. "Don't worry, I got me one too, except mine is a dolphin." We hear the shower turn off, and in a few minutes our boy emerges, dark and shining like a seal. "My turn!" says Analise, giving me a wink as she enters the bathroom, one hand over the other with her new toy.

I hold my arms out to my baby boy, the towel around his waist like a sarong. "Ready to go home tomorrow?" I ask.

He nods and climbs into bed with me. "But when will you and Analise come back?" he asks with a yawn.

For the millionth time today, I think about the tumor my doctor found in my breast. The one secret I've kept from everyone, even Analise. "Oh, we'll be back before you know it. We might have to fly you out to California. Grandpa Ruben left a message saying how much he hates his job with the assemblywoman because he misses out on all the fun."

Horatio sighs, and I realize he's already falling asleep. I bury my nose in his wet blond locks, my Aveda shampoo perfuming his hair with rosemary mint. I caress my baby boy and wonder what loves and heartaches he'll have. Who will arrest his heart? Will growing up among brave loves ensure his own bravery? Will he remember two old ladies who loved him with wild abandon?

In the middle of my thoughts, I hear Analise exit the bathroom. "Well?" I inquire.

She looks disappointed. "So much for 'family' connections. She sold me this one without batteries." I chuckle. She notices Horatio tucked in my arms and whispers, "Shhh. Our baby's asleep."

Behind her, the orange glow of the evening sun sets her skin ablaze. I watch her remove her bathrobe, her pubic hair a prickly patch of white. She is a dazzle of spots. "We've both become leopards over the years," she says, reading my mind.

"Sleep with us tonight," I beg.

She puts on her one cotton nightgown, the one she wears for the boy's sake. Otherwise she sleeps nude. "Gretchy, are you all right?"

I nearly want to burst, but I sigh instead. "I just miss you. Even when you're in the same room with me, I just miss you sometimes."

She walks to my side of the bed and cuddles behind me. Her thin body is warm and soft next to mine. She gives me a playful bite on the neck, and whispers, "Go *mimi*." Our code name for sleep. The three of us lie together, in croissant fashion. But I can't sleep. My head is swarming with thoughts, as if I'm going to explode if I don't just say it, just take the chance. I bring her warm hand, which is resting over my tummy, to lie between my breasts. I analyze my feelings a little more before I speak.

"Analise, I don't think I ever loved anyone else in this life the way I love you. I know you know this. But what I've never told you is that I wouldn't have married Ruben if you had stopped me. I think I was falling in love with *you*. I mean, I know…I know now I wanted to be your lover. I mean, after all, they say you're supposed to marry your best friend. Silly, huh?"

Again, I've waited too long. My lifelong friend is snoring gently, while my grandson sneezes in his sleep and then nestles his head into my soft belly. Outside, palm trees shake their heads like doddering old men. Analise and Horatio. How sweetly their bodies hum against mine.

I am drifting off to sleep with Analise's warm breath against my ear when she whispers, "I heard that." A tender bite on my earlobe. "I love you too."

A Very Nice Woman
Sally Bellerose

It's been two years since I started keeping track, and I've only been able to come up with thirteen dykes who actually live in this little town. That's counting the seventy-year-old women who rent the apartment across from my sister. They walk their cats on a leash, not exactly proof that the old ladies are queer.

But one night a week my neighborhood is crawling with lesbians. There were six standing in a gaggle, talking and passing around a beer right across from my place when I stepped out my front door tonight. It's because I live on a side street near a bar that's called The Keg from Sunday to Friday. On Saturday night the club's name changes to Frenchie's. I'm guessing about a tenth of the population of this Massachusetts town has French-Canadian blood. I don't know, maybe the bar owner thinks that Quebecois spawn a lot of dykes. I come up with five, including myself, which, if you do the math, *is* a high percentage of my total figure of thirteen.

Today is Saturday, and they've hung a big sheet across the front of The Keg that says FRENCHIE'S—WOMEN-ONLY NITE. There are a couple of nicer bars in the bigger towns around here that have "women-only" night, but The Keg is the only one I've heard of that gives up Saturday. The other clubs turn queer every other Tuesday or the third Thursday after the full moon. Me and Frenchie's are tucked out of the way in a pretty deserted part of town—you have to be looking to find us—but we're always there on Saturday night.

This Saturday night I'm doing what I usually do: hanging in the shadows inside the club—watching the girls dance, play pool, make eyes at each other; wishing I wasn't so backward, when the lights flicker for last call.

I finish my beer and button my pea coat. Not ready to go home to my empty bed, I walk in the opposite direction. I keep checking my hands and head to make sure my mittens and hat are on. I feel good. Not so drunk that I don't know enough to bundle up. Not so sober that the cold really bothers me. My sister is baby-sitting both our kids. As long as I show up in time for her to serve the ski crowd at IHOP, everything will be just fine.

I scramble up a four-foot-high snow bank and balance on one foot on top of the hard-packed snow. Just drunk enough to be proud of this achievement, I slide down, land on my knees, and laugh. I hear a car pull to the side of the road, so I get off my knees and look up. Anne, an older woman, thirty-five at least, with a pouf of red hair that spills over her shoulders and halfway down her back, and makeup that looks better in bar light than in the street-light she's parked under, is leaning out the open window of her beat-up Camaro. Her chin is in her hands. Her hair hangs down below her propped elbows. Exhaust pours out her tailpipe.

"You're tipsy," she says with approval.

She seems to be flirting with me. I try not to dwell on this because if I do it'll scare the hell out of me and I won't be able to talk to her.

"You look like a movie star. Is it warm in that car?" I'm flirting back, on the verge of being forward. I've made up a poem. Life is good.

She opens the passenger door. I'm amazed to find myself sitting next to her. Her heater is broken, but it's still warmer in the car than it was on the snow pile. The car starts moving. She studies me while she drives. Anne doesn't seem to think driving requires two hands on the wheel or two eyes on the road.

"Pretty cute, isn't she?" she asks.

"No." I look straight ahead. Stella, the "she" Anne is referring to, the to-die-for girl who changes partners every couple of months and shares a few words with me on occasion if there isn't anyone more interesting around, is not cute. She's good to look at, hot, handsome maybe. I suppose I should pretend I don't know who Anne is talking about, but what would be the point? Stella already knows I'd suck her through a straw if I weren't so shy and she'd let me.

"No," she agrees pulling a Heineken bottle from under the seat. "*You're* cute. Baby dyke," she says fondly.

I'm not sure how I feel about being called "baby dyke." I'm almost twenty-four. I don't get called "cute" much, so I smile back.

Her hand, in a soft leather glove, twists the cap off the beer. She brings the bottle to her lips and passes it to me. I take a slug. She's very curvy and her clothes play it up. Her green earrings match her green sweater, which goes real nice with her leather jacket. She's trying hard to be pretty. I appreciate that.

I know how it feels to want to be attractive. I don't know what to do about it myself. I don't think I'm homely. Nothing about me is distinctive enough to qualify as ugly. I'm very plain: dirty-brown hair, medium build, medium height, B cup. It's hard to find anything in particular to play up. A lot of people have a hard time remembering my name, which is Jenny, or even that they've been introduced to me. I should rob a bank. I'd get away with it. The witnesses would never find any distinguishing characteristics to describe me.

Anne moves and talks and acts like she's beautiful. The longer I sit next to her, the better-looking she gets. I check myself out in the rearview mirror and run my hand through my hair. Slicked back tonight, it makes me look like an adolescent boy looking for trouble. For my job, I feather it forward like Mary Martin in *Peter Pan*. Either way I feel like I'm impersonating somebody. I glance at Anne's gloved hand, which rests on the eight inches of thigh exposed between her knee and her short skirt, and I'm glad I combed my hair back tonight.

She grins. I'm afraid she might be getting ready to pull over and tell me it's time to hit the sidewalk, but she touches my lips with one of her gloved fingers and kisses my cheek. She does all this while driving with one hand. Experience. Her musk cuts through the yeasty beer smell. She smells powdery, clean, as if she just stepped out of a bath, not a bar. I get rigid when she touches me, but lean a little toward her when she draws away.

The smell of her inspires me. Why can't I have a crush on *this* woman? Maybe I can just will my horniness onto a different path, transfer it from Stella to Anne. I don't have to have a thing for a girl who makes me sweat but barely gives me the time of day. I could have a thing for a girl who makes me perspire by squirming in the seat next to me and touching me with kid gloves. It's not as if I'm not attracted. My sweat glands have already switched over. Maybe I'll ask her out somewhere, like dinner. I could get my sister to baby-sit a little earlier, and we could go to a movie too. Then after the movie we'll go to Frenchie's and slow-dance. She'll sigh and call me honey, and I'll say, "Let's go, baby," real confident because the evening has gone so smoothly and it's obvious…

"Tell me," she says, slow and throaty, her voice cutting right through my feeble daydream. "I like you. You like me?" I feel as if I got the wind knocked out of me. Right in mid fantasy I've stumbled up against the real thing. The sound of her goes up my pant leg and stays there, still vibrating after she's finished talking.

I say, "You make me nervous." A pathetic answer, but at least it's not "Let's go, baby."

"Not necessarily a bad sign." She continues unfazed. "Because I'm forward?"

"I don't know. No offense, it's just…you flirt with everyone. It's hard to know if you're serious." Oh, my God, I hope she doesn't think I mean *serious* like I expect her to marry me because she said she likes me. "I mean…"

She pulls her head back and laughs. "Serious. I'm very serious about women, and I love sex. How about you, Jenny?" She's teasing me, but she asks it like a real question, as if she's interested, not just mocking me. She gives me a minute. I'm not quick to answer, so she cuts me a break and says, "I see you at that club every week, but you always go home alone. Makes me wonder if you really like girls. I think you do. I think you're very shy." She gives me a look that makes me think she could have two of me for a snack. "Or are you just so serious about big bad Stella that you can't even *think* of any other girl?"

I'm in way over my head. "I'm seriously drunk," I lie, hoping it'll explain my lack of witty comebacks.

She drives without comment for a few minutes. "You're not *that* drunk," she finally says cheerfully, like she's been thinking about it and her conclusion pleases her. "Stella, just so you know, is bad news. As soon as she knows she's gotten your attention she loses interest. Also, if you want some friendly advice, she's drawn to lipstick and ankle straps." She wiggles a high-heeled boot in the tight space between us to illustrate what Stella likes. I stare at her foot, which comes to a rest against the chunky boot on my own foot.

"Where are we going?" I've never been on this street, and I want to get off the subject of Stella. With each passing second I'm getting less interested in what attracts Stella. I'm a little annoyed that she keeps bringing her up after accusing *me* of not being able to think of any other girl.

"My place, unless you say no. Which you certainly can. In which case, I'll drive you home." She tilts her head and arches her eyebrows. "Really. Shall I drive you home? Where do you live?"

"I've never said no to anyone. Not that I've been asked much."

I want to let her know that I'm green, but I have a short, solid history of saying yes when asked directly.

"You've really never said no to *anyone?*" This fact seems to excite her. I don't have the heart to tell her I've only been asked by one person, my ex-husband. "Tell me, are you attracted to every woman you meet who you happen to know is a lesbian?" I shrug. "You've never been with a woman, have you?" She pulls to the curb in front of a big brick apartment building. "Home," she says, yanking the emergency brake. "How long since you and the hubby split?"

"Two years," I answer without checking my annoyance. "How do you know I was married?"

"Oh, please." She rolls her eyes. "I bet you know the names of half the girls who were in that bar tonight, where they live, whether or not they're cheating on their girlfriends. And you're as shy as they come. People talk. People snoop around and listen in on conversations. We all do it. A cute, shy, young woman, always alone. Somebody knows someone who knows your sister. Somebody else went to high school with you. The girls fill in the gaps for each other." She leans over me, not bothering to stop her arm from brushing against my jacket, but not pressing into me either, and swings open my door. She pats my leg, smiles, and says, "Two years is too long for a case of coming-out jitters. There's a cure."

Twenty minutes later I'm on my back on her satin bedspread, fully clothed, hat and scarf tossed beside me on the bed, boots still on, my pea coat a lump by the door. One of my arms is still inside my brown sweater. My white collared shirt is hiked up around my neck.

I adjust my bra and shirt and make a futile stab at the sweater. Anne is still pretty much clothed too. Her own green sequined sweater is disheveled, her skirt unzipped. She bends over, rummaging through an old steamer trunk at the end of her bed. The slit of her skirt is ripped almost up to her waist. There's a run in her shimmery green stockings. I grin, remembering the easy ripping sound of the silk lining, the more resistant popping as the stitches in the slit of the skirt's fabric gave way one stitch at a time in rapid succession as I groped for her, too impatient to wait until my fingers found the zipper. In a sex-crazy frenzy I ripped the skirt of a woman I barely know. Tore her stockings. In the morning maybe this will seem seedy and stupid, sinful even. Jesus, what a relief to have done something to feel guilty about. By tomorrow I'll probably be too exhausted and too busy with the kids to feel much of anything. Right now Anne's gazing at me as if I'm the most desirable woman she's ever laid eyes on, and I can't wipe the grin off my face.

I already came twice and my boots aren't even unlaced. I'm not sure if Anne came at all. There was a lot of heavy breathing, a lot of moaning in a short span of time that didn't all come from me. I'm not sure exactly what the sounds coming from her meant. She smiles over the curve of her butt, straightens up, pulls the green sweater over her head, and throws it on a chair. Her hard little nipples, visible through the mesh lace of her pink bra, point downward as she bends toward the contents of the trunk again and pulls out a negligee yellow with age, a man's velvet smoking jacket, and fishnet stockings. She discards them in a pile at her feet, then holds up a silk kimono. "Here's what I want." She rubs the silk against her cheek.

She unhooks her bra and lets it fall to the floor. I stare at her breasts. I've never stared at breasts before. Between my job as a nurse's aid, high school gym class, and my three sisters I've seen plenty, but never stared. Her nipples are strawberry-pink. She shakes her long red hair and throws the kimono over her shoulder. It covers one pale breast. Naked except for her boots, she walks to the bay window. She faces the street and pulls down the shade on the small cluttered studio apartment.

One foot on the trunk, she unlaces her knee-high leather boot slowly, watching me watch her reflection in the cracked oval mirror to her right. Her breasts dip and bob from two different angles as she performs for the glass, herself, and me. She walks back over to the bed. Kneels in front of me. "Here, let me help." She slides her hands inside the sleeve of my sweater, pulls it off my shoulder, unbuttons my shirt slowly from the bottom, looking straight into my eyes the whole time. With her hand in the hollow between my breasts, she lifts the bra. Kneads my midriff, works her hands up my sides to my shoulders, pushes me back down on the bed, kneads slowly down each of my arms, holds me by my wrists, sucks one nipple then the other with her insistent moist lips, nipping the hard tip of each puckered nipple. The bra cuts into me above my breasts.

I come in my pants for the third time in twenty-five minutes.

She pulls back, pleased with herself, and places the kimono in my lap. "You might be more comfortable in this."

A gurgling noise comes from under my still-zipped jeans, the last of the beer babbling its way to its logical conclusion. I feel a spasm in my gut. Anne slides onto the bed, straddles me, rests her butt on my thighs. She arches her back so that if I were naked our pussies would be touching. I lean back on my elbows and focus on the curve of her belly and the mound of her red bush surrounded by a halo glow from a candle burning on her night table. She twists one finger in the bush of hair right above her clit; otherwise, she sits very still and lets me look.

There's another gurgle, louder, and a slight cramp. I sit up in a panic, as if the vice squad has switched a searchlight on us. Anne balances with the flat of her hands on the bed so she doesn't tumble off my lap. A wave of nausea comes over me. "I'm sorry. Maybe I should go home." I realize how selfish this is. Anne is just warming up, but the beer is wearing off and every fear and feeling of inadequacy I've ever had seems to be converging. What if she wants me to get naked from the waist down?

She puts one hand around my neck. "Stay," she says softly, but it feels like a command. I'm afraid of her. She takes her hand from the front of my jeans and slides it to the back. "Don't worry, I'm a very nice woman. I'm curious. Aren't you?" She rests her middle finger in the crack of my ass and massages. "And I'm *so* turned on," she adds in a deliberate moan. Her voice is soothing and arousing, and I believe every word. "Don't be embarrassed. You're lovely. You're sexy." She lies down on the bed, pulls me down next to her. "You're whatever you want to be."

I say, "I need the bathroom."

"Of course." She rolls over. "I'm sorry, I wasn't thinking," she says sincerely.

When I come back she's straddling a pillow, rocking, riding like Lady Godiva on her horse. Her hair is draped over her breasts. "Keep your pants on if you want too. But please don't leave. Not yet." The quake in her voice, the raw loneliness, starts a tremor in me. Brave, to let somebody see you like that, to let someone know how badly you want something. I sit next to her. Slowly, shaking like a leaf, I take off my pants.

She sits on my lap and straddles me, one hand on my back, the other hand massaging my ass just like before I got up to use the bathroom except there's no denim cutting into me now. She curves her upper body into me, her breasts an inch from my breasts. Leans closer, braces herself on the bed, sways so her nipples graze mine. Moves her hips like she's pumping on a swing. She holds her breath. Her long lashes are dark with mascara and moist with sweat. They flutter for moment before she shuts her eyes. Her breath comes back in a sharp gasp.

Possibilities

Wendy Caster

Cleo took a left onto 11th Street. She could have turned right. She could have continued walking north. But she took a left. The sidewalk was jammed. A group of pierced and tattooed teenagers dressed in leather and studs pushed past two suburban couples gawking at a shop window bondage display. As Cleo jaywalked to the food co-op, she heard one of the suburban women say, "Should we go in? We can't go in!" and giggle.

Cleo perused the food co-op bulletin board. She never actually went into the co-op—she believed that if God wanted us to eat green things, He would have made green chocolate—but she always read the notices and announcements outside. Cleo sympathized with Natalie, "single nonsmoking female college student," in search of "studio apartment, $500 a month." To achieve that goal, Natalie had two options: move a thousand miles away or go back in time twenty-five years.

A sign offering singing lessons caught Cleo's eye. Someday she would have the money, the time, and the nerve to take singing lessons.

An extremely cute long-haired woman came out of the co-op, lit a cigarette, and stood next to Cleo. Cleo resisted the urge to bum a smoke—after six months she still wanted one—and got involved in an eleven-by-fourteen handwritten tirade against "the fascist management of the food co-op."

The woman with the cigarette said, "What that jerk doesn't realize is the food co-op doesn't have a management. We have committees and boards. Fascism means saying 'yes' and something happens. The food co-op means saying 'maybe' and in six months changing the decision to 'possibly.' "

Cleo laughed. "That's why I freelance," she said.

"Lucky you. Freelance what?"

"Human resources consultant. I go in, I give a seminar, they pay me, I leave."

The woman with the cigarette examined Cleo from head to toe, taking in her red high-top Keds, faded jeans, black tank top, and close-cropped hair. Cleo explained, "I look very different in my corporate drag and makeup."

"I'd like to see that."

Was she flirting? Was she gay? It wasn't clear. Cleo remembered her "date" last year with Marion from her karate class, when she discovered—after six lovely hours of conversation and laughter— that Marion was happily, even enthusiastically, heterosexual.

The woman put out her cigarette against a section of the wall speckled with ash prints. She threw the butt in a trash can, rubbed her right hand against her black slacks, then stuck it out toward Cleo. "Roxanne," she said. Cleo took her hand. It was warm with a friendly grip.

"Cleo."

"Two more hours of work and then a hot date with my laundry. Some Saturday night, huh?"

"Hey, clean laundry can be a beautiful thing." Cleo was embarrassed at her dumb response.

"I guess." Roxanne smiled, shrugged, and went back into the food co-op.

Tuesday morning, on the bus to Powerhouse Inc., Cleo tried to read a cutting-edge article about problem employees, but her mind kept drifting to Roxanne. Was there any possibility?

Maybe Roxanne was gay but not out yet. Yes, that could be it. Maybe Cleo could be Roxanne's first lover. That was a possibility! *Maybe,* Cleo thought, *maybe…*

I sit in my ancient faded red armchair, Roxanne on the newish faux leather Ikea couch. Roxanne says, "I've never been involved with a woman, but I've always wondered..."

I say, my voice calmer than my heart, "Can I brush your hair?" Roxanne's hair is French-braided, thick and dark down her back.

Roxanne says yes and smiles a nervous smile. I move to the couch. Roxanne pulls a brush out of her backpack and starts undoing her hair. "No," I say. "Let me."

My hands tremble as I gently unravel the intricate braid. I can hear Roxanne breathing.

I comb Roxanne's hair with my fingers, long strokes I feel through my own body. I brush the back of Roxanne's neck, and Roxanne quivers. "Yes," I think. "Yes."

I hold Roxanne's hair to one side and kiss her neck. Roxanne moans. I nibble on her shoulder and stroke her breastbone and breasts in circles that go almost to her nipples but do not touch them. She arches her back and leans against me.

It was Cleo's bus stop. Time to be a neutered professional grown-up. Damn.

On Saturday, Cleo decided it wouldn't kill her to buy some broccoli.

The food co-op was dark and cool and smelled of nectarines and peaches. Cleo spotted Roxanne at the first cash register. She really was cute.

Cleo roamed the small crowded aisles. She pondered why the world needed five different brands of veggie burgers—or one brand, really. She grabbed some broccoli, a can of soup, and a box of raisin bran, then got in Roxanne's line. Roxanne was very fast, but friendly to the customers. Occasionally one of the other cashiers interrupted to have her sign something. Cleo hoped Roxanne would remember her.

"Hey, Cleo," Roxanne said. "How ya doin'?"

Cleo put her three items on the counter. "Fine," she said. "How are you?"

A muscular teenage cashier bristling with energy thrust a piece of paper in front of Roxanne. "You said it was OK on Tuesday," he said.

Roxanne answered, "Don't worry. I remember," and signed the piece of paper.

"Do you live around here?" Roxanne asked. She looked Cleo right in the eyes, and her voice was creamy and deep. She was flirting. Wasn't she?

"About a mile away," Cleo said.

A woman with dozens of tiny braids came over to Roxanne. "This guy's check cashing card is out-of-date and he's pissed."

Roxanne said to Cleo, "Excuse me for a second."

Cleo watched Roxanne deal with the angry customer. Roxanne smiled and listened, then spoke quickly and quietly. The customer shrugged and pulled out cash. Roxanne thanked him and went back to Cleo.

"Sorry 'bout that," she said. "It gets hectic here."

Roxanne checked out Cleo's three items and Cleo paid.

Cleo knew she needed to say goodbye and leave, but she didn't want to. What should she say next? Something, she had to say something. Preferably clever. She pointed to chocolate bars stacked next to the register. "They seem so un-food-co-op-y," she said, feeling foolish as soon as the words left her mouth.

"They're organic, made from happy cocoa beans, with no refined sugar." Roxanne grinned. "But they're still rich as hell and very fattening." Roxanne tossed a few into Cleo's bag. Cleo went to pay, but Roxanne waved her money away. "A little thank-you for being patient while I dealt with that guy." Roxanne's voice was deeper than ever. She was definitely flirting. Wasn't she?

The muscular teenager was back, asking Roxanne to OK a check, so Cleo said goodbye and left.

Roxanne had been flirting. Cleo was sure of it. Well, pretty sure.

But was she one of those women who just flirted with everyone? Or was she actually interested in Cleo? Cleo liked how Roxanne had dealt with the angry customer. Roxanne had a presence that people respected. She'd make a good butch, Cleo thought. Yes, that was a possibility. Maybe . . .

I say goodbye to Roxanne, glad that we had a lovely evening full of talk and laughter, but sad that neither of us made a move. I close my door, lock it, and get ready for bed. In a few minutes I'm in my sleeping gear—underpants and a tight red tank top. There's a knock at the door. I look through the peephole. It's Roxanne. I think of running to get a bathrobe, but I don't. I open the door. She looks me up and down, grins, and says, "Oh, my." In one quick, smooth movement, she steps in, closes the door, pushes me against the wall, and kisses me deep and hard.

"I wanted to do this all night," she says, and kisses me again, running her hands hard over my breasts. I melt under her insistence. If I weren't up against the wall, I would fall down.

Still kissing me, she runs circles around my nipples with her fingers. They jump up to her touch, hard and luminous. I realize I'm digging my fingers into her back.

We stagger into the bedroom weak-kneed and panting. We fall onto the bed, and she lies on top of me, her leg between mine, rocking against me as we bite each other's necks. She takes my hands and holds them against the bed next to my shoulders. She kisses me hard, then pulls away. I strain to reach her, but she keeps her mouth about an inch from mine, still rhythmically rubbing her thigh against me.

"Cleo! Cleo!" Cleo's best friend Jimmy hugged her hello. "What's with you, honey?" he said. "I've been chasing after you and calling your name since you passed my corner three blocks ago! And now you look like you have a fever. What's going on here?"

"I met this woman."

"Oh, you *do* have a fever."

They walked to the park as Cleo told Jimmy the whole story, every word she and Roxanne exchanged, every nuance, leaving out only the fantasies. When she finished, Jimmy said, "There's one way to find out. Ask her out."

"But she's always at work, and there are people around, and what if she's not even gay, or what if she is and just doesn't find me attractive? What if I make a fool of myself?"

"Join the human race, honey. We're all fools. Ask her out."

Cleo wasn't sure what to do, so she called her other best friend Diane and brought her up to date. Diane said, "Don't bother. She's straight."

Cleo called her third best friend, Leslie, and asked her advice. Leslie said, "She gave you chocolate. She wants you."

I go to the co-op just as it's closing. Roxanne says, "I have to close up. Can you wait?" I sit on a crate near the books and magazines while she goes into a small office and works on the computer. I'm trying to figure out how the woman in a yoga magazine got her feet behind her head when I realize that Roxanne is behind me. She runs her hand across my brush cut, then grazes the back of my neck with her fingertips. She leans down and nibbles on my earlobe. The yoga magazine flutters to the floor.

I turn to face her and we taste each other's lips with delicate, lingering kisses. Her hair is down and I run my hands through its silky thickness. She kneels and kisses my nipples through my T-shirt. I figure that if I ask her out, she will probably say yes.

Cleo kept shopping at the co-op. She had even developed a taste for broccoli, but she still couldn't get up the nerve to ask

Roxanne out. There were too many interruptions, not enough privacy. After all, Roxanne was at work whenever they saw each other. Cleo finally asked Jimmy if it would be too damn wimpy to ask Roxanne out by leaving a card. Jimmy laughed and said, "Honey, whatever works."

Cleo called Diane. Diane said, "Don't bother. She's straight."

Cleo called Leslie. Leslie said, "She gave you chocolate. She wants you."

Cleo found a beautiful card with a close-up of a giraffe's face. The giraffe's eyes were deep and dark and somehow sexy. She wrote, "Thanks for the chocolate bars. Can I take you out for coffee sometime?" She included her phone number and E-mail address.

Only two registers were open. A long line of people stood grumbling at each one, shooting dirty looks at Roxanne at one register and the muscular teenager at the other. The old man paying for his groceries at Roxanne's register pulled out his bills one at a time, straightening them and counting them over and over. The next person in line, a super-thin woman in jogging clothes, radiated impatience. Roxanne smiled when she saw Cleo. Cleo handed her the card. Roxanne said "Thanks!" then looked around her and shrugged at the chaos. Cleo smiled and left.

Within a block, Cleo felt terribly embarrassed. What had she done? She didn't know if Roxanne was remotely interested. She didn't even know if she dated women. Cleo pictured Roxanne being pleased when she opened the card. She pictured her being annoyed.

Cleo called Jimmy. He said, "If she calls, she calls. If she doesn't, she doesn't. There are lots of fish in the sea, and you're a heck of a sexy fisherwoman!"

Cleo called Diane. Diane said, "You won't hear from her."

Cleo called Leslie. Leslie said, "She wants you. It's just a matter of time."

Roxanne lies on the bed, naked, her long hair draped across the pillows. I look up from between her legs at the landscape of her beautiful body, the rolling hills of her breasts and belly, the brush of her pubic hair. I kiss her thighs, rub my cheek against her. I'm finally going to lick her and I can't wait, yet I also want to stop time at this perfect moment of anticipation. Her lips glisten with moisture. Shall I start slow, with long liquid licks, or quick, with the shock of the sudden? I want to have ten first times, twenty first times, so I can try every variety, every approach.

I kiss her tenderly, slowly, all over her triangle of hair. She moans so deeply that she raises my temperature. I leisurely open her lips with the tip of my tongue. She moans again, a long, deep sound that follows my movements. She is swollen and wet and smooth and salty and sweet, and I lick her with the flat of my tongue to get as much of her as possible. And again. And again. I want to lick her forever.

I slip two fingers a tiny way into her. She squeezes me hello. I lick her clit as I stroke her opening with my fingers. Then I thrust my fingers all the way in. She gasps. I pull out most of the way, still licking her. I move my fingers in and out a tiny bit, a tiny bit, in and out, a tiny bit, and then I thrust them in. Her gasp is shocked, thrilled. I pull my fingers out again, still licking her. Again I tease her. And again. And again. And again. I thrust my fingers in. This time, her gasp is practically a scream.

Keeping my timing and pressure steady on her clit, I move my curved fingers in and out, in and out, deep, hitting her G spot again and again and again. When I think she's about to come, I reach up with my other hand and roll her nipple between my fingers. Her moans quicken and deepen, and her thighs tense and her clit vibrates under my tongue. I suck on her clit, pulling her orgasm into my own body. She comes for a very long time.

A day passed and then another. Cleo jumped every time her phone rang. She checked her E-mail frequently, but not so frequently that Roxanne would get a busy signal if she called. And she talked each day to Jimmy, Diane, and Leslie, not quite willing to admit how much she wanted Roxanne to call but not quite able to change the subject either. She read each of them the note she had left, asking if it was too forward or not forward enough, too obvious or not obvious enough. They teased her, but they were also patient. They too had waited for phone calls.

She ended each conversation by saying that even if Roxanne did call, it could be to say "No thanks." And each time, Jimmy said, "Whatever happens is fine," and Diane said, "Forget her," and Leslie said, "She wants you."

Cleo sat in her red armchair and thought about what each of her friends had said. She thought about Roxanne.

Roxanne holds her arms out to me, and I go to her. We fit perfectly, with our heads tilted to the left, our right arms around each other's necks, our left arms across each other's backs, our breasts and bellies and thighs pressed together. We hold each other for a long time. We've been together a year, a full year, and it just keeps feeling better and better.

We go into the bedroom. Roxanne lights the candles we keep on the dresser. I set up our CD changer with Bonnie Raitt and Annie Lennox and Sade and Diana Krall and press RANDOM. On comes Diana's Krall's voice singing, "They Can't Take That Away From Me."

We turn to each other and kiss. In our year together, we have developed a choreography of kissing, a dance in which no one leads and no one follows, yet the steps get more and more intricate. We're at the unhurried waltz stage now, tasting each other's lips and mouths and tongues. Each kiss melts into the next, feeding the fires in our bodies.

It strikes me that one year is the perfect moment in a relationship: new enough to be hot and surprised but old enough to know each other's desires and needs. I know that if I nibble on her ear, she will shiver with delight, but I also know that it is too soon. I want this night to take forever. So we kiss, and we kiss, and we focus on the kisses as though they are the center of the universe. Which they are.

Roxanne unbuttons my shirt. I'm not wearing a bra. She holds her hands a quarter of an inch from my nipples and heats the air around my breasts until my nipples cry out, "Touch me, touch me!" But I say nothing. She takes my shirt off and just looks at me. It is all I can do not to throw myself at her. "Beautiful," she whispers. She reaches out and strokes my left nipple once. Both nipples jump to attention so quickly that we laugh. My laugh is half moan.

Roxanne kneels and unties my shoes. She removes my shoes and socks and kisses the tops of my feet quickly. Then she reaches up and opens my slacks and pulls them down toward her, taking my underpants too. I lift one foot and then the other as she removes my slacks, and then I am standing there naked. She is completely dressed.

I reach toward her blouse, but she shakes her head no. This is something new. I feel more naked than I have ever felt with her, and it's a delicious, slightly scary feeling.

Roxanne lowers me onto the bed. She lies on top of me and kisses me hard. I feel the buttons of her shirt, her belt buckle, the zipper of her jeans. I feel even more naked and very vulnerable and very, very turned-on. We kiss for a long time.

Roxanne gets up. I start to ask where she's going, but she says "Shhh" and goes into the bathroom. I'm a little cold, but I feel as though it would be wrong to get under the covers. Roxanne left me naked and waiting, and I'll stay naked and waiting. I want to touch myself and feel how wet and swollen I am, but I wait for Roxanne. Annie Lennox sings about sweet dreams.

When Roxanne comes back, I'm a little disappointed. I'd expected something—a change of clothing, a sex toy, something. She lies on top of me, and I realize that there's a bulge between her legs. Now I know what my anniversary gift is.

Roxanne kisses me on my neck, down my shoulder, to my breasts. She blows on my nipple then licks it once, quickly, as though to see what mood it's in. My moans answer her question, and she takes my nipple in her mouth and sucks it until it is a hard, happy mountain of flesh. She sucks rhythmically until my hips are following her rhythm. She moves to my other nipple with her mouth, playing with the first nipple with her fingers. My hips move faster and faster, pushing against her crotch, pushing against the surprise waiting inside. When I feel as though I might come just from what she's doing to my nipples, I reach down and unzip her pants. She reaches down and holds my hand away.

"Do you want me inside you?" she whispers.

"Yes!"

"Then ask nicely," she answers.

I moan, "Please.

"Please.

"Please."

She releases my hand and I unzip her. The dildo is lavender and curved. When I realize where it will hit me inside, I moan again.

Roxanne reaches to the night table and pulls out some lube. I take it from her, pour some on my hand, and start stroking the dildo. Now we are both moaning. It is almost a flesh-and-blood part of her.

I wrap my legs around her and pull her into me. She tries to enter me slowly, but I push up against her. She says, "You want me, don't you?"

"Yes," I say, as I push up against her again.

"Yes.

"Yes.

"Yes."

We buck against each other in a frenzy of sensation. We kiss and bite each other. Our hair is matted against our heads with sweat. We stare hungrily at each other then close our eyes as emotions overtake us. Bonnie Raitt is burning down the house, and so are we.

Soon I realize that I have to come. Roxanne realizes it too and pulls out of me, slowly, tiny bit by tiny bit. My insides don't want her to leave, but I need to come. Roxanne starts to slide down my body to lick me, but I stop her. I push her on her side, facing me, then I flip over so that her mouth can go between my legs while I lick the dildo clean. When Roxanne sees what I'm doing she laughs; a husky, sexy laugh.

Roxanne starts licking me. I'm very close to coming, but somehow I manage to suck the dildo while pushing the base against her so she'll feel the movement. We get into a rhythm of licking, the dildo in and out of my mouth, her tongue back and forth on my clit. It is only minutes until I come, a muscular orgasm that clenches my fists and curls my toes and arches my back. To my delight, I realize that Roxanne is coming too.

We lean on each other, heads on each other's thighs, breathing deeply. Roxanne kisses my thighs then starts to lick me again and—

The phone rang. Cleo took a deep breath and picked it up. "Hello," she said.

"Cleo?"

"Yes."

"It's Roxanne."

Cleo took another deep breath and said, "So, Roxanne, how ya doin'?"

Now she would know.

What I Learned in Yeshiva
Raphaela Crown

It's not like my family is super religious or anything. Yes, our home was kosher ("for Grandma"), but we ate whatever we wanted at the Chinese restaurant we went to every Sunday night—except for spareribs, for some reason. I mean, I went to public school, plus twice-a-week Hebrew school, which was a real drag. But I must have talked about my friend Christopher a little too much, because the next thing I knew, it was goodbye freshman year at Barnard, hello yeshiva—in Jerusalem! Little did my parents know that I was hanging around Christopher because of his twin sister, Christina. But somehow I didn't think that piece of information would help distract them from the looming threat of intermarriage.

So here I am in yeshiva. Well, it's not exactly a yeshiva, since that's just for guys. I'm at "Midreshet Lippenschmuckler," which means...well, I'm not sure what it means, except that it's like a yeshiva, only for girls, and some people named Lippenschmuckler gave a shitload of money to have the place named after them. If my name was Lippenschmuckler I sure wouldn't go around advertising it. But everyone calls the place "Lipsmackers" anyway.

And speaking of names, I'm not Suzanne anymore—I'm Shoshana—and my frankly hot body is completely hidden in these stupid long skirts and long sleeves. Well, you're allowed to roll them up to your elbow. Big whoop. But suddenly I'm looking at elbows in a way I never did before.

The other girls are actually pretty nice, especially my roommate, Tzipporah, formerly known as Tiffany. She's kind of a

Jewish Southern belle; she's from Atlanta and has the cutest accent. We look a little like Mutt and Jeff. She can't be more than five-foot-three, this side of plump but not an ounce over, and with her firm, bouncy tits she actually looks sexy in these clothes. She's all pink and blond, while I'm five-nine and strongly resemble the illustration for "Rebecca the Jewess" from that book *Ivanhoe* we read in senior English. You know, olive skin, dark brown hair, green eyes, and what my mother claims is a Roman nose. It just looks long to me. Tzippy's, on the other hand—she claims it's really hers—is so cute I want to... But that's definitely not on the program here. Instead we spend all morning reading *Chumash* (the first five books of the Bible) and the prophets, who are always wailing about something or other, then all afternoon talking about modesty and "family purity" (that means sex) and which *bracha* (blessing) you're supposed to say before you eat which food.

I tell you, there's nothing like talking about modesty all day to make a person obsessed with sex. When we go out—careful to keep our elbows covered; you just know what a bare elbow can do to a susceptible man—I feel like a huge sign saying SEX! SEX! BUT DON'T TOUCH! Tzippy's brother is in the guys' yeshiva (those Lipsmackers were definitely into putting their name in large letters on the outside of buildings) and says it's even worse for them. They're always getting hard-ons during the Talmud discussions.

Take "Practical *Halacha*"—religious rules and stuff—which we have in the afternoons. It can get pretty graphic. If Mom and Dad only knew. For instance, the *ketuba,* the marriage contract, not only guarantees a woman's right to have sexual relations but actually entitles her to sexual satisfaction! And it's a *mitzvah*—a really good deed—to have sex on *Shabbat.* So all those people who won't desecrate the Sabbath by turning a light on are actually screwing like rabbits. But according to Jewish law, a woman isn't supposed to have sex when she's having her period or for the seven days afterward. In the Bible the prohibition is just for the time that you're actually bleeding, but later the rabbis tacked on extra days. "Probably at the request of their wives," Tzippy leaned over and whispered to me.

Today we talked in excruciating detail about how a woman knows exactly when her period is over and it's time to go to the *mikvah* and get immersed so she can start having sex with her husband again. Sometimes a woman can't tell if she's "clean" or not, and she actually has to show her underpants to the rabbi for a ruling. Can you imagine? All of this stuff about underwear and cleanness and "discharge" and everything made me kind of sick but also excited, in a way.

"I'd check *your* undies, honeybunch," Tzippy whispered, wiggling her blond eyebrows like Groucho Marx.

"While I'm in them?" I wanted to say, but I lost my nerve. If I didn't know better, I'd swear the girl was flirting with me. She's always touching me when we talk. And when we have *havruta* (that's studying in pairs) she always looks at me with those big blue eyes of hers. "What do you think?" she asks. "I really want to know what you think." Or "Oh, Shoshi, you're so smart! I never would have thought of *that*."

It drives me crazy just to be near her. She's so delicious I want to nibble on her neck or suck her fingers, but of course I'd never do any of these things. At least during the day. Last night I had the most wonderful dream. Tzippy was in it, of course, whispering in my ear, like she always does, only this time she was saying, "Yes, do it, do it." Tzippy said I woke up with a huge grin on my face, but I refused to tell her what I'd been dreaming about.

Fortunately, since nobody takes girls' learning all that seriously, we can go out whenever we want to (provided we're with another girl, of course) to shops, cafés, even aerobics classes. Yesterday we went to the Arab market—the *souk*—in the Old City. "Come look, pretty American girls, it doesn't cost anything to look!" the shopkeepers kept saying. Tzippy was a huge hit. Several men offered to marry her on the spot.

"Yeah, your parents would really go for that," I said.

"I can think of something they'd like even less," she answered, looking right at me, "and it would definitely be more fun." I'm not sure what she meant, but I got a funny feeling somewhere in the midsection of my long denim skirt.

One word about those skirts: It's hard to walk without tripping over yourself. As we were wandering through the *souk*, I twisted my ankle and ended up falling right on top of Tzippy. I was mortified, of course, though despite my embarrassment I managed to register the fact that she felt pretty soft and wonderful. But the weird thing is that I could have sworn she pulled me tighter just as I was trying to scramble off her.

"You'd better take my arm," she said. "We can't have you falling for these Arab guys, now can we?" But though I tried to tease her back, all I could think of was how deliciously plush she felt and how good she smelled and how my arm seemed to rub against the side of her breast with each step we took. She insisted on buying me some lavender-scented oil to rub into my twisted ankle.

Actually, my ankle is fine; it's my heart that feels like it has an Ace bandage wrapped around it. But I'd better recover in time for aerobics today. It's a women's-only club. We can't have men watching us prance around in next to nothing, now can we? I'm amazed, though, at what these *frum*—super religious—ladies wear when there aren't any guys around. They come into the club in hats, long skirts, long sleeves, and high-necked blouses and then emerge from the dressing room wearing slinky spandex cut all the way up the side. Tzippy has a cute two-piece number that holds her body tight and firm, and as she sweats, two perfect circles start to form around her breasts. And her butt is almost a perfect match: high and round, like a couple of beach balls. I love the way the Lycra hugs the bottom of each cheek. Frankly, it's all I can do to follow the instructor and not Tzippy's ass. Fortunately, I'm pretty athletic. I ran track in high school, so I can keep up without too much effort. Sometimes Tzippy calls me "Legs."

Today, after "Funky Step," we decided the shower at the club looked kind of gross. So we headed back to the dorm with our sweaty workout clothes underneath our skirts, feeling very daring.

So get this. While we're in the shower, Tzippy asks me to scrub her back. That old line, I think to myself. Can the Georgia Peach really be that oblivious? But of course I'm delighted to help my fellow Jew, so I take the bar of soap and run it up and down her downy back. I wish I could soap the crack of her ass. Those globes are pretty much irresistible. Is it my imagination, or can Tzippy actually be groaning as I drop the soap then slowly stand up? She does seem to be rinsing herself awfully carefully down there.

"Shall I do your back?" she asks.

"No," I say, embarrassed that my nipples are standing straight up and that I have goose bumps all over even though the water is nice and warm.

"You could be a model," she says approvingly, "so trim and muscular. I've got myself a little belly. See?"

I groan silently. I can't look, or I'll be rubbing my hands all over the slight but delicious rise of her stomach. So we towel off and put on clean underwear, but somehow we don't get around to getting dressed. We agree it was a great workout, but Tzippy says she's kind of tight and would I mind rubbing her back with those big, strong hands of mine? Again, I think, even a girl from Georgia can't be this naïve, but of course I agree, using the lavender oil she bought me at the *souk*.

"Any place in particular?" I ask. At first I simply try to sit at the edge of her bed and lean over, but it's kind of awkward.

"Well, just sit on me, darlin'," says my delightful roommate, which of course makes sense, so I start kneading her lovely back, still soft and warm from the shower. But her lacy white bra is in the way. I definitely don't want to get oil all over it, so I ask and Tzippy agrees—well, of course she should take off her bra. But the thing opens in the front, not the back. So I reach around to unsnap it, trying not to actually touch her breasts, though of course I want to.

I notice her delicious peachy tits seem to stand up as I brush against them—inadvertently, of course—and it's all I can do not to cup them in my hands. God, to put them in my mouth, to suck those nipples…I can't even think about it.

So like a good girl, I go back to her back. But I'm heading slowly but surely for her ass. She literally feels like putty in my hands. I can sense her muscles smoothing and lengthening underneath my fingers, and I'm getting closer and closer to her crack and the light brown hair between her legs. I slip my hands under her white lace panties, trying to push them down a bit. I mean, it would be a shame to soil such beautiful underwear, but I'm afraid if I actually ask if it's OK, Tzippy will come to and realize what's happening. So I gently slip my fingers under the lace and slowly slide the panties down her legs. As I pull them free of her feet I can't help giving the crotch a little sniff. I can smell her delicious peachy cunt, Tzippy's cunt.

My nose is wet. My God, her panties are soaked with peach juice. Does Tzippy know what's going on here? I can't help it, I've got to explore that delicious ass, so I scoot down to the end of the bed and part her cheeks, then push my Roman nose down between her lips and give a long, satisfying lick. She opens her legs for me—peach or not, she knows how to be eaten—and lifts her beautiful belly off the bed so I can put my fingers into her. First one, then two, she is groaning for me, coming against one hand and grabbing the other to pinch her pink nipples.

Suddenly she throws me off. *Oh, shit,* I think, *expulsion! Exile! death!* Well, it was worth it. But instead Tzippy lies on her back and pulls me down onto her.

"I want to taste you," she says. Not bad for a beginner, I think. She moves so her lips are next to my sopping panties and pulls them aside so she can lick my clit. "Like this?" she asks, and I don't know if it's the question of a novice or a seasoned lover, but I'm so turned-on I know I'll come if she just breathes on me. Besides, I haven't even gotten to kiss the girl. So I sit on top of her, slowly wiggling out of my sports bra, my brown skin and red-brown nipples an amazing contrast to Tzippy's golden pinkness. I lean my head down over hers. For a modest girl, she's one hell of a kisser. Suddenly she's running the show, pulling me down, biting my neck, then rolling over so she's on top of me, her hands gripping my wrists and holding me tight. She works her way down my body, giving little kisses and swirls with her tongue, till she makes it to my promised land. "*This* is manna," she says, sucking and licking.

As we lie there panting with huge grins on our faces, we have to interrogate each other. "When did you first know you wanted…" I start to ask but trail off, embarrassed.

"I've been trying to get you into bed for weeks!" Tzippy complains. "The oil, the soap, the back rub… I couldn't tell if you weren't interested or just totally clueless."

I can't believe it. All my attempts not to even look at her glorious body and *she's been trying to seduce* me.

"Do you feel bad about this?" I ask, wondering how such a thing could be possible but knowing that Tzippy takes this religion business more seriously than I do.

"It's OK," she says confidently. "In *Vayikra*"—that's Leviticus—

"it's written that a man shall not lie with another man as with a woman. But it doesn't say anything at all about two women!" Even so, it turns out the guys in the yeshiva are all busy giving each other hand jobs. I guess as long as you don't actually lie down together it's kosher.

"But actually there is one problem," she adds. Oh, no, I think, my heart sinking. "How do we find out the right *bracha* for eating pussy?"

Want Ad

Dawn Dougherty

*Old-school butch seeks fierce and tender femme to set her heart on
fire. Me: late forties, well-established with good manners. U: intelli-
gent, funny, and likes to dance. Age/race unimportant. Box 1749*

Abby read the personals every Thursday when the weekly gay
rag came out. It gave her something to do between customers.
Old-school butch? She liked the way that sounded. Abby took a
sip of her decaf and scanned down the list. They all sounded either
desperate or miserable.

*Willing to travel far distances and pay for dinner.
Help save this jaded heart from complete destruction.
Lonely? Sad? Me too!*

Abby clicked the pen against her teeth as her eyes wandered
back to the first ad.

"Looking for a date?" Michael squeezed behind her with two
trays of muffins.

"Maybe. Listen to this one." She read him the ad.

"You dykes are all the same with your 'set my heart on fire' crap.
Give me that paper, I'll find you a date." He put the muffins in the
display case and took the paper. "Here you go: 'Well-hung, uncut,
hairless Italian boy, 5'9", 175. Seeks daddy to suck my sausage all
night long.' Now that's how you write an ad."

"Suck my sausage?" Abby looked at the paper to see if he was
telling the truth. He was. "Men are pigs."

"True. But at least we're honest." Michael grabbed a towel and wiped crumbs off the counter. "You need a girl who wants to polish your pelvis, honey."

A customer came in and Michael took the order. Abby topped off her coffee and sat up on the counter. Maybe she needed to start dating like a gay man.

Fierce and tender femme.

The ad drew her back like a blinking road sign.

"Hey, babe," Michael broke her concentration. "Can a girl get a little help here?" Abby looked up and saw a line almost to the door.

"Ooh, sorry!"

***

Sydney read the ad from her office and felt mortified. *Well-established with good manners?* She sounded like an investment firm. Maybe she should have sexed it up a little. The phone rang. "Sydney Auto. Can I help you?" There was a pause. "Yeah, hold on one sec. Vick, when will the Honda be done?"

"Hold on." Vicky stuck her head out into the garage. "Tess, when will you be done?"

A scruffy blond head poked out from underneath the car. "Half hour. Tops."

"Half hour," Vicky said.

"Half hour," Sydney echoed into the phone. "OK, no problem." She hung up. "My ad is in." Sydney handed the paper to Vicky, who read it and smiled.

"You're a charmer, Syd." Vicky sat down on the vinyl couch in the corner of the office. "Come out with me and my friends if you need a date. We'll hook you up."

Sydney could imagine that scene. Vicky was ten years younger than Sydney and went through women like a hot knife through butter. Every Monday morning was spent listening to her latest conquests. Even if half of what she said was true, she was having twice as much fun as Sydney.

"Thanks for the offer," Sydney said. "But I'll be fine on my own."

Sydney thumbed through the schedule of appointments for the week and then checked to see if the parts she ordered were in yet.

The chime above the door rang, and a short girl with cutoff denim jeans and a tiny white shirt came in.

"Can I help you?" Sydney asked.

"Is Tessie here?" She wasn't wearing a bra.

"Tess? Yeah, hold on." Sydney smiled. Tessie? Must be her new girlfriend. "Vick, would you get *Tessie*, please."

"Sure." Vicky opened up the glass door from her spot on the couch and sang, "*Tessie*, someone's here to see you."

Tess rolled out from underneath the car and peered into the office. Her face broke out into a sheepish grin when she saw the girl.

"Hi," Tess came into the office. "This is Melanie. Melanie, this is my boss, Sydney, and this is Vick." They said their hellos, and then Tess and Melanie went outside.

"That must be the new girl," Vicky said. They both watched them. Melanie was leaning up against the wall, and Tess was whispering something in her ear. She had her hand on Melanie's stomach. Melanie giggled and then planted several kisses on her neck.

From her spot behind the desk, Sydney watched the two lovers. She sipped her coffee and hoped the personal ad would get her out of her slump.

Sydney left the shop in the semi-capable hands of Vicky and Tess (once Tess had untangled herself from her girlfriend) and drove home with all the car windows down. The weather was warm and clear. When she got home, she ate in front of the television and then grabbed a quick shower, checking out her face in the bathroom mirror when she was finished. Her short, cropped hair had only a few stray grays. There were definitely wrinkles around her eyes, but she thought it gave her a nice Paul Newman look. She got to the gym fairly regularly and considered herself a pretty good catch.

"All right, here goes," she said out loud. She picked up the phone and dialed the number to her personal ad mailbox.

An automated voice came on: "You have...no...new messages."

Sydney sighed, hung up the phone, and went back to the bathroom. Upon closer inspection there were deep grooves under her eyes and around her mouth. What could have passed for laugh lines fifteen minutes ago were now most assuredly wrinkles. Sydney clicked off the light and went to bed early.

When the alarm went off at seven A.M., Sydney hit the snooze bar four times before crawling out of bed. She made some high-octane coffee and ate her toast as she walked back and forth from the bedroom to the bathroom getting dressed. She grabbed her keys and her jacket and opened the door to head out, when she thought about her ad.

Should she check once more?

Who would have called her between last night and now?

She paused at the door then abruptly grabbed the phone off the wall and dialed the number. The same voice came back on: "You have...three...new messages." Holy shit. "Press 1 to hear your first message," the voice said. Sydney followed the instructions.

"Received Monday at 9:01 P.M.": "Hey, old-school butch." The woman paused to giggle at something Sydney had obviously missed. "My name is Mindi and I just loved your ad. Umm, let's see, I'm definitely fierce, not so sure about that tender part, but I am funny." She let go with a torrent of giggles that made Sydney cringe. "So call me. Oh, yeah, I'm bisexual and I'm fifty-three—which, since you said age and race were unimportant, I guess is fine." Bisexual was neither an age nor a race, Sydney thought. She didn't like the giggling bit but wrote the number down anyway and moved on to the next message.

"Received Monday at 9:45 P.M." Sydney checked her watch and figured she'd be late to work. "Hi, my name is Max and, uh, I know you, uh, said you wanted a femme and all, but I thought maybe you'd give me a try." Max's voice was deep and husky. "I'm an old-school butch too, and I know if you gave me a chance I could light your heart on fire. I bet a dyke like you deserves it. Give me a call." Sydney was glad she hadn't given her number out on her voice-mail message.

"Received Monday at 1:15 A.M.: Hi, my name is…" There was a pause, like the person was trying to decide what name to use. "…Abby." Another pause. "I guess it's a little late to be calling, huh? Not that you'd know since you're not exactly on the other end. Oh, God, I'm rambling." The woman was nervous. "I've never answered an ad like this. But yours was just so intriguing. I'd like to meet you sometime and learn more about those good manners. I also love to tango and salsa. Call me."

Sydney wrote down the last number and put the slip of paper in her breast pocket. She locked her door and drove to work whistling.

***

"Morning, sunshine!" Michael was a morning person.

Abby muttered hello and went into the back of the shop to drop off her bag. She liked that Michael got there before everyone else and made the coffee.

"So I have some news." Abby poured herself a drink and then started to fill the sugar containers.

Michael was taking the muffins out of the oven. "Give it up."

"I called the well-mannered butch."

"Ooh, you did not!" He put the pans on the counter and practically skipped out to see her. "And?"

"Well," Abby hesitated. "I was an idiot."

"Did you tell her you loved her already?"

"No. But I think I rambled. I don't know. She had a nice voice, though."

"What did you say?"

"I said her ad sounded intriguing and that I would love to meet her. I told her I could salsa and tango."

"Why?"

"Because in the ad it said that she wanted somebody who liked to dance."

"Oh." Michael didn't look convinced. "Can you?"

Abby finished filling the sugars and started restocking the napkins. "Well, I did take tango lessons. Once. Five years ago."

Michael cringed. "That'll make for a rough first date."

"And once I went to a salsa night at Chaps."

"One night of gay salsa does not a salsa dancer make."

Abby didn't want to think about it anymore. "She could like blubbering idiots."

"Sure. Anything is possible." Michael looked at his watch. "OK, time to roll." He unlocked the door and let in the first customer of the morning. Abby was glad for the distraction. It meant she could put off thinking about what a dope she was.

Abby checked her messages obsessively for the next three days. By the end of day two, she decided that the butch in question was not going to call. But on the third night, as Abby was stuffing her dirty clothes into her laundry bag, the phone rang. She was expecting her mom and answered with a friendly "Hey!"

There was a pause. "Hi, is Abby there?"

The voice wasn't familiar, and Abby worried it was a bill collector.

"This is Abby," she said tentatively.

"Hi, this is Sydney." In the split second it took her to say her name, Abby knew who it was. "I'm returning your call about my ad."

Abby's hand immediately flew to her hair as if Sydney could see her messy ponytail. "Oh, hi."

"Hi."

They had now said hello four times.

"I'm glad you called back," Abby said.

"Well, I'm glad you called." There was a pause. They weren't getting far. "So, tell me about yourself."

Abby felt an apple forming in the middle of her throat. "Uh, well, let's see." She felt like she was on a job interview. "I'm between jobs at the moment." She knew it sounded a little sketchy. "I just left a job of two years"—that gave her some stability—"and I'm looking for something where I can use my public policy degree. But for now I work at a coffee shop and do some volunteer work."

"That's great. Must be nice to have the down time."

"It is. So what do you do?"

Sydney told her about the shop, and Abby was impressed that she actually had a job where she had employees. Maybe she could fix Abby's windshield wiper.

"So how old are you?" Sydney asked.

Abby took a breath and paused. "Thirty-one," she finally said. She was biting the skin around her thumbnail. "How about you?"

Sydney paused as well. "Forty-eight."

They both did the math.

"Seventeen years, huh?"

She could have been Sydney's daughter.

Abby felt a twinge of panic. "I hope you meant it when you said age didn't matter."

But seventeen years is a serious chunk of change, Sydney thought. "Age is a state of mind, Abby."

Abby liked the way she said her name. "Right."

They made plans to get together for coffee the following Thursday night. When Abby asked how she would know who Sydney was, she said, "Somehow, I don't think we'll have a problem picking each other out. I'll be the forty-eight-year-old butch dyke with short hair." Abby laughed. Sydney was charming. "So how will I know you?"

Abby thought for a moment. "I'll be the one looking for the forty-eight-year-old butch with the short hair." Then they hung up.

Abby had a date.

***

Sydney was trying to get Alice off the phone, but they hadn't talked in three weeks and had a lot to catch up on.

"So how did the date go?" Alice asked. Alice was the first woman Sydney had ever hired. They'd worked together for five years until Alice and her lover Nancy bought a house and moved to the country.

Sydney was filling Alice in on the details of her last date with Mindi. "She raises Pomeranians," Sydney said.

"Those little yippy fluffy dogs?"

"Yeah, can you believe it?"

"So was she cute?"

Mindi had worn a red skirt with pink nylons, a pink sweater, and red shoes. She had very short blond hair and massive red earrings that dangled to her shoulders. She looked like a Christmas tree from the '80s. "She was OK."

"I know what that means."

"It's safe to say we won't be going out again."

"So what's the woman like tonight?"

Sydney checked her watch. She had to leave in half an hour. "She sounds cute. A little young, though."

"How young?"

Sydney knew what was coming. "Thirty-one."

"Holy shit, Syd! That's like twenty years younger!"

"Seventeen, actually."

"You could be her mother."

"No, I couldn't."

"You know what I mean," Alice laughed. "What are you going to talk about over dinner?"

"It's not dinner, it's coffee. And I think I can manage to keep up a conversation. I don't have Alzheimer's, for chrissakes." Sydney was starting to get a little nervous. What was she going to talk about?

"Hey, Nance," Alice called her lover. "Sidney has a date tonight with a woman seventeen years younger than her." Sydney heard Nancy say "Holy cow!" in the background.

"All right, I gotta go."

"Hey, have a great time, and be sure and call me in the morning. Unless, of course, you have company, sugar daddy."

"Goodbye, Al."

***

Abby grabbed a pair of black pants out of her closet, pulled them over her hips, and looked at her reflection in the mirror. Then she picked up a blue sweater and yanked it over her head. The sweater didn't fit right, and Abby thought she looked better in the black skirt. But then she'd need to find nylons. She was starting to sweat.

"What are you going to wear, Abby?" Her roommate Jill was home.

She surveyed the landscape of clothes. "Nothing, I'm going naked."

"I'm sure your geriatric butch would like that."

"Shut up, Jill."

She came in and stood in the doorway. "My suggestion would be pants with the low-cut shirt. Although the skirt is nice, it seems a little soon for such easy access."

"Is this your way of being supportive?"

"Give the girl something to look at, honey. That's all I'm saying."

***

Sydney didn't know whether to be late or early. If she got there early she might look too eager. If she got there late she risked offending her date. Plus, then she couldn't check her out first.

Sidney parked around the corner from the coffee shop and checked her watch. It was exactly seven o'clock.

***

Jill told Abby to get there early and sit in a dark corner.

Michael said be late and make a big entrance.

Abby was praying she could just find the place. She'd never been there before and got lost. Then she had to park two blocks away. She checked her hair in the rearview and smoothed out her lipstick. She was fifteen minutes late.

***

Abby had the voice of a woman who couldn't get out of the house on time. Sydney knew she'd be late. She ordered a coffee, sat in the corner, and waited. Two kids on skateboards came in and went up to the counter. The bell on the door rang again, and a woman with a shaved head and four rings in her nose came in. She joined two other women already at a table. Sydney sipped her coffee and tapped her thumb on the table nervously. The bell rang again, and in walked the woman Sydney was waiting for.

***

Abby stood in the doorway. She was so nervous she was about to jump out of her skin. The woman wasn't there. She had the wrong place. She was too late. The woman had probably arrived before Abby and ditched already. She had seen Abby and thought she was hideously ugly or too young and ran out the back door.

"Abby?"

Abby spun around.

"Yeah." The sound of her voice startled her.

"I'm Sydney."

Abby definitely had the right place.

***

Sydney couldn't believe her luck. She was gorgeous. "I'm back here in the corner." She extended her hand, and they shook briefly. It was oddly formal for a blind date. Abby's hands were like ice cubes.

"Oh, I didn't see you."

Sydney stepped aside to let Abby walk to the table. She watched her ass as she went. It was a total package deal. Sydney was feeling a little dumbfounded. She was not prepared for beautiful. What was this woman doing answering ads in the paper?

Abby knew Sydney was checking out her ass. She was glad she hadn't worn underwear.

"Can I get you something to drink?"

"That would be great. Coffee. Cream and sugar." Jill was gonna eat her words; Sydney was hot.

Abby chewed on the corner of her thumb as she sat by herself. This was not the kind of dyke she was used to hanging out with. She watched as Sydney took her wallet out of her back pocket to pay for Abby's coffee. There was something erotic about her buying Abby's drink. Abby was feeling way out of her league.

"So," Abby said.

Sydney put the drink in front of her and sat down. "So."

They both looked at each other and smiled.

"Sydney's an interesting name. As in Australia?"

"Yep. My mother spent a summer there before she met my father. She fell in love with the city. She thought it would make me sound cosmopolitan."

"It does."

"I'll let Mom know you approve," Sydney said, and Abby smiled.

"Where is Abby from?"

"Grandma Abigail. Not nearly as interesting as your story." Abby was flirting. "Although I could make up something if you like."

"Try me." So was Sydney.

"I am a direct descendent of Abigail Adams and the eighth Abigail in my family. Oh, and we spell it A-B-B-I-G-A-I-L-L-E."

"That works for me." Sydney smiled and leaned in a little closer. Things were going well. They talked about Sydney's job and where they both lived and what kind of job Abby was looking for. When they started on their second cup of coffee they launched into the merits of the local lesbian poetry scene and the advantages of owning versus renting. They finished their second cup of coffee and both got quiet. Sydney decided to take the risk. "This is nice."

Abby's stomach flipped. "Yeah, it is."

"How do you feel about the age difference?"

Abby thought about it for a moment. "Well…I was worried. There are a lot of ways to be forty-eight." Sydney nodded. "I'm sure you were worried what kind of thirty-something I would be. Did any of your friends give you a hard time?"

"Well," Sydney said. "Maybe. A little."

"Plus you said 'old school' in the ad. That made me curious but a little nervous too."

"So what do you think now?"

"About what?" Abby found herself staring at the space between Sydney's ear and collarbone. Her neck was incredibly sexy.

"The age difference?"

"Oh, right." Abby's face turned red. She needed to pay attention. "Well, fine. I feel fine. Very fine."

Sydney liked her answer. "Great."

They walked to Abby's car slowly.

"So should we do this again?" Sydney didn't want her to get away.

"I think so." Abby emphasized the 'I.' She liked the way they looked walking down the street together.

"Me too. I had a great time," Sydney said.

"So did I."

Then Sydney leaned in, kissed her gently on the cheek, and said good night.

***

The flowers arrived at Perk Up with a note that said, "This is what 'old school' means."

"Oh, that's good," Michael said.

Abby couldn't believe her eyes. It was a massive arrangement of wildflowers. The customers gathered around to find out who the lucky girl was.

"That's a fifty-dollar arrangement, honey. Very classy."

Abby stood beaming in front of the flowers.

"That's very good," Michael added.

***

The next date was a real date.

A real live, Saturday night, new-pair-of-shoes, open-my-car-door date. Sydney picked Abby up at her apartment and came up to meet Jill. Jill was beside herself.

"You have got to be kidding me!" Jill had crammed into the bathroom while Abby was putting her earrings in. Sydney waited in the living room. "Where has she been hiding?"

"I know! Can you believe how hot she is?"

"Are you sure there isn't something wrong with her? She doesn't look almost fifty. Maybe we should run a background check. Do you think she has a sister?"

Sydney brought more flowers. Abby wore the black miniskirt.

Sydney picked the restaurant (Thai) and paid for dinner and parking. Abby happened to love Thai food but was feeling a little off-kilter. Where were Abby's feminist politics? It wasn't like her to let someone make all the decisions. Sydney walked Abby up to the door at the end of the date and kissed her good night in the entryway.

"Do you want to come in?" Abby tried to sound cool.

"I'd love to. But it looks like your roommate is home."

Shit, Abby had forgotten about Jill.

"Maybe next time you can have dinner at my place instead."

Abby felt her thighs turn to jelly. The thought of being with

Sydney at her house was mouthwatering. "Sounds nice."

The next date was not at Sydney's, though. The next time they saw each other they decided to go dancing, much to Abby's dismay. It didn't take Sydney long to realize something was wrong. "Umm…I have a confession," Abby finally said after a third failed attempt in the middle of the dance floor.

"You can't dance, right?"

"Well, I'm sure I could if someone taught me."

Sydney laughed. "You lied to me, Abby?" she said in mock indignation.

"Well, I wouldn't say lied…I just stretched the truth a little."

"No salsa?"

Abby shook her head.

"No tango?"

Abby shook her head again. They both cracked up in the middle of the dance floor.

The date after that they had dinner out again and ran into one of Sydney's ex-lovers. Her eyes nearly popped out of her head when she saw them together.

"Sydney, is this your new…friend?"

"No," Sydney said. "She's my daughter." The woman walked off in a huff.

After each date Sydney dropped Abby off at her door with a kiss and nothing more. Abby was feeling a little confused. And a little frustrated.

"What are you waiting for?" Alice asked Sydney.

"Jesus, we've only been out a few times!" Sydney was getting it from both Alice and Vicky. "I'm taking things slow. Working my mojo."

"Mojo, my ass. Sounds like you're scared. Worried you might throw your back out?"

"Being naked really helps those years melt away," Vicky said.

Sydney ignored their comments.

It took her two more dates to finally arrange for them to have dinner at her house. Sydney cooked. Abby brought wine. Over dinner Sydney confessed she didn't know who Lauryn Hill was. Abby told Sydney that she was hoping she could fix her windshield wiper. It was after the dishes were done when Abby was standing and looking at some family pictures on the wall that Sydney walked up behind her and put her hands on Abby's stomach. She pushed Abby's hair aside and inhaled the smell of skin and soap and perfume that lingered around her soft neck.

Heaven, Sydney thought.

They stood there for a long time with Sydney's arms wrapped around Abby and the hum of the dishwasher and lingering music in the background. Sydney kissed her neck and ran her hands over Abby's stomach and up and around her breasts.

Heaven, Abby thought.

Abby had no idea what to do next. This woman had seventeen years' experience on her. She felt her knees shimmy back and forth a little. She wasn't sure if it was because Sydney was breathing hot and heavy on her neck or because she was so scared she was about to fall over.

"Will you spend the night?"

They still hadn't moved from their position facing the wall.

"Do you need to ask?" Abby said.

"I want to make sure you aren't planning on leaving anytime before breakfast." Abby thought Michael would appreciate that line.

Abby turned around to face Sydney. She put her arms around Sydney's neck and gave her a deep, soft, wet kiss. "Depends on what you're cooking."

Sydney peeled off all of Abby's clothes off right there in the living room. Abby was completely naked, and Sydney hadn't even taken her watch off yet.

Vicky was right: Sydney relaxed considerably once Abby was naked. So did Abby. Sydney noticed her knees shaking, but once her clothes were off and Sydney had cupped one hand around her ass and one hand on her breast, Abby took a deep breath and melted in her arms.

***

Sydney was determined to wait until the next weekend to see Abby. She didn't want to screw her every night for three weeks then never see her again. But Abby surprised her and stopped by the shop on Wednesday after work.

"Hi," Abby waltzed in like she owned the place. Sydney was a mess and had grease and dirt all over her. Vicky and Tess materialized from nowhere.

"Hi!" Sydney said.

"Thanks for the flowers." Abby thought she must have had stock in some company.

"You're very welcome."

Sydney felt Tess and Vicky chomping at the bit for an introduction. "Ladies, this is Abby. Abby, this is Vicky and Tess."

They each put out their hand for Abby to shake.

"Nice to finally meet you," Vicky said.

"Same here."

They all stood there staring at each other for a minute. Sydney broke the ice. "Come into the office."

She motioned for Abby to follow her. Sydney turned around and gave a silent 'stay' order to Vicky and Tess. They both gave her a thumbs-up as she walked away.

The office was cool and quiet when Sydney shut the door.

"I was in the neighborhood."

"I'm glad."

Sydney pinned her against the counter. "I also think I'm having trouble with my car." Sydney ignored her and kissed her shoulder. "I also have this broken windshield wiper." Sydney started to unbutton her shirt. "I also have this really difficult relationship with my much older mechanic." Sydney unhooked her bra and pulled her right breast out. "She doesn't seem to understand the newer models," Abby giggled.

Sydney unzipped Abby's pants and let them fall to the floor. Then she lifted Abby up onto the counter and sat her right on top of the appointment book. The phone rang. Sydney picked up the receiver and hung it up again.

"Service doesn't seem to be very important around here," Abby said.

Sydney spread Abby's legs. "I must speak…" Sydney put the flat of her tongue on Abby's clit. "To the owner." Abby shut up and put one foot on the back wall and the other at the edge of the counter. The phone rang again, and without missing a beat Sydney picked up the receiver and hung it up again. She heard the radio playing in the shop and Tess and Vicky dropping tools and talking. Abby looked down at the top of Sydney's head just as Sydney wrapped her arms around her ass and pulled her in closer. Abby dropped her head back just as she came. She threw her arm back and accidentally knocked over a jar of pens and a stack of papers. The phone rang and Vicki shouted, "Do you want me to get that?" Sydney picked her head up and shouted back, "Yes!" Abby and Sydney both started laughing.

"Damn, girl," Abby said, "you sure work well under pressure."

"Well, I'm not usually doing this many things at once."

"I have to say, I am pleased with this service." After she pulled herself together they headed out. Vicki and Tess stopped what they were doing.

"I'm sure they'll be wanting an update."

Abby was feeling very pleased with herself.

"Can I talk you into dinner tonight?" Sydney asked.

Sydney put her arms around Abby's waist when they got outside.

"You can talk me into anything." They kissed. Abby started to walk away and stopped. "Are you going to stare at my ass as I leave?"

"I was hoping to."

"Good," and she turned around and walked very slowly away.

Wild Iris

Jane Futcher

Makeup is wrecking us, Lulu thought, her heart kicking against her ribs from the assault of the telephone. She pulled off her silk sleeping mask and took out her earplugs while Roxie reached for the phone, knocked a glass of water on the floor, and found the lights. *She doesn't have a film job till next week. This can't be a wake-up call.*

Lulu was right. "Your water broke fifteen minutes ago?" Roxie said, her voice clear and full of love. "Any contractions yet?"

At that moment, Lulu knew Roxie was leaving and would be gone for weeks because Dharma, Roxie's daughter, was having her baby, the baby that wasn't due for another month.

"I'll call the airlines right now and phone you back, sweetheart," Roxie was saying. "I love you. Hang on till I get there."

"Hey, Lulu!" Roxie jumped up, turned on the shower, and dialed the airline. "We're going to have a baby. Want to come to Tucson with me?"

"Wish I could," Lulu said.

An hour later, they were chasing the airport bus down Highway 101 to Mill Valley. Roxie was in the passenger seat, her brown leather backpack on her feet, their red long-haired dachshund, Glenda, trembling in her lap. Wizard, also known as the Wiz, Glenda's black-and-tan brother, lay curled in the backseat sleeping.

Halfway to the bus stop, Roxie handed Lulu a huge red card. "Happy Valentine's Day, Lu." She kissed Lu's cheek.

"Wow," Lulu said. She pulled out a heart-shaped box of See's chocolates and a card. "Here's yours."

Roxie brushed a strand of her streaked blond mane from her eyes. "I'm sorry I won't be here for your birthday."

"Baby comes first," Lulu said, opening the card with her teeth as she followed the bus off the freeway and into the parking lot. The card was one of Roxie's handmade specials, a lacy doily decorated with sparkly red glitter around a heart-shaped photo of Roxie, Lulu, and the dogs.

"So you don't forget me." Roxie leaned over to kiss Lulu.

"It's beautiful," Lulu said. "When'd you have time to make it?" Roxie barely had time to breathe these days, doing makeup on the crew of a police series that traveled all the time.

"There were some kids on the set this week. Their teacher was helping them make valentines. So I joined them."

Lulu lifted Glenda and Wiz from the car and waited with Roxie by the steps of the bus. Despite the rain and cold, Roxie was wearing her Southwest clothes—a straw hat, white linen pants, a beige pullover, and a woven tan scarf from India. She looked terrific, her freckles still dark from their week in Mexico and her green eyes sleepy but warm.

"I'll call from the hospital," she said, kissing Lulu on the lips as the bus driver waited impassively for her ticket. After she boarded, he scanned the parking lot for stragglers, climbed into his seat, and whooshed the doors closed behind him. From inside the bus, Roxie blew a kiss to Lulu and the dogs.

Lulu looked at her watch: six-ten A.M. She'd never get back to sleep, so she might as well walk the dogs. A light rain was falling by the empty college ball fields. Walking the dogs was hard without Roxie because Glenda spent the whole time turning around to look for her, and the Wiz, who hated rain, dug his heels in and only moved if Lulu coaxed him with doggie treats. Lulu didn't have any doggie treats this morning, so she had to croon words of encouragement with every step they took. *I can win this war by outwaiting him,* Lulu thought, standing up straight and tall, gazing up at the hills, at the green coastal oaks ascending to a ridge on the far side of the soccer fields.

As they crossed the wooden style into public open space and started up the hill, Lulu felt like crying. Roxie was gone more than ever these days: on location with the TV crew; taking care of her grandson in her spare time; flying to Arizona whenever she could to see Dharma, whose pregnancy had been horrible, with morning sickness and hypertension that required bed rest at the end. *If Roxie and I survived life with Dharma, who did not speak more than a sentence to me in the two years we lived together and whose beautiful upper lip curled whenever I entered the room, we can survive anything.* Now Dharma was married to a dermatologist in Tucson, and she and Lulu no longer fought over who got the last swallow of milk in the morning.

"Wooowwrr." Glenda wheeled around, her bark so shrill Lulu's ears hurt. A woman in a brown felt hat, red down vest, and blue jeans, hiking solo, was climbing up the hill behind them.

"That's quite a greeting."

It was Grace, the textile designer she and Roxie often saw on the trails. Lulu called her her guardian angel, because she'd helped Lulu find Wiz once last fall, when she was by herself and Wiz disappeared into the hills chasing the scent of a deer. Grace was leaning over now, letting Glenda sniff her hand between barks. Wiz lay docilely on his back, tail wagging. When Grace rose, Lulu realized she was much taller than Roxie, with perfect posture and straight brown hair.

"I'm turning up this way," Lulu said. "Want to come?"

Grace assessed the hill on their left. "It's awfully steep."

"It'll make your heart pound and your pulse soar. It feels good."

"OK," Grace said skeptically, following Lulu. This time the

dogs came without Lulu pulling them. "Where's Roxie?"

"Gone to Tucson. Her daughter's water broke at two A.M., and she's going to the birth."

"How exciting," Grace said.

"I guess." Lulu chewed her lip.

"My daughter is way too obsessed with her Internet start-up to think about kids. I wish she would."

"I guess it's natural to want grandchildren," Lulu said, although nothing about children seemed natural to her. For one thing, Roxie's kids—and now her grandkids—had long been the biggest source of trouble in their relationship. Lulu resented how much of Roxie's time they took, and Roxie begged Lulu to stop being so insecure and jealous and realize there was enough love to go around.

"You don't like children?" Grace's eyes were brown and penetrating, set deep behind her brow, taking everything in.

Lulu stared at the rivulets of water streaming down the deep grooves in the road.

"Another grandchild means Roxie will be gone more."

"You miss her when she travels?"

"I…" What did Lulu feel? She missed her. She resented her. She was glad to be free of her. "I like being by myself."

Grace stopped to catch her breath. "You don't have to wait for me if I'm going too slow."

Lulu looked down at her scuffed brown leather boots and blue jeans covered in dog mud. "The dogs are much better with two people. They're used to two people." The Wiz had stopped directly in front of Grace to sniff some owl scat, and his leash had twisted around her legs. Lulu stepped close to her, unwinding the leash, lifting it over Grace's shoulders and head in a little dance, noticing as she did that Grace had a nice smell of green apples and soap.

Grace squinted at Glenda. "I love the way she runs. When I master my animation program, I'd like to draw her."

"Glenda would love to be in a movie," Lulu laughed. "She believes herself to be a star and is generally disappointed with her supporting cast." They had reached the crest of the hill, a green, open meadow where tufts of blue iris burst up from the ground on both sides of the road.

The trail sank, then climbed again, narrowing as it entered a forest of coast oaks. "Is learning animation hard?"

"It's hard, but not as hard as it was in the old days. Come over and play with my software sometime."

Lulu blushed. "I'm terrible at computers."

"You have one?"

"For writing. That's all."

"I'm online too much," Grace said. "I think it comes from living alone. I talk to more people online than I do in person."

The road narrowed through the woods, zigzagged to the left, looped back around the hill.

Seasonal streams bubbled across the path in low spots, but Wizard leaped over them without Lulu having to drag or coax him.

"They're being uncharacteristically cooperative," Lulu said. "I think they like you."

The woods had a sweet, fresh smell, of rain and sage and fallen leaves from the madrones and coast oaks and bay laurels. They passed the pond, where a woman was tossing a stick for a golden retriever, then back down to the playing fields. At the car, Lulu cradled the Wiz in a towel and, sitting on the back bumper, wiped the dirt from his belly and paws.

"So adorable," Grace said. "Hairy little beasts."

"Thanks for coming with us." Lulu put Wizard in the car and wrapped Glenda in a dry towel.

"It was fun walking with you guys."

"We're here every morning," Lulu said.

"Maybe tomorrow, then."

"Sure," Lulu said, thinking that by now Roxie was halfway to Tucson.

Roxie called at nine P.M. to say Dharma was seven centimeters.

"Great," said Lulu. "Give her a hug from me."

"She's...another contraction. Gotta go."

At six A.M. the phone rang. "It's a girl," Roxie said. "She's six pounds, two ounces, and sweet as an angel."

"Congratulations," Lulu smiled. "What's her name?"

"Doesn't have one yet."

"How's Dharma?"

"Exhausted. But very happy."

"She's lucky to have you there," Lulu said.

"I'm so glad to be... Oops. The other line. Love you."

"Love you too," Lulu said. But Roxie was gone.

It was raining again at the parking lot by the ball fields. Glenda trembled and stared accusingly at Lulu for bringing her out in such weather again. She lunged at the red Jetta that pulled up next to them, then wagged her tail furiously.

"Hey," Grace smiled. "Hey, Lulu. Hey, Mister Wiz. Hey, Glenda." She was wearing her red jacket and army-green floppy hat.

"You're so upbeat this morning," Lulu said.

"Am I?" Grace climbed out of the car. "I guess I am. I'm happy to see you."

Lulu blushed.

"And happy to be out on this glorious wet day. And happy because I solved a design problem as I drank my morning coffee."

Glenda began to paw the ground on the fire road, preparing to roll in something evil.

"No!" Lulu begged, but the dog rolled anyway.

Grace laughed. "Maybe I should take her."

"Sure." Lulu handed Grace the dog's leash. Suddenly Glenda was prancing along beside them like a show dog. So was the Wiz.

"You've got magical power over them."

Grace glanced at Lulu as they climbed breathlessly up the fire road. "What do you do?"

"What?"

"For a living."

"Work at the *Sunrise*."

Grace looked at her curiously. "Are you a reporter?"

Lulu nodded.

"Have you ever seen a dead body?"

Lulu laughed. "Not on the job."

Grace frowned. "I always imagine reporters arriving at crime scenes stumbling across corpses."

"I saw my mother dead, but she wasn't on the floor."

Grace looked embarrassed. "Was it terrible?"

"It was OK. I was holding one hand when she died, and my father was holding her other one, and then the undertakers came and put her in a plastic bag. She had cancer."

Grace stopped on the hill. "Look." She pointed to the grass beyond the road. "Wild iris. Beautiful, beautiful iris."

The flowers were cobalt against the green grass. Lulu felt her insides soften to the blue.

"All yesterday I was thinking about you," Grace said. "I realized I wanted to know more about you, and Roxie. I just wanted to talk, talk, talk with you."

"Talk, talk," Lulu repeated, flustered. Grace was such a beautiful woman, that mass of brown hair and those brown eyes and her strong, imposing body, that it was hard to find words.

Every day for two weeks they walked and talked on the trails as spring gushed up through the earth, bringing red warriors and monkey blossoms and more wild iris.

"I've been walking every day with Grace," Lulu told Roxie when she called one morning.

"The dogs are much better when she's there."

"Great," Roxie said.

"Glenda's in love with her. She's totally well-behaved with Grace."

"I'm glad," Roxie said. Did she have a clue that Lulu was falling in love with Grace too?

Grace told Lulu that her husband had died twenty years ago, when their daughter was six months old, in a motorcycle accident in Berkeley. Four years ago she'd broken up with the man she'd lived with, then had a hysterectomy, then lost her business, sold her house, and moved here. Now she was coming out of hiding, she said. Lulu told Grace about the land she and Roxie had bought up north, in the country, where they planned to build a house.

Lulu noticed she was taking more time than usual getting dressed for her hike in the morning, trying to decide whether to wear the red bandanna or the purple one, the L.L. Bean boots with the shredded toe or the new, expensive pair of Eccos from Macy's Christmas sale.

One morning, a deer leaped across the brush ahead of them and Wiz tugged on his leash, fighting to be free.

"When I lived in Sebastopol," Grace said, "my house bordered a huge state park, and deer took refuge from the sun under our deck. One day a buck, sick and dying, sheltered himself beneath the deck. We heard him down there, bumping, dying, and one day we heard nothing, and then the smell began, putrid in the summer heat. Pete, the painter I lived with, went under and pulled the dead buck out and laid him down by the stream below the house. A few months later it was nothing but bones, shiny, picked away by the vultures. Pete took the bones and made a sculpture with them."

"I once pulled a dead raccoon out from under our deck," Lulu said. "Roxie had to hold my hand because I was afraid it might come back to life and bite me."

Grace laughed. "I used to feed the raccoons too, and later the squirrels. I fed the squirrels every day for two years and I fed their babies and the babies brought their babies back and those babies matured and brought their babies back. I learned my lesson." She paused ominously.

"What lesson?" Lulu asked.

"It's a long story."

"I love long stories," Lulu said, enjoying the purr she felt in her legs as Grace talked.

Grace always told complicated stories with haunting twists and cosmic significance. Roxie's conversation was always very down-to-earth and practical.

"Soon I was feeding hundreds of squirrels peanuts and vegetables and kibble. They'd stand on their little back legs and beg at the kitchen door and glass windows. I was so proud of all my animal friends. I thought I was St. Francis of Assisi."

"What happened?" Lulu asked, intrigued.

"One day, we went to Hawaii for two weeks, my first vacation in years, and my daughter and her boyfriend stayed at the house. They decided they didn't want to feed all the animals, and the squirrels got restless and hungry and then angry and chewed through the screen doors when Rachael was at work and came into the house and rooted through the kitchen looking for food. They began to have horrible fights over the food, or lack of food, and one died in the kitchen. Rachael didn't tell me what was going on, didn't want me to worry about it, but it was driving her mad. When I came home and saw the damage from the squirrels I realized how foolish I'd been, and I've never fed wild animals again."

Grace's voice was turning Lulu on, warming her legs and stomach. She didn't know why exactly. Maybe it was just that after Roxie being gone so long, and always so busy when she was at home, and always so matter-of-fact and practical, Lulu wasn't used to anyone telling her stories, craved the murmur of a woman, soft and open and excited by her side. Sometimes she had to beg Roxie to talk to her, tell her things, details, things that happened at work, ideas, theories, anything.

"Is this boring you?" Grace's brown eyes studied Lulu's. "If it is, I'll—"

"Not at all."

"Well, so, that was the beginning of my daughter Rachael's queer squirrel karma. Squirrel things kept happening. At Christmas I always have a tree, get kind of carried away with handmade ornaments and stringing the lights, which can take days— very obsessive, but I love doing it. I had a squirrel ornament, and my daughter was still mad at squirrels, and she glued a jalapeño pepper onto it. The kids all thought it was very funny because it looked like a penis. But soon after that, at her college, a squirrel leaped on her for no reason and bit her as she was walking to class. And then she won a grant to go and study squirrels in South America. Not long after she returned from her studies, she began to feel very badly. By the time we got her to the hospital, she was in a coma. She stayed in a coma for a week. It was meningitis; the doctors said she might not come out of it. But she did." Grace looked at me. "This is the really weird thing: While we were in the emergency room waiting, we looked up on the TV in the waiting room and there was an image of a skinned squirrel pinned to the side of an old cabin."

"Strange," Lulu said.

"I told my daughter, half serious, that all the bad stuff happened after she glued the pepper to the Christmas-tree squirrel. I think that's when it began. Or probably it began when I started feeding the squirrels. Sometimes they were all staring at us, begging for food. Sometimes we were afraid to go out. The squirrels hemmed us in."

"It should be an Alfred Hitchcock movie."

"It was like a movie," Grace laughed.

They were back at the parking lot.

"Tomorrow's my birthday," Lulu said suddenly. It was only raining lightly. "Roxie's coming home on Tuesday."

Grace looked at Lulu quickly. "I'll make you a birthday breakfast after our walk tomorrow."

Lulu blushed. "Tomorrow's Saturday."

"Is that a problem?"

"No. It's good."

"You don't work tomorrow, do you?"

"No," Lulu said.

"You can see my house."

The next morning, Roxie called from Tucson. "Happy Birthday, Lu," she said. "I wish I were there."

"Me too," Lulu said, because she needed supervision.

"Are you having a party?"

"Grace is cooking me breakfast after our walk. And Stevie is taking me to dinner and a movie."

"That's great." Lulu could hear the baby through the phone. "Dharma's sleeping. The baby kept her up all night." Lulu heard a tiny wail. "Gotta go, Lu. She's cranky this morning."

Lulu knew she should call Roxie back, tell that her that something was happening with Grace, that she didn't trust herself to be alone with her, that all their walking and talking on the trail, among the wild iris and red warrior flowers and grass and gurgling water, had stirred some sort of lust jungle inside her. Something about Grace's stories and her artist's eye and her originality. Plus, Grace was open and willing and available, not called off to a grandchild or some film location in Seattle or Cleveland. She listened when Lulu told her stories, like about her reclusive sister who lived in a mobile home in Georgia with no electricity and twenty sick cats. But Lulu didn't call Roxie because she was a coward, and besides, nothing had happened, and furthermore, Lulu was pretty sure Roxie had affairs when she was on location. So why should Lulu confess?

Still, she felt guilty the next morning and stole one of Roxie's Valiums, prescribed for neck spasms, to help get her through the walk and breakfast with Grace.

When they met in the parking lot, the Valium was starting to make Lulu's tongue stick to her mouth and slow her heart and numb her nerves, but other than that she felt great, like she was about to slip down into silk, into the fabrics Grace designed, to see where this narrative would take them.

"Hey," Grace said, getting out of her Jetta. Lulu nearly asked her right there if Grace felt the same way she did—light-headed and excited and sticky and hot. But Grace kept filling the silences with stories, this time about her niece who capitalized the names of all common nouns and put semicolons where commas should go. The Valium took away Lulu's jitters, allowed her to enjoy the hike and the rhythm of Grace's words and the not knowing where they were going. At the parking lot she and the dogs followed the red Jetta to Grace's townhouse in the woods.

"Scrambled eggs, tofu bacon, and waffles," Grace said, placing the plates on the circular oak table. "And fresh-squeezed OJ."

"Yum," Lulu said, looking at Grace's breasts in her red T-shirt. She had never seen Grace with her coat off.

"Shall we take a nap?" Lulu asked as soon as they'd eaten.

Grace laughed. "Are you sleepy?"

"No," Lulu said. "I'd like to hold you."

Grace studied Lulu, and Lulu wondered if she were going to be angry. "I'd like to hold you too," she said softly, somberly. She took Lulu's hand and led her upstairs, to the sunny bedroom and wide bed with white linen sheets and a white linen down quilt. Lulu pulled Grace next to her, the three cats staring at them from positions around the room, then lifted herself on top of her.

"God," Grace whispered. "I wondered what this would be like."

"What's it like?" Lulu said, her lips inches from Grace's mouth.

"Great." She paused. "Fantastic."

"I like you," Lulu said. She lifted Grace's red T-shirt over her shoulders. The sight of full white breasts and flat stomach and tattoo of a ying-yang symbol on her left shoulder made Lulu want to swim inside her. She wanted to wear Grace's body on her face and suck her stories from inside her and feel Grace fucking her with her smart, hard, kind, strange words. Now Grace was on top, sweaty and sticky, breasts slipping against hers. She slid something inside Lulu: a long, green, sleek cucumber from the refrigerator; a big, fresh, organic, pesticide-free cucumber that split Lulu open. Grace was tilling her, turning her old soil over and planting new seeds of sex and squirrels and imagination inside her.

"I've never fucked a woman before," Grace whispered. "I think I like it."

"You're a natural," Lulu gulped. "Please. More."

"You're going to have to stay right here and let me fuck you until Roxie comes home," Grace said, face beaming, eyes bright and amused.

Grace was savage, all wet and tough and talkative, coming and sweating and loose, aggressive, womanly, hard and dominant. Lulu couldn't remember the last time she and Roxie had had circuit-breaking orgasms, couldn't think of anything now but Grace coming inside her and biting her nipples and stroking her to life.

"I'm fucking you," Grace whispered.

"I know it," Lulu moaned. "You're a fucking genius."

Lulu came again. They lay sweaty and close, then Lulu drew her cheek across Grace's breasts, opening her legs and inhaling her sweetness.

"God," Grace swallowed. Lulu sucked and ate and slid her tongue over and over across her as Grace clutched her hair and arched and yelled and came like a gurgling creek.

In the afternoon they drank peppermint tea in bed, with the three cats grooming themselves, one venturing as far as the bottom of the bed, and Lulu gazing at Grace's full, white body next to hers.

"I haven't been in bed with anyone in four years," Grace said.

"Let me again." Lulu kissed her.

"I didn't realize you were so sexy," Grace whispered. "Sort of butch in those boots and jeans, but sort of not."

Lulu smiled. They slid down again, and Lulu wiped her nose in the sweat of Grace's armpit and sucked the soft hair. The sun had left the room. Grace pushed herself up and found a green T-shirt. "I can hardly stand up," she smiled.

Grace's legs were endless. "I might be in love with you," Lulu said.

"Don't tease me," Grace said, suddenly serious.

"Take me apart," Lulu said. It must be the Valium.

She pressed Lulu back against the kitchen counter and drew her artist's hand between Lulu's legs, her touch peeling back Lulu's layers of protection, of disappointment, of longing and loneliness. Lulu was loving her, loving Valium for letting her let Grace love her, undo her. Grace was on her knees, licking slowly, an artist finding just the right color and stroke, one hand holding Lulu's ass, the other opening her labia. They found their way back to the bed, where Grace mounted her, pushed her fingers inside Lulu again, her breasts slipping against Lulu's, her sweat dripping into Lulu's eyes, smelling of sweet grass and squirrels and green apples. Lulu could feel herself falling, like the raccoon, like the deer, like Glenda, into the comfort of her lair.

"Put all of yourself inside me," Lulu begged. "Give me your art. Give it all to me."

Grace pinned Lulu's shoulders to the bed. "I'll be your whore and your master," she said. "I'll be your fucking john."

Lulu laughed and then came and then sobbed. She pounded her fists against the pillow, sobbed for Roxie and for this betrayal and for the love she had not felt in so long.

Then they lay silent in Grace's white sheets, breathless, breast to breast, lips chapped, legs trembling from taking so much of each other.

When it was dark, Lulu got up and showered with Grace, their nakedness a holy gift. Grace dried Lulu off with fresh towels, touching her so tenderly Lulu held back another sob.

"Does it matter that we don't know each other?" Lulu asked finally.

Grace laughed. "We'll get to know each other." Then more seriously, as Lulu pulled on her jeans, she said, "Do you have to go?"

"My friend Stevie is taking me to dinner and a movie."

"Will you come back?"

"Yes," Lulu said, gazing at the brown eyes.

Grace was waiting, in black jeans and a black T-shirt. They fell over each other. "I missed you so much," Grace said, pressing Lulu close, lips covering her lips. "I was afraid you might not come."

"I'm moving in." Lulu just plain old wanted to fuck Grace.

Grace frowned. "Don't tease me."

Lulu pulled up Grace's T-shirt, her legs tingling at the sight of the white breasts topping out of her black bra. She bent over Grace, unfastened the clasp bra, tasted her nipples, which hardened in Lulu's mouth, against her teeth.

"Let me die now," Grace said, her brown eyes unfocused, back arching as Lulu pressed her fist inside her.

Glenda and Wiz danced and pranced and leaped on Lulu when she brought Grace home at three A.M. There were six messages from Roxie.

"Guess what?" Lulu told Roxie the next morning as she held Grace in her arms. "Grace gave me a birthday present."

"What was it?" Roxie said.

"She...you know. We..."

"What?"

"We...were lovers."

Roxie was quiet for a minute. "You fucked her?"

Lulu laughed. "She's really hot. She's right here, in fact."

"Jesus, Lulu. Do you still love me?"

"Of course I love you."

Roxie laughed nervously. "Then I guess it's OK."

Lulu was amazed and happy.

"But get it out of your system fast, because I'm coming home in three days and that'll be that," Roxie said.

"You're not mad?"

"Of course I'm mad. You can't fuck her when I get home."

"OK," Lulu said. "I love you."

"Love you too."

Grace sat up, her breasts uncovered. "You told her?"

"She said we can fuck all we want till she gets home."

"Really?"

They stretched back down under the covers as the rain pattered down on the marguerites in the garden, and Lulu traced her soul over Grace's torso.

The first morning Roxie was home, she and Lulu and Grace walked together in the hills with the dogs. Lulu told Roxie they were falling in love, and Roxie told them about her grand-daughter, and then they all went out to breakfast and drank large cappuccinos and fresh OJ and shared spinach quiche at the downtown café.

Heartwood

Sacchi Green

Anya surged ahead up Mount Tamalpais, her bright hair luring me onward like a sun-burnished grail. Grail? Too many Renaissance Faires must have warped my mind, but nothing less than her loosely braided red-gold beacon could have distracted me from the looming void of the sky. That and the earthier seduction of fine, round buttocks thrusting against denim overalls, not to mention memories of her body moving in her belly dancing outfit. And out of it too, when she tried to challenge my resolve. The past two weeks had been filled with delectable torment; just thinking about it ought to be enough to get me through an hour of suppressed panic on a mountain trail.

Anya paused just before the summit, gazing out over golden hills descending toward the blue waters of the bay. The fierce elation on her face made me forget the impulse to crouch in the stunted bushes for shelter. Then she moved her fingers sensuously over the carvings I'd made on her walking staff, and my senses jerked to attention as though my body felt her touch.

"Robin," she called, "doesn't it make you want to fly?" She clamped the staff between her thighs and spread both arms, winglike; my own thighs clenched, and more than sweat dampened my jeans. I moved closer to her without noticing the steps in between.

She grasped the staff with both hands and worked it more firmly into her crotch, flashing me an innocent grin I didn't believe for a minute. She knew what her erotic moves did to me. "You must have carved some kind of spell into this," she said. "I'll bet I could fly it like a broomstick!"

She spread her arms again and leaned into the breeze, tendrils of bright hair working loose and lifting like tongues of flame. The winged-victory pose thrust her breasts forward until the denim overalls seemed scarcely equal to the strain; she leaned even farther, glancing sidelong to make sure I appreciated the view.

"Don't!" I said harshly, even though the drop-off below wasn't all that abrupt. She caught the tension in my voice and on my face, and stepped back at once, all teasing abandoned.

"I'm sorry, Robin. Are you...are heights a problem?"

A diplomatic way to put it. I answered more or less honestly. "Not heights, exactly. It's more like...exposure, I guess. Too much space on too many sides. Too much vulnerability to...well, whatever. The wrath of the gods, cosmic rays, lunatic fringe fundamentalist snipers. I don't know—it's nothing rational. I'm just more of a woods and caves and canyons girl."

"A perfectly reasonable attitude," she assured me. "Probably better for survival than my obsession with high places. Mountain peaks feel almost...well...sacred, but you shouldn't have let me tease you into coming up here."

"Just tease me on up a little further, now that we're here," I said, hoping she didn't know how much further her blend of sensuality and wicked imagination might drive me.

She shifted obligingly back into vixen mode. "How about if I tell you my deepest fantasy is to be fucked on a mountaintop?"

OK, so maybe she did know. I called her bluff, twisting my hand in the bib of her overalls and yanking her close, enjoying the pressure of her breasts against my knuckles. I pretended to ignore the approaching Cub Scout troop. "Seems a little public," I muttered against her ear, "but if that's what turns you on... Won't the view be kind of a distraction, though?"

"Not if we're doing it right." She grinned up at me, then pulled away. "OK," she admitted, "a free show for the tourists isn't quite what I had in mind." She wriggled her assets against me again for the benefit of an Asian couple's camcorder, then turned and climbed toward the summit.

Once there, in the shadow of the fire-watch cabin on the peak, I felt secure enough to take in the panorama with only a faintly pleasurable frisson of anxiety. Wavelets on the bay sparkled, and what was visible of San Francisco shimmered in the sunlight, but a fog bank muffled the seacoast and a tongue of mist nudged into the Golden Gate as far as where the Marin Headlands blocked our view. Nothing turns me on quite like the tenuous touch of fog.

"Would it help," Anya said, mischief in her voice, "to visualize the whole Bay Area as a woman opening her thighs to the sea?"

I almost choked on a burst of laughter. "What does that make all the ships and boats? Sperm?"

"Well, you can't carry the metaphor *too* far," she admitted. "I mean, would that make Tiburon the G spot? And what about Sacramento?"

"And you accused *me* of having a twisted imagination!"

"Some of your carvings do make a case for that," she said, "like the one with the warrior babe slicing her way out of the dragon's belly. But *this,*" as she raised her staff and rotated it lovingly, "is just absolutely, magically beautiful. I'm jealous that you made it before you met me."

I watched her caress the finely detailed feathers of the hawk's head at the top, then turn it to reveal the woman's face looking out from the hollow of the bird's throat so that its fierce beak jutted above her brow like a peaked helmet. The undulations of the female body were perfectly placed for the grip of a woman's hand; I felt my own palm and fingers tingle. Crisscrossing strands of chain linked by tiny inlaid gold stars followed the contours of her breasts without concealing them. Golden lightning bolts linked the strands draping her hips, with one bolt, larger than the rest, poised strategically just where a wandering finger might most wish to probe. I knew Anya was already planning to work my motifs into her Middle Eastern dance costume.

"How could you create something like this," she said, "without being a wide open sky–loving type? Your wolves and gnarled trees and murky caverns I can understand, but this?"

"I must have guessed a sky lover would come along someday," I said, and turned abruptly away. My face felt flushed, and not from sunburn. I was afraid there'd been more in my voice, for an instant, than the fantasy game of seduction we'd been playing all through the Ren Faire. "Take your time," I said brusquely over my shoulder. "Enjoy the view. Really. I'd just as soon you didn't hurry. I'll be in the van."

I started down, hoping she wouldn't try to match my pace. A quick backward glance showed her still at the summit, watching me. Her sensitivity to my need to be alone made things even more complicated. Why couldn't sex be simple? Hardly an original thought.

I loosened my tied-back hair and let it blow across my face for whatever illusion of shelter its dark length could provide and looked at nothing but each patch of ground my feet were about to hit. I groped for the semblance of cool control I'd struggled to maintain ever since Anya had invaded my life.

Anya hadn't been the first to seem to think the ROBINSWOOD sign over my wood-carving booth bore some kind of secret message along the lines of "Bi-curiosity satisfied here." Many a plump bosom spilling over a tightly laced "Renaissance style" velvet bodice had been pressed suggestively against my counter, undeterred by caped, booted escorts of the masculine variety. The guys, attention riveted on the explicitly lesbian eroticism of some of my carvings, didn't notice their dates looking me over or see the flirtatious glances when the girls came back later, alone.

When Misty had been on the scene, with her unpredictable bouts of drama queen jealousy, I'd been careful to conduct nothing but business at Ren Faires. Now that she was gone, I still hadn't been tempted. Until Anya.

Anya seemed to light up the interior of my booth like afternoon sunlight slanting through a redwood grove. As soon as that image occurred to me I knew I was in trouble.

It was no use trying to make her think I was impervious to her seductive charms, since she'd caught me enjoying the view, all too overtly, the first time she'd passed by. Her costume had been right out of the Arabian Nights, all scanty scraps of chain and bells and beadwork covering less than most laws allow, with some token veiling of cloth so sheer it intensified rather than obscured the sheen of her flesh.

And then she danced. Damn, could she dance! The performance area was close enough for me to watch and still keep an eye on my merchandise, but once she got to working her luscious body I wouldn't have noticed if Ali Baba and the forty thieves had been shoplifting. Artistry, sensuality, total and passionate evocation of the joys of a woman's body. It made me wonder whether Scheherazade had known another 1,001 tales she didn't reveal to the Sultan.

But Anya had been trailing a boyfriend when she first arrived. I don't do rebounds. Especially that kind. They'd broken up on the second day, fairly publicly—well, everything is public at a Ren Faire, which is a major incentive for me to tend only to business. Still, I could hardly turn her away on the evening the guy, drunk and all too close to being abusive, pursued her into my booth.

I stood up from my workbench and stepped between them. "Anything I can do for you?" I asked neutrally. He scowled and tried to dodge around me, and I gripped his shoulder with one hand hard enough to hold him off. He reassessed the situation, not too drunk to notice my height and reach. A glance at my carvings seemed to impress on him my proven dexterity with sharp tools like the one in my other hand; he swore and pulled away, and moved off into the twilight.

"Sorry," Anya said, a bit breathlessly. "Do you mind if I hang out here a little longer?"

As it turned out, she hung out there most of the next two weeks, whenever she wasn't performing. After she got a close look at the hawk-woman staff, which she clearly coveted but couldn't afford, I offered her a job tending the booth during peak business hours and times when I wanted a chance to see more of the Faire.

Not that anything was more worth seeing than Anya. She was good for business, especially in costume; sometimes she'd draw a crowd by dancing out front while I played one of my hand-carved flutes. She was a skilled role player, as we were all supposed to be for the benefit of the paying public. Her Circassian-slave act with me as "mistress" may not have been quite what the organizers had in mind, but it sure got attention.

When the public wasn't within earshot, she sketched caricatures of some of the more extreme specimens and entertained me with a wit so wickedly satirical that I almost wished we could have been just friends, without the complications of sexual tension. Almost.

After the first day of a slightly tentative approach, Anya had driven that tension mercilessly. I'd been foolish enough to let it develop into a challenge.

The night after she'd started helping at my booth I was putting away my tools, watching her reach up to release the canvas flap to close the entrance, and speculating on whether even her belly dancing getup could possibly be as sexy as the plain cotton T-shirt clinging to her full breasts. As she raised and lowered her arms the tantalizing points of her nipples teased at the thin fabric—and teased at my senses. I enjoyed the sensation a little too long and looked up to see her watching me watching her.

"Robin," she said, then hesitated. "Do you think you might…" She paused, and a slight flush rose from her throat to her cheeks. Then she took a deep breath of resolve, which had a nice effect on the T-shirt, and went on. "Would you like me to do some modeling for your carvings? I've posed for art classes plenty of times. Not that you don't do just fine without me," she gestured at the shelf where the more erotic pieces were displayed, "but if I could help out…in any way at all…" She started to pull her shirt up. There was no way I could bring myself to stop her before at least getting a look at how deep a shade of rose her nipples were. Then she yanked the shirt all the way off and shook her hair out of her face, which made her creamy flesh quiver and set off quakes all through my body. I hoped it didn't show.

"Hold on," I said, and then, clearing my throat and rephrasing, "Wait a minute!" She was unzipping her shorts by then, but I grabbed her hands and somehow kept mine from traveling any farther. "Just where do you think you're going with this?"

She tilted her head back to look up into my eyes. Hers were the amber-brown of a woodland stream. Woodland stream…redwood grove… Right. Deep, deep trouble.

"Somewhere I've been wanting to go for a long, long time," she said, "but never…never quite managed…"

She was being honest, but I had to resort to brutality to maintain any kind of self-control. "If it's an introductory course you're after, I can recommend a bar in Sausalito and several in San Francisco with a smorgasbord of instructors to choose from."

A flash of anger lit her eyes. Her submissiveness didn't go beyond role playing. "Hey, if you really don't want to jump my bones, forget it! My mistake."

She knew damned well there was no mistake. "Nothing

wrong with your bones," I admitted. "Fine, fine structure there. And the flesh isn't bad either." I allowed myself a leisurely stroke across the delicious curves of her ass before stepping back and jamming my hands into my pockets. "But I don't do rebounds." *Or bi-curious* was the unspoken subtext I was pretty sure she'd caught, since she didn't bother to challenge the "rebound" part. It had been obvious that she'd dumped him and he hadn't given up hope of getting her back.

"You don't look old enough to be so set in your ways," she said, anger replaced by a spark of something else. She knew already that she had me. The only question was how long the game would take. She bent to pick her shirt off the floor, pulled it on slowly, sensuously, with a bit more wriggling than absolutely necessary, and demonstrated that putting clothes on could be just as sexy as taking them off.

Then she began to zip her shorts, paused, and lied blatantly with a wide-eyed look of innocence. "My zipper is stuck. Maybe you could help. Your hands are so strong."

It was a good thing I wasn't holding any sharp carving tools. I yanked up the zipper and backed her against the counter, not removing my hand from her crotch. "I also don't do anything but business in an anthill of gossip like a Ren Faire." Passersby had been bumping the thin walls of the booth every minute or so; she knew just what I meant.

"I could stay a day or two afterward before I have to go back to San Diego…but I can be really, really quiet…" She arched against my fingers and raised her hands to my shoulders. I shrugged them off. A day or two, and then gone. Right. Why the hell not? Except that it was asking for grief.

"You think you can be quiet?" I moved my fingers slowly against her, working the denim seam of her shorts into her dampness. "This is just a test," I muttered against her lips, and she caught her breath, stifling little whimpers. She tried for a kiss, but that would have been cheating, and besides, my self-control couldn't have survived.

I moved my mouth down to the hollow of her throat, and then over the upper curves of her breasts. She tried to pull her T-shirt up, but I caught her hand. "Just a test," I admonished, and flicked my tongue across the cotton stretched over one taut nipple. Her response was gratifying but still silent. When I took my hand away from between her legs her guttural note of complaint was barely audible. Then I cupped her heavy breasts in both hands, working her flesh through the fabric, and she began to undulate the way she did in her dance routines. I caught one moving nipple in my mouth and played it for a while before switching to the other. Anya's frantic breathing could hardly be called silent anymore. Then I bit, gently and not so gently, and as my saliva soaked the thin cotton and made it cling, I sucked hard enough to make her thrusting engorgement show dark-pink through the fabric.

She tried hard to subdue the sounds she couldn't help making. It was a losing battle. "I'm sorry," she gasped, "but don't stop, don't stop, please…" She yanked the T-shirt up suddenly, and my mouth was full of sweet, demanding flesh and her hands were in my hair, pulling my head harder against her. I kept on until such shuddering sobs wracked her that I realized she was one of those rare women who can come from breast play alone.

It almost pushed me over the edge, but someone stumbled against the outside wall again. I eased off, and she began to catch her breath. I pulled down her shirt.

"There's a lot to be said for wet T-shirts as an art form," I said, not altogether steadily, and gently touched the darkened patches still clinging to her peaks.

She caught my hand and tried to pull it down toward her crotch, but I yanked it back. "I guess I failed the test," she said, still breathing hard. "But maybe with practice…"

"You didn't fail that one," I said. "You did just fine." I nudged my sleeping bag out from under the counter with my foot. "You can stay here tonight. I'll be in my van." Another minute there with her and the musk of arousal in the atmosphere would be thick enough to use for lube. I left abruptly and made my way through tents and booths and faux castles to the vendors' parking lot. It did-n't matter that the van was too full of gear for me to stretch out— I'd have spent the night curled into in an aching knot anyway, sleeping fitfully, dreaming of Anya, racked by sub-orgasms, more torment than relief.

I can play games as well as anyone. I just can't tell whether I'm winning or losing.

The climb back down to the parking lot wasn't all that long, since the road extended most of the way up the mountain. I'd parked facing inward, but now I swung the van around to an over-look and tried to come to terms with the gulf of space below.

I got out and focused at first on the hawks wheeling on invisi-ble pillars of air, but my gaze slid away to the faded psychedelic swirls on the sides of the van. I'd been meaning to replace them, now that Misty had drifted on, as I'd always known she would, to find another version of her own private fantasy. Vermont, this time, "because it's *real* there!"

She'd left me the old van, with its all too real foibles, since I was the only one who could keep it running. I had no doubt that Misty herself had found someone to keep *her* running, someone as young and biddable as I used to be.

Something with a pre-Raphaelite flavor appealed to me for the van, maybe Lord Leighton's *Flaming June*. But, as I envisioned that reclining body, sheer orange draperies doing little to conceal the luscious thigh, even less to obscure the soft, perfect roundness of breasts and sweet thrust of nipples, Anya's face and hair became part of the picture. Not such a stretch, really; her features had something of the same clarity, though her expressions usually showed wit and passion rather than pensive serenity. If she'd been conventionally pretty, I wouldn't have looked twice, no matter how enticing her body. Cheerleader types gave me nightmare flashbacks to high school.

To blazon a reminder of her across my van was just asking for another kind of nightmare. That particular self-torture, at least, I could avoid. Maybe van Gogh's *Starry Night*? I had an awful suspicion that I would see her in that too. Maybe it was time to outgrow whimsy and settle for an all-over forest-green.

Maybe it was too damned late to worry about it. I climbed into the driver's seat, feeling her aura already clinging to the interior. Keeping my breathing deliberately slow and steady, I extracted a packet of latex gloves from the aptly named glove compartment and slid it into my pocket. I had tacitly promised to fuck her, now that the Ren Faire was over, to move her well and truly past the dreaded "curious" stage, but I wasn't going to do it in the van and be tortured by her lingering scent long after she was gone.

I tied my hair back and leaned out the window to check on Anya's progress. She'd been standing by the big map board where major features of the view were outlined. Now, as though she'd been waiting for a sign, she started toward me. When she got close I realized she clutched a handful of bay leaves from the tree I'd shown her when we arrived.

"Souvenirs?" I asked.

"No, seasonings," she said, coming up right against the van, her face close enough to mine for vagrant tendrils of her hair to brush my cheek. The keen, savory scent of bay filled the air between us as she crushed the leaves and rubbed them on her throat and then unhooked the straps of her overalls and thrust the leaves down under her tank top and between her breasts. "I want to make sure I'm appetizing enough."

I reached in to retrieve the leaves and kept my hand there. "You get any more appetizing," I said, "and your second-deepest fantasy had better be to get fucked in a parking lot."

"Anywhere," she murmured. "Anytime." She opened the door and eased around it, tossing her staff gently into the backseat. I pulled her close, and closer, until somehow she was straddling me on the seat.

"Nice," I said, "really nice, but not quite *my* fantasy. Maybe sometime when there isn't a Cub Scout troop approaching. Again."

She laughed and squirmed around until she could clamber into the passenger seat. I began to seriously doubt my ability to pay enough attention to driving to get safely down the winding road. Then I considered the incentive and got the van rolling.

The sun shone through the windows onto her hand resting on my thigh. Heat flowed through me from knee to cunt to belly and beyond, and even when we descended into the fog bank and the sun gave way to swirling fronds of mist her hand still seared me.

"Robin, where are we going? How far to your fantasy?"

How far. How far, after all, into myself was I going to let her see? "From the mountain to the valley," I said. "From one sacred place to another." The road switchbacked down the steep slopes, green treetops showing through gaps in the dissipating fog. When I pulled into a deserted corner of an extensive parking lot Anya looked around in puzzlement and then growing comprehension.

"Redwoods!" she said. "Huge ones!"

"This is Muir Woods National Monument," I told her. "Definitely worth seeing. The fog is lifting, but it's still pretty cold and damp. We don't have to get out if you'd rather not. We could just go on to the campground as planned."

"This is another test, right?" she said.

"No," I said, but she knew it was a lie. She opened her door.

"Wait a minute." I rummaged in the back. "Wear this. It'll be cold for a while yet." I handed her a long hooded homespun cloak, my major concession to the costuming conventions of a Ren Faire. She burrowed her face into the brown bundle and breathed deeply, and a warm flush spread across my skin as her teasing eyes lifted to mine.

"Mmm," she said, "a woodsy bouquet, notes of oak and moss, with fruity undertones and a hint of sweat. A jaunty little vintage, tangy on the palate. You've been sleeping in this, haven't you?"

I reached for her, but she was out the door and well along the path to the park entrance before I could extricate myself. "Is there a rest room here?" she called back. "I'll find it and meet you outside."

She'd become almost subdued by the time I found her, looking like a storybook waif lost in an enchanted forest. The dark cloak was clutched tightly around her, and the hood slipped back from her bright hair as she gazed upward in awe.

I took her hand without speaking and led her along the wide pathway among the trees. The fog had lifted from the ground, but mist still drifted among branches so far above that it seemed only natural for them to be cloaked in clouds.

"It's beyond beautiful," Anya said at last. "Overwhelming. Don't they make you feel infinitesimal?"

"No," I said, "they make me feel infinite. Connected to life and time." I steered her onto a side trail. On an even fainter track made by deer, I held rhododendron branches aside for her to pass through, and in minutes we were alone together in a primeval world.

Anya stepped ahead of me into a narrow shaft of sunlight. "This must be it," she said. Across the small clearing a single huge redwood loomed, half hollowed by fire from a long-ago lightning strike, still lifting its green, living crown high into the sky.

"I wanted you to see this place, to feel it," I said, "but we don't have to…"

"Yes, we do," she said, and stepped up through the ragged archway into the living cavern. I followed, and she turned, still clutching my cloak tightly around herself.

"Are you sure?" I asked, not even knowing how many questions were tangled into one.

"Oh, yes. As long as you're sure you won't be distracted by the view." She spread her arms wide, and the cloak fell open. Warm air musky with her scent flowed from her naked body. Her skin seemed to glow in the shadowy space as she drew my hand first to her lips and then to her breasts. Dreams and fantasies dissipated in the urgent reality of Anya, here, now, open.

"No wet T-shirt games this time," she said. I just had to catch those quirked lips in my mouth, to eat that wicked little smile. The taste was so good I pressed harder, probing for her willing tongue. Before I was ready to move on she began to rub against me, gyrating with even more passion than in her dancing, and then, of course, I was so ready, it was a struggle not to rush things.

I slid my lips from her mouth to the curve of her cheek, then downward over her chin to the tender hollow of her throat. I ran my hands lightly across her breasts, feather-brushing her nipples, teasing just the rigid tips even when she tried to thrust harder against my touch.

"Please, Robin, please," she begged, forcing my head downward from her throat. I nibbled at the full outer swells of her breasts but, despite her little whimpers, continued downward. I knelt to savor her gently rounded belly, as succulent as I'd imagined when I watched her dance. Now she danced too, to the music of her own soft moans and my ragged breathing and the pounding of blood in both our bodies.

Down ever farther then, distracting her with the progress of my tongue through her tangle of coppery curls as I stretched a latex glove over my hand, knowing I should be even more prepared.

She caught her breath when my hand pressed into the heat between her legs. Her gasp when my thumb circled her clit became a series of sweet-harsh cries as I worked her slippery folds, pushing a little farther in with each stroke. "Yes…more, please Robin, yes, damn it, more…" I gave her more, and more, and had still more left to show her another time, but now she was on the verge of surging over the edge. I gave in to temptation and lowered my mouth to taste her hot, wet flow as she spasmed against my tongue and the waves of her coming swept from her body all the way through to the core of mine.

Later, by moonlight, in a tiny private campground far up a little-traveled canyon, she demanded another installment, and afterward I assured her that there was still more to be learned.

"Robin, I have to go back to San Diego, but sometime…whenever I can…and then after I get my degree maybe I could…" She wasn't all that coherent, but I knew what she meant. "And I don't mean just for this," she went on, writhing against my body, "except oh, my God, when you get me going there isn't anything else in the world!"

"You have a permanent invitation to my cabin in the Feather River Canyon," I told her. "I have a special, um, friend there you might like to meet."

The startled expression on her face turned into a grin as I went on. "Wood isn't the only thing I can carve. Latex, for example, is a tree product, after all. It can be worked, if you know how. And I do."

"Does your, um, friend, have a name?"

"I've never told anyone else, never needed to, but yes. I'd really like to introduce you to Dragontongue."

To see her laughing face, feel her closeness, breathe the lingering aura of her ecstasy was worth even the risk of loss. And loss was by no means inevitable.

"I'd be honored to meet Dragontongue," Anya said. "I'll be counting on it. Dreaming of it too. You and Dragontongue and some deep, deep conversation."

Then she rolled over onto me and persuaded me that lessons were fine, but the best way to learn is by doing. And she was a very, very good learner.

First Rites

Myriam Gurba

When you join a gang, it's kind of like getting baptized. At least that's how it was for me. It transforms you. Your homies become blood to you. They're your new family. You know they'd die for you, and in return you'd die for them. You've got to pledge your loyalty to your new *familia,* but instead of water being poured over your head, it's their rage and anger that makes you one of them. You come out of it a new you with a new name. Your *clicka,* the new family you've just joined, picks this name out for you. Bye-bye Jose, Johnny, or Fernando. Hello Puppet, Smiley, and Snoopy. Forget Lupe, Lorena, or Beatriz. Remember Shady, Shy Girl, and La Green Eyes. See, your homies watch you. They know you better than anyone else, better than your mom or even her old lady, *tu abuelita.* They watch you, and they give you a name for who you really are, for what your actions and the little things about you tell about your soul. You laugh all the time—*boom,* you're Giggles! You score things from the corner store without ever getting caught, hey, we know who you are—you're Bandit. And if you have a distant look in your eyes, like you're somewhere far away from the barrio and you ain't never coming back, they call you Dreamer. That's how it goes.

I knew who I was before I officially joined the *clicka.* My name had been picked out a long time ago 'cause what my true nature was showed through and through. Since I went to junior high, they'd been calling me *La Payasa. Payasa* means *clown* in Spanish. You might think I got this name 'cause I'm funny, some kinda joker. But that's not why they call me *La Payasa.* They call me

Payasa for my drag, homes. How do you tell a clown apart from everyone else? They got that crazy costume that makes them stand out, that makes them different. I got my costume too. I'm always in drag. I call it my *loco* drag—khaki Dickies with sharp creases ironed into the pants, three sizes too big, with a cotton belt holding them up high; my bright white wifebeater with a blue Pendleton over it, one button buttoned at the very top; and old-school Nikes on my feet. Oh, and my head's shaved completely bald, *puro pelón*. That's me, that's my outfit, my drag. I'm the *Payasa*. The only *loca* in the Latin Playboys.

That's the name of my *clicka, Los Playboys Latinos.* I was the first *loca* to ever join the Playboys. Usually, the way it works, if you're a guy, the Playboys jump you in. If you're a girl, the Playgirls take care of business. But not me, I'm a different kinda gangster. The *Payasa* is a straight-up *loco,* no doubt. The truth of that is what makes me *La Payasa.* My homies know me through and through. It's like they can see right through me, and they don't see the soul of a playgirl—they know I got the soul of a *loco veterano,* an old-school gangsta. That's why it was the *locos* who jumped me in, the *locos* who showered me with their rage and their violence and beat the shit out of me to prove that I was one tough macho, worthy of the *familia* Playboy.

It went down where it always does, under the bridge behind crazy Momo's house. It's dark back there, and Momo's shack covers the field up real good so the *jura* can't see nothing. And if they do wanna see anything, they gotta shine a bright light from their squad cars through all the bushes, and once we see that, we know to split. *Pinche* LAPD don't know this barrio like we do, and once we start running we can disappear into this neighborhood like hoodlum magicians into thin air.

We all met back there before midnight. All the *locos* were there. They were quiet. One of them, the one we call Azteca 'cause he's so dark, had a lead pipe in his hands. The field that we were in was totally still, and I could hear the traffic whizzing by on the freeway on the other side of the bridge. The moonlight bounced off Azteca's pipe like some kind of crazy magical glow, and I knew right then that it was gonna start. I didn't even see it. I just felt that cold lead crack against the back of my knees and my whole body gave out and I hit the ground. They beat me for a whole fifteen minutes. I took every second of it, everything they had to give me. After a while they were all kicking me so hard that I started to puke up blood. Then someone got on top of me—I don't even know who it was, but he straddled my hips while I was on the ground and just started boxing the shit out of my face. I felt my cheek tear and blood came spilling out of it. One of my eyes was swelling up. The air smelt heavy, like blood, puke, spit, and sweat. And then it stopped. One of the *locos* reached out his hand and helped me up. That was it. I was in.

The next day I went to Sammy's house. Sammy does the best tattoos in all of east Los Angeles. He learned in prison. Sammy is an artist.

I gave myself my first one, three dots on my hand, on the flesh between my thumb and my other finger, that soft part. I cut open the little holes with the sharp edge of a paper clip and filled them in with ink. When my mom saw them, she went crazy. "Do you know what you're getting yourself into, *mal creada*! Those three little dots are gonna get you killed!" My three green dots. *Mi Vida Loca.* "My Crazy Life," the original gangster motto that I wear proud and true. I'd write it on my body if I wanted to. Maybe that made me an evil girl, an evil creature like my mom said. I didn't care. All I knew was that the words made me feel branded, and I liked the way that felt.

Sammy was gonna ink my name across my stomach that day,

Payasa curving over me across my hips, cut into me in Old English. I was so excited that I got to Sammy's pad hella early, but he didn't care. He was ready for me. He was up cleaning his needles and getting the ink ready when I got there.

"Sit down, *Payasa.* I gotta take care of some shit and I'll be right back."

I sat on his dirty couch, staring up at a velvet painting of a big puma. I heard his voice, and it sounded like he was arguing with someone. He came back after a minute. He had to tell me something. At first I was pissed, but then when he explained, everything was cool. See, he wasn't gonna ink me—his sister was.

"What the fuck, Sammy!" I yelled at him. "I didn't come here to get inked by no girl. What the fuck is wrong with you?"

Sammy looked at me, "*Calmate, Payasa*—take it easy. You don't understand. Heartbreaker knows what she's doing. Serious, dude. My sister has got the soul of an artist, man."

Sammy sat down to explain everything. He told me about how when he was locked up in *la pinta,* he got a letter from Heartbreaker every week, just like clockwork, and that those letters were what kept him alive and hoping for the next week to come around. She'd send him these envelopes with mad drawings all over them and pages of poetry with walls of roses climbing around the words. He pinned the scraps of paper to the walls of his cell like some kind of inspirational wallpaper that wrenched his heart each time he stared at it for too long. There were *Virgenes* who looked down from the walls with eyes of redemption and bleeding *Corazones Sagrados* to make you cry and give you hope that maybe when our moms and *abuelitas* lit candles at church for us, there might be some greater thing out there that really was watching out for us. He quit fucking around while he was doing his time and decided to leave the gangster life behind him. He started going to the prison library and reading and working out. After a while all he did was study, lift weights, and practice his new hobby, tattooing. Most of the guys in the *pinta* have someone from their own *clicka* that does everyone's tattoos. But since he wasn't down for the life anymore, it was OK for him to work on anyone. Even the *puto* faggots from the Aryan Brotherhood got inked by Sammy. He perfected his art, and he knew that when he got out he would come home to his barrio and teach his little sister the art that could make her work live and breathe. He started her practicing on the skin of dead chickens. Their skin is best. All plucked and smooth, it's pale and tight. It doesn't jiggle around too much. When she was ready, Sammy let his sister work on his own arms.

He rolled up his sleeves to show me his biceps. I looked at his arms and couldn't believe what I saw. I couldn't believe that La Heartbreaker, the most beautiful *loca* in our barrio, was responsible for the ghetto art dancing across her brother's arms. His body featured drawings of *Jesus* with thorns piercing his head and blood pouring from them like you could taste it. Flowers surrounding the feet of *La Virgene,* and Christ's mother with a look on her face like she was so proud of all the beauty and pain created by her son. I reached out and traced the pictures with my finger, feeling the lines that were carved into his arms by the hands of his kid sister. When I looked up, Heartbreaker was standing in the doorway. When I saw her I knew I couldn't say no to Sammy's proposition.

La Heartbreaker was true to her name, like we all were. She was the finest *heine* in the barrio, the one all the homies wanted to get with and put a baby in. This girl had green eyes, big and glassy, like emerald obsidian or smoky glass. She had long brown Mexican hair that hadn't been cut since she was seven years old and looked red when it was in the L.A. sun. Long, lo-o-ong eyelashes. Fine-ass body. Tight, smooth skin stretched across her cheekbones. Pretty Latin freckles. Her body was long. Everything about her was long. And she had this voice. It was like the sound of crystal.

"Hey, *Payasa*. You don't mind that I'm gonna work on you, right?"

"No, no Heartbreaker, that's cool. Let's get on with it then."

She sat down with her brother watching over her, master and apprentice on dirty old chairs, and she showed him the stenciled letters that would be etched into me.

"Nice job, Heartbreaker."

She applied the letters to me with Speed Stick then peeled off the stencil slowly. She turned on the power to the needle and then she touched me.

"Take a deep breath, *Payasa*. Don't forget to breathe."

I did like she told me and breathed. I saw her hair fall around her face as she came at me with the needle. It pierced my skin, but she stood her ground, her hand firm and steady, unmoved by my rippling skin, the thin layer of fat that sits on my belly. I tried to do like she told me, keep breathing, but it was hard. I bit my raw lip and drew blood from it. She never stopped to comfort me, she was so into her work. I looked down and saw blood mingle with black ink. Every once in a while she'd turn and dip her needle for more paint and then get right back to work on my skin. I felt some of my skin rising up to form my name, burning and seared, torn into fancy scars. I loved it. It was a pain that I owned. I couldn't believe I was actually trusting La Heartbreaker with a tattoo as important as this one, but with each stroke she proved herself.

When she got to the last "A" in my name, my T-shirt that I had refused to take off was covered in blood and ink. She finished up and stared at her own work. She was just as in awe as I was.

"Heartbreaker," Sammy said, "I'm gonna take off. I gotta go meet Spooky at the park. You know how to show her how to take care of it, right?"

"Yeah, Sammy."

"OK, *pues. Cuidate, Payasa*. Watch your back. I'll see you later."

He left and we were alone. I lay back on the couch. My body had this rush that I'd never felt before, like I was high. There was just this rush, like when you get all fucked up on whippets or meth. I feel stupid saying it, but I felt so fucking happy, like I could do anything. It was like all the pain took me somewhere else. That tattoo took up so much of my body; it outlined my name, smooth and clean.

Heartbreaker got out a metal tube and squished some stuff all over her fingers. She pulled up my shirt and told me she was gonna rub it on me. It would keep me from getting infected. It felt cool when she rubbed it on me, and then she asked me if she could trace the lines of her work on my stomach.

"Sure." She followed each letter with her finger, tracing it and then jumping to the next one, over and over like she could hardly believe she'd done that to me. My tummy felt so tender. Then she looked me in the eye, and I knew something between us changed with that look. She kept her hand on my stomach, all lubed up, and slid it down to my belt buckle. At first I was scared, but when I saw the flash of green from her eyes, I knew it was OK. She worked her hand down my pants, through my boxers, and stroked my pubic hair. She squeezed me down there, getting that goo all over it. She rubbed it onto my thighs and got them all slick. They were hot and slippery. She started rubbing, slow, then faster. Her arm kept coming down on my stomach and it would burn with pain but it felt so good down there, I didn't want her to stop. She pulled her hand out real quick, and I was worried for a second that she was gonna stop. Then she flipped me over real fast and pulled my pants down. I had my legs apart and I was on the floor, kneeling with my head on the couch. She took one of her wet, slimy fingers and slipped it into my ass crack. She got it all wet and slippery like my stomach and started to play with my asshole. It felt so good. She played with the skin around the hole, teasing and pulling it, and then she slipped a finger inside and pumped it. I'd never had anything inside my asshole before. Then she put in another finger and then another. She had three fingers inside me, moving all crazy like she wanted to rip me open, and I was moving back and forth down there with her all crazy on my ass. I felt her middle finger jamming way up inside of me. I started to scream and breathe real hard, and she reached around and touched me in front. She rubbed on my thing up there, and it got hard like a dick. She was touching me on both ends, and I started to shake all crazy. I felt like I was losing control, and for a quick second I got scared again and thought of my cousin, the one who shook all the time, but then it was like I just ate her hand, right up inside me, and I was just an extension of her and her art and her beauty.

She took her hand out of me and bit me on the neck and collapsed against me. She kept rubbing my ass, dirty from the lube stuff and my shit and some blood. She kept biting me until my shoulders were marked from her teeth and they were like tattoos from her mouth.

She breathed real softly in my ear. I hadn't touched her once. She was the girl all the *locos* wanted.

She whispered in my ear, "How did you like it, *mijo,* eh li'l boy? How did you like your first time?" My first time.

Mrs. Sullivan Takes Off
Ilsa Jule

Blindy brought the wheeled carry-on bag to a dramatic halt at the bar. She collapsed the handle inside it and let out a loud protracted sigh meant to get attention. She sat right next to the young woman who was the only other patron in the airport lounge.

Blindy wasn't sure why, but today she needed to get a lot of attention in public. She had argued with the male flight attendant over the ice cubes he'd served with her complimentary can of ginger ale. She knew she was being preposterous when she told him, after inspecting the ice, that it wasn't cold enough. He rolled his eyes and said, "The ice is frozen. I believe that meets FAA regulations."

Blindy acted as if she hadn't heard him and said, "While this ice may be as cold as water gets when it assumes a solid state, ice can become much colder."

The more she frustrated the attendant and her fellow passengers, the more glee she derived from making a spectacle of herself. This was how bored she had become lately. Where she used to take pleasure in distancing herself from others, she now took pleasure in watching herself annoy them. She continued her informed diatribe: "Ice at the polar caps," she explained, "where the annual mean temperature is minus-eighteen degrees Fahrenheit, is obviously far colder than the ice I have been served." She looked to the two passengers seated beside her, noted their spirits sink, inhaled to signify that she was not quite done, and concluded her monologue by stating, "Glacial ice, while not only extremely cold, often turns a lovely hue of blue." She then exhaled.

The attendant seized the opportunity to interject and quipped,

"We ran out of both glacial and polar-cap ice on the last flight. You'll have to rough it like the rest of us." He then directed his attention to the woman who occupied the middle seat.

Instead of taking offense at the barb, Blindy regarded it as the small reward due for her inspired commentary on ice. In her head she began to quickly draft a letter of complaint to the airlines, wherein she would forego any mention of her remarks on glacial ice; rather, she would complain that her polite request for clean ice after she had been served dirty ice was met with a rude refusal.

She inspected the top of the can of ginger ale she had been handed and noted that except for a few small particles of dust, it looked clean. She opened it, and with a flourish she pushed the cup with the low-grade ice to the side, then drank straight from the can.

As the two passengers who sat next to her continued to exchange looks, she turned back to *People* magazine, a guilty pleasure reserved for in-flight reading, and pretended to read. In fact, she couldn't concentrate. Her mind wandered aimlessly. She was beginning to sense that her recent languor was indicative of something greater than boredom.

Now seated at the bar, Blindy realized that the young woman had noticed the bumping of the carry-on bag as it was brought to a stop but had not become agitated. Blindy felt unsatisfied by her nonreaction.

The bartender, a weary Irish man with a fifties-style haircut now gone completely white, took a last drag off his cigarette, stubbed it out, and walked toward Blindy.

"A champagne cocktail," she said as he came to a stop in front of her.

She'd never had a champagne cocktail. but she liked the name. It sounded annoying. Would she annoy the bartender with this request? He shrugged as if to say *Suit yourself* and began mixing the drink.

For a moment Blindy wondered if bartenders went home to their wives and smelled like a bar in the same way that a cook smells like a kitchen. Could a bartender smell of anything more than smoke, emptied ashtrays, and stale beer?

Blindy's thoughts turned to Sandy, the female chef she had dated for several years in San Francisco. Sandy often came home with the smell of long hours spent in an active kitchen, lingering on her hair and clothing. It had not been a pleasant smell. What was impressed upon Blindy's memory even more than the smell was the condition of Sandy's hands and forearms. They were chronicles of bumps into hot pans and nicks to the flesh from knives. According to Sandy, both dull and sharpened knives were hazards in their own ways. Sandy's arms and hands never quite healed; while bruises and burns faded, fresh ones appeared daily. Her skin was mottled by her vocation. Sandy didn't care about the branding of her flesh; she pleased herself and the eaters with a continuously evolving menu. Blindy also recalled that Sandy had been a bit of a grump.

After the breakup, Sandy went on to open a successful bistro in the wine country of Northern California, and Blindy made a habit over the years of flipping through food magazines in hopes of finding mention of her. Sometimes she was rewarded with small articles. Sandy appeared in the black-and-white photos that accompanied the stories, a little older and somewhat heavier, in the way one expects a middle-aged and successful chef to fill out. Blindy's past association with Sandy pleased her.

"I fucked you," she'd say softly to the photo in the magazine. "You fucked me. You fucked me and cooked for me. Why didn't it work out?"

Blindy turned her thoughts back to the woman seated beside her. The woman had flawless white skin, and her dark brown hair, pulled back, into a ponytail highlighted the soft, angular features of her face. A small forehead, high cheekbones, a thin narrow nose, a thin mouth, and a fine jaw and chin. Blindy felt she was appraising the woman as one might a purebred dog or horse.

This woman wasn't pretty, but she was very attractive. Her looks, a combination of conventional attributes, were imbued with a sense of the unknown as attractive, not scary.

The woman looked straight ahead at the bottles of alcohol that rested in rows along the mirrored wall. As the bartender placed a napkin and the champagne cocktail in front of Blindy, the woman turned to look. Blindy couldn't catch the woman's eye, which frustrated her. *Not until I have annoyed you will I feel satisfied,* she thought.

Blindy let out another protracted sigh and kicked her high heels off her feet onto the floor so that one of them rolled under the woman's chair. She massaged her feet through her knee-high stockings and groaned slightly. The woman finally turned. Blindy rubbed her toes, made eye contact, and said, "Bunions."

The woman formed her mouth into a meager smile, and Blindy ruled this response: not good enough. *You are bothered but not completely. You will not go home and complain of your dealings with me to a lover or friend. My work here is not done.*

Blindy picked up the shoe that was nearest to her with her toes and then said, "Excuse me," and nodded in the direction of the other shoe.

The woman leaned over, picked up the shoe, and handed it to her.

As the woman gave her the shoe, Blindy thrust the question "Where you coming from?" at her.

The woman hesitated in answering, but Blindy persisted, "Or is it going to?"

Blindy smiled a warm broad smile. Something about using honey versus vinegar to attract flashed through her mind. She felt herself pulling more of a spider-and-fly routine. *You will be caught by me,* thought Blindy.

"I like dick," the woman said icily and tossed her head so that the ponytail moved back and forth.

The corners of the smile shifted, and now Blindy's lips were drawn into a thin, even line. A surge of adrenaline coursed through her veins. In her mind she railed against the woman: *I haven't attended dyke marches, gay pride parades, Take Back the Night vigils, and volunteered at a rape crisis center to have you, Miss Prissy Straight Girl, throw your sexuality in my face.*

Blindy offered, "I have one in my bag," and nodded to the carry-on at her feet. "If you're not too busy, I'd be more than happy to show you how it's really done."

In fact, she did not have a dildo in her bag. She had stopped traveling with one after catching the questioning looks of the guard examining the X-ray of her luggage as it was scanned at the security checkpoint. Blindy left her dick at home unless she traveled with baggage to be checked.

She took a large drink from the cocktail and concluded that it was too sweet. Now she longed for a double bourbon, straight up, both for the taste and to reverse the impression that she was a sissy. Blindy would show this chick who was boss.

The woman snickered, turned toward Blindy, and stood up to leave. Blindy couldn't say whether she meant to block the woman from departing or not, but her leg moved behind the woman and, as she attempted to back out she met with Blindy's knee. Blindy smiled, placed her hand gently on the woman's arm, applied pressure, and said, "Why don't you take a seat?"

The woman would have had to make an awkward climb in the opposite direction to get out. She knew she was trapped, so she sat down again, her cheeks flushed slightly pink.

Blindy snapped her fingers to get the bartender's attention. He looked up from the newspaper or racing form he was reading. "Another round." Blindy waved her fingers over the two glasses.

The woman sat facing forward, her eyes shining with anger. Blindy looked at her in profile until the bartender placed fresh napkins and drinks in front of each woman.

Blindy took a sip of the cocktail. "Drink up," she said, and lifted her glass.

The woman turned and said, her voice cracking, "I know all about you. You're trying to recruit me."

Blindy smiled at this charge. She matched the woman's piercing gaze but said nothing.

"I'm married to a man," the woman said, and waved her left hand at Blindy.

Unlike a vampire who recoils at the specter of the cross, Blindy did not shy from the wedding band. Instead, she took the woman's hand and held it so that their palms met. The engagement ring, a large diamond in an attractive setting, was worn beside a wedding band that was tasteful in its simplicity.

Something had passed between them while their palms were in contact. Blindy let the woman's hand slip to the bar. "Platinum?" she asked.

The woman nodded.

"Drink up, sweetie. I am going to fuck you," Blindy boasted and took a long drink of champagne. The sugar in the drink was giving her a buzz. She had forgotten all about her boredom.

The woman looked at Blindy and smiled. "You seem awfully sure of yourself."

Blindy nodded and wondered if she really wanted to go through all the trouble of fucking this woman.

"What's your name, Miss I-Like-Dick?"

The woman took a sip of her drink, then stated matter-of-factly, "Mrs. John Sullivan."

Blindy leaned in close to the woman so that both of their faces seemed quite large and said, "Blindy," extending her hand.

The woman took Blindy's hand, and Blindy held it instead of shaking. Mrs. Sullivan shook her hand free of the grasp.

Blindy liked the feel of the smooth, warm, dry skin and the small bones in the fingers of Mrs. Sullivan's hand.

They looked at each other. Blindy noted that the woman had velvety blue eyes. Mrs. Sullivan broke her reverie with the question, "What makes an anonymous fuck between women any better than one between a man and a woman?"

Blindy was taken aback by this.

After a pause, in a playful tone she said, "I give up. What makes anonymous sex between women better than between a man and a woman?"

Blindy's urge to annoy was being assuaged. Blindy looked at Mrs. Sullivan's small breasts underneath the gray sweater she was wearing. She asked herself: *Have I been too well-behaved? Do I need an hour with this woman to change all that? Could hand-holding be enough? When can I declare a victory? Do I want war, or will a few battles appease me? Will a kiss? The feel of this woman's tongue in my mouth?*

As the list of questions in Blindy's head increased, Mrs. Sullivan interrupted her thoughts. "Pride," she stated.

Blindy flinched at this. Could Mrs. Sullivan be right?

Blindy looked at her fingers as she traced small circles in the condensation on her glass and replied, "Maybe."

"You want to crush my pride," stated Mrs. Sullivan, and Blindy saw tears well up in the woman's eyes.

"I don't want to crush your pride. I want to keep mine in one piece."

Mrs. Sullivan, in an angered tone, said loudly, "And what? Your rubber dick inside me, that keeps your pride intact?"

Blindy looked at the bartender. If he heard the question, he acted disinterested.

"Shhh. Don't get all excited," Blindy said. She felt a small headache coming on from the champagne. She snapped her fingers to get the bartender's attention. "A glass of ice water," she said.

When he placed it in front of her she asked him, "Don't you have some tunes? This place is a crypt."

"CD player's broke," he answered, and headed back to his newspaper.

The women sat in silence for a few minutes. The roar of jet engines broke in at intervals. Blindy wondered about Mrs. Sullivan. Were there tiny particles of Mr. Sullivan sprinkled about her? Something from a kiss, a caress, a fuck? Where was Mr. Sullivan? What kind of a fool was he? His wife was not the kind of woman to be left unattended in an airport bar.

Mrs. Sullivan looked at Blindy, and Blindy noticed an unmistakable "yes" being conveyed to her. Her heartbeat quickened and her mind flew into gear. They needed a plan, and they needed it within the next two minutes.

They heard a jumble of voices approach the lounge. Shortly a group of people, male and female, in matching uniforms entered the lounge. They were a flight crew. Someone yelled, "First round is on me." Then the bartender was addressed by his first name, Henry, and the somber mood of the lounge was disrupted by the commotion.

Blindy looked at Mrs. Sullivan and said, "Let's get out of here," and tucked a fifty-dollar bill under Mrs. Sullivan's glass. Blindy gently took the woman's elbow, releasing it once Mrs. Sullivan had taken a few steps toward the door. As they stood next to each other, Blindy noticed they were of equal height, but Mrs. Sullivan was slender with a boyish figure. Blindy was voluptuous. Mrs. Sullivan wore a short-sleeved charcoal-gray wool sweater, dark-gray slacks that zipped up the side, and black heels.

Blindy picked up Mrs. Sullivan's bag from the bar and, handing it to her, said, "You're traveling light. Did you lose your luggage?"

She didn't answer the question, and as they exited the lounge, Blindy noticed a dark mood come over Mrs. Sullivan. Blindy grew concerned. Her own mood was equally erratic. She still wanted to fuck this woman, she had said as much, and the boredom that she had tended to so carefully for so long was interrupted, but what to do about this situation?

As they left the terminal on the street level, the last light of day faded from the sky and Mrs. Sullivan's silence spoke of impending misfortune. Blindy wasn't sure she wanted to be let in on the details, but trained as she was in crisis intervention, she knew Mrs. Sullivan should not be left alone. When the Marriott shuttle bus pulled up, without thinking about it Blindy guided Mrs. Sullivan on board. Upon arriving at the hotel, Blindy led Mrs. Sullivan to a seat in the lobby and secured a room, with two double beds, for the night.

Once in the room, Blindy cracked open the bar. "Were you drinking gin or vodka?"

Mrs. Sullivan mumbled, "Vodka."

Blindy mixed a weak vodka tonic and opened a Heineken for herself.

She placed the drink on the table beside Mrs. Sullivan, then she began to undress, carefully removing her skirt and blouse. She sat at the edge of one of the beds in her bra and slip. As she rolled off the stockings she felt a little self-conscious in her underwear. She also felt, and she couldn't say why, happy. Here she was, sitting in a hotel room with a gorgeous and disturbed woman. Only hours before, she had been mulling the possibilities to quell the dullness of another Sunday night. She had come up with the thoroughly unoriginal: Clean the kitchen and rent a video.

"He left me," said Mrs. Sullivan.

"Did he?" asked Blindy.

Their eyes met. "Yes, he did."

Blindy thought, *You have beautiful fucking eyes,* then asked "When?" and took another sip of beer.

"Last year."

"Hmm," said Blindy, and wondered, *Is this just sinking in?*

"I'm coming from my sister's wedding."

"And?"

"And I haven't told anyone."

"And?"

"I feel awful about lying to everyone."

Blindy stood up and stretched. Her mood now switched tracks, and she thought, *What the fuck do I care if you've been left?* "Well, I'm going to take a nice, hot bath. Are you hungry? I want some room service."

Mrs. Sullivan continued to brood while Blindy walked to the phone and placed an order for a burger and a small salad.

Once in the tub, Blindy heard the sounds of the TV. As she relaxed in the bubble bath she heard a knock on the door and called out, "Will you sign for that?" Blindy heard the sound of the tray being placed on the table in the other room. She hoped that Mrs. Sullivan gave the guy a good tip. She couldn't stand meager tipping.

After a moment or two Mrs. Sullivan peered her head around the door and asked, "Enjoying yourself?"

"Quite," replied Blindy, swishing some of the bubbles.

"Good," replied Mrs. Sullivan, and then she hurled the plate with the burger on it at Blindy. Blindy raised her arms to protect herself. The plate rebounded off Blindy's forearm and landed with a crash on the floor. Blindy was unhurt and not shaken. She had once protected a woman at the shelter from an ax-wielding former boyfriend. It took a lot to get her worked up.

The burger had fallen onto the bath mat. Blindy fished the soggy bun out of the bubbles. She reached over, took a bite of the burger, decided it was still edible, and rested it on the edge of the tub.

The lettuce, tomato, and slice of onion lay on the floor.

Blindy stepped out of the bath and stood on the bath mat, in no hurry to dry herself. She watched as trails of bubbles slowly slid down her breasts and stomach. Then she rested her palms against the edge of the sink counter and examined her body in the wall mirror. The water dripped from her long, dark pubic hair onto the mat. A rare feeling of admiration filled her. For a second or two she didn't feel middle-aged. As of late she liked that she was older and wasn't even bothered by the slight bulge around her waist and the way flesh had gathered at her hips in recent years. Blindy stooped to pick up the pieces of the plate and marveled that it had been broken neatly in two. She placed the halves back together, producing the illusion that the plate was whole.

She dried herself off and wrapped a towel around her body. Her breasts swayed as she went into the main room in search of ketchup. At that moment she didn't care if she looked desirable or not.

Blindy swallowed hard as she entered the room. Mrs. Sullivan was lying on the bed naked, her white skin in stark contrast to the unattractive dark brown bedspread.

Blindy took a few bites of the burger and turned off the television as she passed it. She stood at the bedside and looked at Mrs. Sullivan lying rigidly on the bedcovers.

"Well, aren't you going to fuck me?" asked Mrs. Sullivan defiantly.

Blindy looked at Mrs. Sullivan's body and licked some grease off her fingers. Was this woman's body an ideal? Yes. She felt her hands begin to speak to her. *Touch her,* they said. *What are you waiting for?* they asked.

"You're not such a big tough dyke after all?" taunted Mrs. Sullivan.

"Who, me?" replied Blindy, and gestured to the curves of her body beneath the white towel. Her breasts sagged under their weight and age. "I never said I was a dyke."

Mrs. Sullivan's bone-white skin gleamed, and Blindy eyed the small breasts with large, dark nipples. Her eyes traveled past the detailed outline of her ribs, past her taut stomach, and rested on the pubic area. Mrs. Sullivan's lips were visible, as she shaved all the hair down there.

"You look taller when you're lying down," said Blindy, and Mrs. Sullivan laughed.

"How old are you?" asked Blindy.

"Twenty-seven. Why?"

Blindy picked up the edge of the bedspread and covered Mrs. Sullivan. She then seated herself and finished eating the burger.

"Why did you ask me how old I was?" the woman asked.

"Just curious."

Blindy had a strict no-fucking-anyone-under-the-age-of-thirty policy. Of course, she had come up with that policy when she had turned thirty. But that was eighteen long years ago. She wondered if twenty-seven-year-old women always had such nice bodies. It had been more than a year since her last lover, and while there were many reasons to fuck Mrs. Sullivan (namely, that she was completely hot and lying there naked, waiting), there seemed to be more reasons for not fucking her, none of which she cared to contemplate at this moment.

Blindy swallowed the last bite of the burger. She then grabbed a fresh beer and sat at the foot of the bed, where Mrs. Sullivan was wrapped up like a burrito. She pressed the cool glass of the bottle to her temple. The headache from the champagne had subsided. She placed her hand on top of Mrs. Sullivan's foot. She'd had a pedicure recently, and the nails were painted a dark blue. The skin on top of the foot was smooth like flour.

Blindy looked up from the small ankle and met Mrs. Sullivan's gaze. Her previous trepidation was replaced with a craving. The roles had switched. Blindy knew she would not be able to resist being wanted.

Blindy's hands, which had found their way under the fold of the cover, moved slowly up Mrs. Sullivan's smooth leg. When her hand reached the top of her thigh, her fingertips edged along the border of the fine stubble. Her fingers pleaded, *Do it, slide up inside her. Go on. Do it.*

She ignored their urgings and continued to move her hand up along the flat stomach. Blindy's towel had fallen open, and when her hand reached the woman's neck she pulled the cover back and pressed into Mrs. Sullivan, her arm resting under the woman's breasts.

Mrs. Sullivan rolled onto her side, pressing her coccyx into Blindy's pubic bone. Blindy thought, *The beast with two backs, indeed.*

"What now, Mrs. Sullivan?" Blindy's lips gently pressed to the nape of the woman's neck.

"Fuck me."

Blindy felt her clit swell and pressed the dense covering of her pubic hair into Mrs. Sullivan's ass. She pulled back and let her fingers, which required no historical knowledge or instruction, do what they longed to do.

She pressed her index and middle finger into Mrs. Sullivan's pussy, the heel of her palm pressed against her anus. With this, Mrs. Sullivan pressed herself deeper into Blindy's embrace. Mrs. Sullivan was either a quick study, or Blindy was one of several who'd attempted to recruit the elusive Mrs. Sullivan. A woman of no experience with other women never seizes fingers in this way and doesn't know which parts of herself to give to a woman.

With her fingers inside Mrs. Sullivan, Blindy felt the desire in both women increase tenfold, or maybe it was a hundred times. She knew this wasn't the time to work on a math problem, but it was clear that Mrs. Sullivan was a whole lot closer to giving in than Blindy had hoped for.

Blindy thought, *Did you get this wet for Mr. Sullivan?*

Mrs. Sullivan pressed against Blindy vigorously. The contractions against Blindy's fingers were strong.

"Your pussy is...buttery," said Blindy.

"I want your whole arm inside me," the woman implored.

Blindy laughed at this request. She pressed her remaining fingers inside Mrs. Sullivan's overwet pussy and noticed the more fingers she pushed inside Mrs. Sullivan, the bigger she got.

Blindy removed her fingers, and Mrs. Sullivan asked, "Where are you going?" "Nowhere," replied Blindy as she rolled Mrs. Sullivan onto her back. Blindy got on her hands and knees so that she was crouched over Mrs. Sullivan, and they looked into each other's faces for a minute or so.

Blindy pressed four fingers into Mrs. Sullivan and thought, *Perhaps my arm will fit inside you.* Slowly she curled her fingers around her thumb, and then with a decisive push her fist was inside. Mrs. Sullivan, who had been sucking on Blindy's forearm, gasped and then closed her jaws into the flesh. Blindy winced and Mrs. Sullivan bent her leg and Blindy rocked her clit against the small kneecap and came in a short, bright burst.

Blindy slowly uncurled and withdrew her fist, pleased she still had it. The air in the room felt cool on her hand up to the wrist. She wrapped her hand in the sheet.

"What was that?" Mrs. Sullivan asked after a moment.

"I don't know," replied Blindy, and thought, *Straight women can be such a chore.*

"Hmm," said Mrs. Sullivan.

Even though the rough texture of the bedspread was unpleasant against her skin, Blindy covered herself and Mrs. Sullivan with it. She lay there waiting for the horror of what had happened to make its way into her thoughts and feelings. The *Oh, my God! What have I done?* failed to materialize. She half enjoyed Mrs. Sullivan lying by her side. Blindy thought it felt nice, and perhaps it was nice.

As she lay there, her fingers twitched for more while the rest of her reposed happily in that doped-up way the body feels after sex.

Mrs. Sullivan spoke. "He said I didn't love him anymore."

Blindy pulled Mrs. Sullivan closer to her, thinking, *What's not to love?* and said, "That sounds like projection."

Mrs. Sullivan said nothing but tugged Blindy's arm, which held her fast.

In an effort to comfort her, Blindy said, "It's hard enough to know what's in one's own heart. Could he really know what was— or in this case, was not—contained in yours?"

"That's the thing of it: He was right," said Mrs. Sullivan, "Not that I had stopped loving him, but I was no longer *in love* with him."

"Was he still in love with you?" asked Blindy.

"Oh, I don't know. Maybe I don't care."

"Then why are you upset?"

"Because my sister is really in love with her husband and seeing the joy in her face made me sad. She was beaming, and I thought, *She can't be serious.* And I felt jealous because I don't have that."

Another straight woman swindled, Blindy thought, but said, "Maybe she isn't as happy as you think. Maybe she was grinning out of a state of nervous exhaustion."

All this patter about straight people was beginning to wear on Blindy's nerves.

"No! She meant it," cried Mrs. Sullivan defensively.

Blindy knew that discussing family could produce the most

heated interchanges between people who have known each other for decades, let alone a few hours. She loosened her grasp on Mrs. Sullivan and the woman rolled away a little.

Mrs. Sullivan pulled Blindy's arms back around her. "Oh, don't do that. Stay."

Blindy entwined her fingers in Mrs. Sullivan's and asked, "Do you have to get going soon?" hoping the answer would be yes.

"No. I'd be returning to an empty apartment. I hate how that feels."

"I kind of like that feeling," said Blindy.

"If it's what you want, then it's fine. I haven't gotten used to it. I was thinking of getting a pet. Something to warm the place up."

Blindy made no reply to this. The idea of pet maintenance got on her nerves. Cats were all hairballs and smelly litter boxes. Dogs were breathing on you all the time and needed to be walked.

They lapsed into silence. Her hands wandered over Mrs. Sullivan's thighs and stomach. She wondered what to do next. She felt a bout of mania coming on and remembered why she hated casual sex. It made her feel lonely. It was an emotional experience devoid of emotional attachment.

Blindy needed to get back to her apartment. She felt Mrs. Sullivan's breathing move into the easy rhythm of sleep. If Blindy were going to escape, now was her opportunity.

Blindy didn't owe Mrs. Sullivan a thing. She felt odd sneaking out, but she didn't want to say goodbye. She just wanted to get home and be comforted by her books. She wanted to lie on the rug that had once been her grandmother's and had been the only housewarming gift from her mother that Blindy liked when she moved into her first apartment. She hated the way the hotel room smelled. She knew if she stayed, the smell would be in her hair, stay on her skin, and give her bad dreams. She felt the panic of not being able to get out of the room fast enough.

Blindy edged her way off the bed, careful not to make a sound. She noted that she didn't have the energy to care about Mrs. Sullivan. She used to feel a sense of guilt after sex, but she used to have a sense of expectation. Tonight she felt neither. She couldn't find anything to latch on to in Mrs. Sullivan. With some women it's the way they say your name or the way they look at you or the way they walk. There has to be something.

With Mrs. Sullivan there was no edge and certainly no hook. She was a confused woman who didn't have the guts to inform her family that she was a divorcée. None of this was any of Blindy's business.

Blindy scooped her clothes off the unused bed and went to the bathroom. After she peed she didn't flush but remained sitting on the toilet. She pulled her weekly planner out of her purse, tore the last page out, and wrote, "Sex between two women who don't know each other can be distinguished from sex between a man and a woman who don't know each other…" Blindy couldn't answer the riddle. She wanted to say, "Because it's just better, damn it!" and in her opinion it was.

She crumpled the piece of paper and stuffed it into her purse. She put on her skirt and buttoned two of the buttons on the blouse. She balled up her knee-highs, panties, and bra and threw them in her bag, alongside the crumpled note.

She flicked off the bathroom light and tiptoed to the door. Mrs. Sullivan snored gently. She carefully picked up the carry-on, as one of the wheels had a tendency to squeak. Even if Mrs. Sullivan did wake up and call out to her, by the time she had enough clothing on to give chase, Blindy could be down the hall and out the door of the main lobby if she took the stairs. It was only two flights. She placed the bag outside the door, and then, fearing drama, carefully pulled it shut. It closed noiselessly.

As a precaution she used the stairs. She hoped the clerk who worked the night shift wouldn't notice that her calves were now bare. As she turned the corner where the sliding doors came into view, she saw a cab waiting for a fare. She hurried toward it. The cool night air kissed the bare skin of her legs and gave her goose bumps. Her nipples hardened, and as she slid onto the vinyl seat, she felt her anxiety begin to fade. She would be home in twenty minutes. She might be bored and alone, but at least she'd be alone.

Lock Bend Exodus
Julie Lieber

I suppose we done the old lady wrong by taking her teeth. Others might say we done more wrong in stealing all her cash. The way we see it, she had no more claim to the money than we had. At least that's what Angie says, though she won't talk about the teeth. I suspect that part of the caper leans on her conscience.

My grandmother's sister Ida raised me. My mother dropped me off at Aunt Ida's house when I was a baby and ran off with some good-time Charlie from up in Virginia. People at church always told me to pray on it and Mama might come back for me. She never did, but I never prayed for it either. As long as I minded Aunt Ida and went to church, we got along just fine.

Then I grew up. When I turned seventeen I got a bit restless and took to staying out late at night with young people who weren't from the church. Aunt Ida called them no-accounts. I had to sneak around a lot. Then last year, when I was nineteen, I got caught for shoplifting, and there wasn't any sneaking around that. Aunt Ida screamed and cried, said I'd better straighten up or she'd turn me out of the house for good. So I didn't have much choice about joining her Prison Ministry for Ladies.

Aunt Ida had been ministering at the Women's Prison in Lock Bend for as long as I could remember. She preached to small groups of inmates. She taught the illiterate how to read and gave away booklets about Jesus. Once a month she hosted a warden-approved gospel party in the prison mess hall. Aunt Ida sang gospel songs, and the warden provided refreshments. All the inmates were invited, and about half of them usually showed up.

My part was in helping with the gospel parties. A lot of inmates came to the parties because the warden let their families come too, and those poor lonely women wanted more than anything to see their kin. The families were so grateful, they testified and praised the Lord and gave generously when Aunt Ida passed around the offering basket.

That's how I met Angie. She turned up at a gospel party a few months ago. I noticed she was staring at me, but she never opened her mouth, not even to say amen. I thought maybe I had spilled something on my bosom, and then it dawned on me that she was taking notice of my shape, which I'm very satisfied with and which Aunt Ida has always warned me about, telling me I should cover myself to avoid wantonness with men.

She never said anything about women. I felt sorry for Angie at first, not having any family to visit with her for the gospel, so I sat next to her one evening to chat. It was partly the way she made me laugh, but more the way she looked at me, that made me warm to her. Pretty soon I was visiting her at the prison without Aunt Ida's knowing about it. I lied and told the guards it was for the ministry. Angie couldn't touch me through the prison windows when I visited her alone. She could only gaze at me and smile, and it was a wicked smile, with mischief in her eyes, like she had her hand under my skirt, and sometimes her smile and her eyes gave me the same feeling as if her hands were on me, and I felt hot.

Of course, by then I knew Angie had no interest in redemption. She just wanted to get out. It was at a gospel party, where we could talk without guards listening in, that she asked me to help her escape.

"I'm here to give hope to your soul," I said. "I'm no jailbreaker."

"Tracy," she said, "you're here to give me wet dreams, and you know it. You want me too. I can tell. So you just drop the angel act and do like I say."

We sat close so that our legs touched, and she leaned in and whispered in my ear and hid her hand behind my back and slid her fingers under the seat of my skirt. I felt her breath on my neck as she talked in my ear, and her voice fell in a whisper. "Are you gonna help me, Tracy?" Her lips brushed against my ear, and I glanced nervously around the mess hall. Everybody was singing praises as Aunt Ida preached. "Don't be scared, baby. Nobody's watching us. We're just chatting." She pinched my bottom over the fabric of my dress. "When you break me out I want you to show more skin. Clothes are like another kind of wall, and I want to take yours down, sugar."

I didn't dare breathe, for I knew if I did I would let go a moan. I parted my legs slightly so she could slide her hand closer to my crotch.

She shuddered, her lips still grazing my ear. "You're wet. I can feel it through your skirt. I can't even kiss you. I'll carry your scent back to my cell tonight and lay awake in misery for wanting you so much. If you don't get me out of here, I'll do something desperate, Tracy. You've got to help me."

My whole body broke out in sweat. "Anything," I mumbled.

"What?"

"I said I'll do anything."

She glanced over her shoulders to make sure nobody was watching. Her voice was low and steady. "I'm on a work crew near the south field. You don't where that is, so listen up." She gave clear directions on where to go and what to do, and made me repeat after her.

I said, "I don't have a car."

"How the hell do you visit here alone?"

"That's the ministry car. Ida's Cadillac. She thinks I take it for shopping."

"They'll recognize that," she said. She looked deep in thought.

"My cousin Vern has a truck," I said on a sudden thought. "I can take it."

She smiled. "Do it. Only don't let on like it was you. Make like it gets stolen. Even if it gets spotted, we can fix it so they don't trace it to him."

Now, there are those who would judge me for spiriting a jailed convict away in a truck stolen from my own cousin. No doubt those same people would question why we flipped the truck in a ravine and set it afire. Angie said Cousin Vern could justly claim it stolen and collect the insurance money in good conscience. Besides, she said, it was a piece of shit.

Nobody saw her leave the penal farm. She figured they never even missed her till head count. She was a trusty from a minimum-security wing on work detail. A prison break was as easy as a smoke break, she said. And that's when she took off: At the very instant a guard turned his back to light a cigarette, she bolted down a hill and hopped over a creek bank, rolling down stream to the south field, where I was waiting in the truck.

She jumped in and told me to floor it. I spun the wheels and kicked back gravel. She told me where to drive, and I stopped the truck when she said so, in an old mining yard with rocky ravines. She grabbed the change of clothes I'd brought her and told me to get out and help her tip the truck down a ravine.

After we set fire to it, I asked, "What are we gonna do now?"

She was looking at the fire and breathing heavy from her labors. She turned to me and smiled. She pulled her straight black ponytail out and threw the rubber band on the ground. She walked toward me as she unbuttoned her shirt, streaks of perspiration gleaming against her brown chest. I started to pick up her new clothes, but her eyes stopped me. They were narrow, black eyes like an Indian's, full of warmth and mystery. She stepped out of the orange-and-yellow glow of the fire below like an otherworldly spirit. She took my hand and led me into an oak grove behind the mining yard.

I fell into her embrace and lost all feeling for a few seconds, but her kiss electrified me. It was like all my nerve endings were exposed, and she had her hands on all of them. She held me tight by my buttocks and the small of my back, and then took her hand up under my skirt. "You bare-assed?" she asked, grinning.

"You said you didn't want no walls."

She lay me down on the moist, smooth carpet of moss and stroked the insides of my thighs. She pulled my legs apart, took her hand inside me, and covered my mouth with hers. It didn't hurt like I thought it might, but I was burning up inside and so wet she couldn't hurt me no matter how deeply she penetrated. I split my legs as far wide as I could and pushed her face into my bosom. All my senses rolled up to one spot laid bare between my legs, and I pitched a fit. She turned me over. I was shaking and breathing heavily into the moss. I heard her unzip her pants and pull them off, and then felt her hand slide back inside me. She pulled my bottom up and rubbed my hip between her legs. She pushed back and forth along a slick track of my hip until she let go a husky cry and unloosed a flood down my leg. I came right along with her, digging my fingernails in the moss and sticking my legs straight out, stiff as line-dried cotton.

She lay down next to me. She was smiling, a sweaty strand of black hair stuck to her lip. I got my breathing steady and asked, "What are we gonna do now?"

"I need to hide out," she said. "I figure I can stay with you."

"I live with Aunt Ida."

"The preacher lady?"

"I thought you knew that."

"Shit."

"It's a big old farmhouse. It might work."

She looked troubled. Then it dawned on me that I didn't just want to help her—I had to. I was an accomplice to escape, and for all I knew she was a killer, a drug dealer, a thief. I didn't know what and I didn't care. "She never looks in on me," I said.

"How's that?"

"Her knees and joints are bad with arthritis, and she can't climb steps. So I stay upstairs. She never knows what I'm up to."

A thick black cloud of smoke billowed up from the ravine. She raised up and said, "We best get out of here."

"How? We just burned up the truck."

"Of course we burned it. We can't be caught in a stolen truck. You ready to hike?" I lay there half naked wondering where my shoes had gone. She rubbed my belly and winked, telling me to sit up. She pulled my dress all the way off and looked at my naked body with something like love in her eyes. I thought she would never take her eyes off me, so lost was she in the sight of my flesh. There was a sudden boom, and she looked over my shoulder. "That fire's gonna attract attention. We best get out of here."

She put on the new clothes I had brought her while I got dressed and wiped my legs clean with her old prison shirt. Drenched in the embers of fire and sex, we walked about two miles out to the state highway and hitched a big old trailer rig. The fellow was real nice and said he was passing through to North Carolina, but he didn't mind dropping two pretty young ladies off at the county line, which was a ten-mile hike to Aunt Ida's.

A waxing moon hung in the sky above us, but it was dark as pitch under the shade of oak trees as we straggled up a hill to the house. Ida was in bed, so sneaking Angie upstairs wasn't a chore. We got to know each other pretty good once we got home, but not the way you're thinking, not at first. We lay in bed and stared at the shadows of willows sweeping across the ceiling as Angie explained how she ended up in prison.

Angie said there was a law against shooting in an occupied dwelling, but she got in trouble for what she called shooting in an occupied person. The law called it attempted murder. What happened was she caught her lover in bed with another woman.

"I snapped. I went for the shotgun and took care to aim for the right one."

"How come you shot the one you loved and let be the one you didn't even know?"

"She hadn't betrayed me." She let go a heavy sigh. "I figured there was somebody else to deal with her, or not to. It weren't my business."

The jury called it aggravated assault. She got five years, and after two years she came up for parole.

"They denied me. Well, I figured I'd learned my lesson whether they thought so or not. For weeks I pondered how I'd get out, without much in the way of a good idea. Then I heard about the gospel parties and how there was a mix of family and friends among the inmates. Figured I'd lay my hooks in somebody on the outside."

"So you laid your hooks in me," I said, but she just smiled in that way that made me want to please her.

She raised up on one arm and faced me in the moonlight. "Naw. It was the other way around," she said low and easy. She tugged at the hem of my nightshirt. "What are you doin' in that thing?"

"You've got one on too."

She sat up and pulled hers off. She had a strong build and a finer bosom than mine. I let her open my nightshirt as I lay still and watched her run her fingers along my skin, and she smiled at me sweetly, without any meanness in her eyes. She leaned over me and tenderly caressed my belly and my stiffening breasts. I turned over on my stomach, almost by instinct, for I knew she wanted to taste my whole body, and I wanted her to. She touched me all over with her hands and lips and tongue, like she was consuming my flesh and spirit all at once. I felt as if I were adrift on some warm south sea.

She whispered, "Sugar, you won't be getting much sleep for a while." She turned me over on my back and parted my legs. She kissed the inside of one thigh as she went down. She parted my lips with her tongue and bore inside, licking me inside and out. She swept her tongue along my clit, long and slow at first, then shorter and quicker as she zoned in on my spot. When she found it, I gasped and rose up on my elbows, wild-eyed. She winked at me and played with it, teasing me by moving away from it and descending inside again, then coming back and sliding all around it. I fell down on my back and writhed while she toyed with me, flicking her tongue closer, closer, until she touched down and drew a tide of rapture.

I brought a pillow to my face. Angie's breath and low groaning rose with the quickness of her tongue, and she gasped mightily when my little rivulet let loose upon her cheeks. I arched my back with the rising swell beneath her tongue, until a white-hot wave of ecstasy rolled over me and I screamed into my pillow like I was going mad.

"Hellfire!" she whispered. "What was that?"

"My muffled screams."

"Damn. You act like you was the one locked up."

"We best not do this in Aunt Ida's house again."

She shimmied up next to me and stroked my cheek. "Yeah, you'll need to keep me scarce around here. That'll be tricky."

It wasn't easy keeping Angie shy of Aunt Ida's notice, except at night. By the mornings, Aunt Ida went on errands and to Bible meetings, and witnessed at the nursing home. I rested after breakfast, though Angie waited till afternoon, when Aunt Ida got home. She whiled away the lonesome hours as best she could without calling attention to herself, but she grew restless.

After Aunt Ida went to bed at sundown, we sneaked outside and ran down to the old barn. It was risky running down there, but Angie said she needed the air. It hadn't been used in years, except for the hay Aunt Ida's farmhands stored in it. I made a little living spot in there for me and Angie. The first few hours of each evening were largely spent in the throes of passion, which seemed to grow with each passing night, though always a bit one-sided.

I felt like there wasn't a square-inch patch of my flesh that Angie hadn't tasted and touched several times over. She made love to me with such fever she wouldn't stop until I came dry. When she came she wanted me facing down away from her, but one night I turned over and pulled her down and thrust my hand between her legs. Her eyes went ablaze. She pushed me off her and looked at me so fiercely I thought she might slap me. My heart pained and my eyes welled up. I started crying.

"What the hell are you crying for?" she demanded. "Stop it, now."

"That was hateful," I said, trying in vain to stifle my sobs.

"I don't want you to fuck me. Besides, you don't know what you're doing."

That broke my heart. I lay down in the hay and felt more sorrowful than I had in all my life. "You're cold-blooded," I said. "I just want to make love to you."

She put her hand on my shoulder. "Aw, baby. I just ain't ready."

"How come?"

"I don't know. I feel like if a girl does that too soon in a romance, I'm liable to lose respect for her."

"Well, you did it right off the bat. I still respect you."

"That's different. Anyway, stop talking about it. It's hard to explain."

"You just don't want to feel beholden to me. That's what it is."

She turned me over and gave me that dark look of hers. "Beholden? You broke me out, so I've been beholden from the get-go. I said I don't want to explain it. Don't act like you know me, little girl. You don't know shit." She kissed my forehead and lay down. "Hey, you still want to go to Canada with me?"

I would have gone anywhere with her. "Yes."

As we lay on old quilts by the light of oil lanterns, it crossed my mind that she didn't love me, and I grew ever sadder. And the more she talked, the deeper my heart sank. All Angie wanted to talk about was plotting her run to Canada. She would need a car and then a switch down the road to keep the law off her trail. And getting all the way to Canada would cost. She needed money.

I knew where she could find money, though I didn't tell her at first. Aunt Ida hid the money from her gospel parties under the floorboards beneath her bed. She never banked the money and never paid taxes on it. She always said "Render unto Caesar that which can be traced" and called the money God's own mercy.

I figured there was no sense in it going to waste. I thought Angie could use some of it to get to Canada, and I waited till Aunt Ida went out on her morning errands one day and sneaked into her bedroom. I moved her bed to one side and lifted the loose pine slabs in the floor. The money was kept in freezer bags, and I grabbed a fat one. I stuffed it in my pocketbook, fitted the pine slabs back in place, and pushed the bed to its centered spot above the secret trove of cash.

That night, after Aunt Ida was in bed, I washed the dishes, which was my regular chore, and warmed up the leftovers from what I had cooked. This was my habit now that Angie was living upstairs. She liked having a cold beer with her supper, and that was tricky, since Aunt Ida forbade alcohol. I crept down to the basement where I kept a cooler full of ice and snatched a beer for the tray. When I had the plate and the beer ready, I took the freezer bag out of my pocketbook and put it on the tray. Then I took Angie her supper.

I put the tray by her bedside, and she squinted as her eyes became adjusted to the dull lamplight. Then her eyes grew wider, and she got a hungrier look staring at the forest-green and ivory tones of those treasury notes.

"How much is there?" she asked.

"A thousand in twenties and some small bills."

"You counted?"

"I sure did."

She tore open the bag and flipped through the bills. "Where'd you get it?"

"Out from under the floor of her bedroom, under the bed."

She looked agape at me. "How much has she got?"

"I don't know," I shrugged. "She's been collecting it for years. I'd say thousands."

"You never counted it?"

"What for?"

"What the hell do you mean, what for? All that cash rotting away under her bed and you ain't even curious?"

"It ain't my money."

"It ain't hers either. This is that money she ripped off from all them poor families at the gospel parties, huh?"

I explained that it was charitable contributions for Aunt Ida's ministry, and Angie had no call to accuse her of thieving. Angie laughed real sarcastically and called Aunt Ida a hypocrite.

She leaned in close to me and said, "Tracy, honey, there's two kinds of people. Them that dwells in the flesh of this world, which is me, and them that dwells in the kingdom of heaven, which is not you, and is not the old lady." That's what she called Aunt Ida, the old lady.

"Which one am I?"

"You're in the flesh, sugar, whether you like to admit it or not."

"And Aunt Ida?"

She grinned savagely. "You have to lay claim to the life of sinner or saint, Tracy. That old lady has herself a cush spot somewheres in between, which is the life of a hypocrite. If there's a Judgment Day, I'll have a better shot at eternal life than that deceiving old bag."

"Don't call my Aunt Ida names."

"I call it like I see it, sugar." She dropped the bag next to her on the bed. "Come here, curly head." She pulled me down on the bed and fixed her black eyes on mine. "You're the prettiest thing I've ever seen. Go on down to the barn and light the lamp. I'll be down directly." She rose up over me and seized me with a deep kiss. "Mmm. I want to turn you inside out. Go on before I do something here that'll wake the old lady up for sure."

Of course, all the while I was keeping Angie company, preparing her meals and plotting her escape, there was a hefty bounty on her head. It was all over the news in nine counties. It troubled Aunt Ida that one of the unsaved souls of the women's prison had broken loose of the just hand of the law, but she only spoke of it once or twice. After a week or so I had grown used to my secret life with a fugitive right under the nose of my dear old aunt. The only worry troubling my head was the thought of Angie taking off to Canada and leaving me behind. I hadn't the shade of concern that Aunt Ida would find us out, as careful as I was. But the old lady turned out to be anything but a fool.

"There's trouble afoot!" Aunt Ida hollered one morning as I fired up the gas for her fried eggs and bacon.

My spine went all rubbery, and devil's fingers tickled the base of my neck. I turned to see her glaring at me through the doorway of the kitchen. "What's the matter, Aunt Ida?" I asked feebly.

She cast me a suspicious eye. "There's been money taken from up under my bed."

I was flush from head to toe, but I played like it was on account of concern over her predicament. "Whatever happened?"

"Don't act to me like you don't know! You've thieved before, though I never thought I'd see the day you'd thieve from your own flesh and blood!"

I couldn't believe she noticed one missing freezer bag among dozens stashed away. I played dumb, still and serene as a lamb. "What are you talking about?"

Her brow sagged. "You've done pilfered God's money from my mercy bank, is what I'm talking about."

By now I was upright and indignant. "I never bother your room and you know it! What's got into you?"

Her features took on a softer look, like she was confused, and she shook her head. She began to cry, and I almost pitied her. "Maybe my mind's going," she sobbed. "But I know how much I had in there. Oh, Lord, I do hope I haven't gone to misplacing things! I do take it out on occasion for a count. Maybe I left a bag in some odd place. Oh, Tracy, child, promise me you didn't take it."

I rushed to her side and took her in my arms, and I comforted her as best I could, telling her not to worry about losing her mind, which was her greatest fear. I felt tempted to tell her she needn't worry, that she was sharp as a tack and had me plum figured out. But I couldn't. For as strong as my feeling was for absolving the agony of Aunt Ida, my desire to please the fugitive lurking upstairs was even greater. Loyalty to the old lady was treachery to Angie, and I had already staked my claim.

Angie says you can't know a person by what they say or how they think. You only really know a person by their gut reactions, when there isn't time to sort things out by word or thought. She knew what she was going to do the minute I told her about Aunt Ida's missing cash.

"I'm leaving tomorrow and that's that," she told me as we lay on the bush-hogged field below the barn. She sat up, leaning into her arms outstretched behind her. "What about you?"

I looked up at the near perfect orb of the moon in a clear autumn sky and recalled the night almost two weeks before, when we had trudged exhausted under its waxing glow to home. The promise of its fullness gave me the idea that we were blessed in some way, that I was meant to leave with Angie when the time came. I said, "I want to go where you go, if you'll have me."

She had her back to me, like she was letting me know the choice was mine. She said, "I'll need your help."

"What do you want me to do?"

"I want you to make the old lady scarce tomorrow. All day long, until suppertime. Can you figure out a way to do that?"

"Yeah."

"At sundown, we'll leave."

"What are you gonna do?"

"Never you mind. Just keep her away, like I said."

It dawned on me that she meant to rob that money. "Don't take all of it," I whispered. "That'd be mean."

She didn't look at me. "It ain't hers."

"It ain't yours either."

"I've learned my lesson," she said, almost prayerfully, like she was talking to that moon. "Now it's time that old lady learned hers. I got the idea when I was inside, after one or two of those gospel parties, that she had a deal with the warden. Ain't no doubt in my mind now. Some old preacher lady running through the pockets of wretches, and a happy warden standing by for his cut. Why the hell else would he let her run a scam like that right under his nose? I've toured the house, Tracy, while she was away and you was resting upstairs. I got real familiar with where y'all keep things about. Especially under the floorboards. You never counted that pile of cash. Well, sugar, it's nigh on thirty grand. Fifty-odd freezer bags packed with donations. After the warden's kickbacks." She snorted. "To hell with them, Tracy. To everlasting hell with them."

She turned and leaned over me. "You still want to go with me?"

"Yes, Angie. I don't care where you end up. I'd follow you clear to jail."

Her dark features looked soft in the scant light. "Let's sleep out here tonight."

"It's getting cold."

"We've got quilts and sleeping bags."

She made us a bed under the moon, and I laid her down to rest. We were warm and naked on top of old sleeping bags laden with quilts. I climbed on top of her and felt snug between her flesh and the weight of the covers.

I felt her legs part underneath mine. "I want you, little doll." She held my hand and moved it between her legs. "Touch me." She gave me a sly look and stroked my hair.

She was warm and wet to my touch. I kissed her desperately, but I was nervous about doing much else, and my ignorance embarrassed me. "I love you, Angie."

She nudged me after a little while and said, "Sugar, just do whatever comes over you. Whatever fuels your need. Shoot. I could come at the sight of you and not much else." I rested my head on her breasts and moved my hand back and forth between her legs. She drew her legs farther apart and gave a sigh. "That's good, baby. No, no. Don't put it in. I'm not so crazy about that. I want you to kiss it."

"You mean your vagina?"

"Pussy, honey. This ain't the doctor's office," she giggled.

Not knowing what I was doing, I surprised myself that it came rather natural to me. I lay down between her legs and felt aflame inside my own skin as I took her into my mouth. I swept about the folds of her tender flesh with my tongue, not trying to imitate how she made love to me but according to my own whim. I parted her lips and found her clit, as firm and full as a huckleberry. I was rapt in her wetness, spellbound by her sex. I heard her breath grow heavy and her voice give out a low moan, and by its pitch I could tell she was smiling. She told me how good I made her feel. Then all of a sudden she stopped me and grasped me by the hair of my head.

I looked up at her. "What?" I asked fretfully. She had barely begun to show signs of pleasure, and now she was staring at me with that old fire in her eyes.

"Come on up here."

I felt uneasy, for her look was stern, and she held fast to my hair, though it didn't hurt. She pulled me up to her and cupped my face firmly in her hands. Her grip was strong, and her breath was heavy.

"Don't be mad," I said. "A girl can't learn everything all at once."

"I can't let you go on till you make me a promise."

I nodded.

"You won't let me down tomorrow."

"No way."

"You'll stay with me to the end. Never leave me, not even after we've made it."

"I'll never leave you."

"I love you, Tracy, and I will love you till the death of one of us." It sounded almost like a threat. Whichever way I looked at it, my fate was sealed.

The next day I cooked a real fine breakfast for Aunt Ida. Biscuits with gravy and sausage and fluffy scrambled eggs and boiled apples. She acted solemn, though, like it didn't even please her a little bit. She stared at me while she poked at her food, and I got a bad feeling she knew something. Like I said, she was no fool.

"Why are you going to the home with me all of a sudden?" she asked.

"I want to minister to the sick," I said.

She dropped her fork and leaned back in her chair. "Is that a fact? That's a might Christian of you, Tracy, child!"

I noticed she wasn't altogether convinced of what she was saying, so I kept my mouth shut with bated breath.

She scooted back and pushed herself to her feet. She disappeared into the hallway, and I heard her walk into her bedroom. Then she came barreling back to the kitchen—shuffling along as quickly as her arthritic legs would carry her—and she burst through the swinging door shaking an empty beer bottle at me. She was a little woman with a little voice, but she could be fearsome. "How long have you been spiriting the devil's poison in my house?" she hollered in a high pitch that chilled me.

It wasn't deceit but curiosity that made me ask, "Where did you get that?"

She clutched that bottle like it she was wringing a neck. "I went looking for my money, like I do every day since I lost it—or you stole it, you foul little sinner—but I'd looked everywhere I could think of except the trash cans up yonder. Don't act like you don't know it! I found half a dozen of these empty bottles. You've been a-drinkin', and I told you back when you ran afoul of the law that I'd not put up with vice in this household."

She pitched the bottle into the wastebasket and said calmly, "I'll not be toting you to no ministry of the sick today, child. You get your things packed, and then we'll spend the morning in prayer before I take you to the shelter for wayward women."

I was shaking from head to toe, though not from fear of a shelter. I feared what Angie would do now, for I knew she was listening. I climbed the stairs to pack my things in accordance with Aunt Ida's wishes and, as fate had it, my own plans for later that day.

Angie was waiting. "I've already packed our stuff," she hissed, her eyes black conniving slits. "I got all your little vanity items and whatnots." She handed me my suitcase. "Go on downstairs and do what I say." Then she told me what to do.

I walked slowly down the steps and looked for Aunt Ida. I spotted her through the doorway to the kitchen. "Aunt Ida? Is that you in the kitchen?" I asked loudly.

" 'Course it's me!" she hollered. "Now come in here and sit down to pray."

I had one task ahead of me after the prayer, before Angie took over. I always drove Aunt Ida when we traveled together, on account of her stiff hands, so it was my habit to ask for the key, which I did. She picked slowly through her pocketbook for the key and handed it to me. "This will be the last time you drive me, unless you fall to the floor and beg for forgiveness."

I felt weak. I took a deep breath and said as loud as I could without shouting, "Let's go, Aunt Ida!"

"Child, I ain't deaf! What's got into you?"

Angie had the stealth of a cat. She came up fast behind Aunt Ida from the shadow of the hallway and wrestled the old lady's arms behind the chair.

"Lord God!" Aunt Ida screamed. "Who's that?"

"Be still, Sister Ida," Angie said low. "Tracy tells me you got a strong heart." She stayed behind Aunt Ida so as not to show her face.

"Go easy on her," I said. "Don't break her arms. Remember the arthritis."

"What?" Aunt Ida gasped. She was hyperventilating. "Tracy! Child! You know this woman?" She looked dreadfully afraid.

Angie was gentle under the circumstances. She held Aunt Ida's arms back and directed me to tie each one separate to the arms of her chair with leather straps she had found in the barn. I did as I was told and whispered to Aunt Ida not to worry, that we didn't mean to hurt her.

Then she got her fire back. "You evil varmint!" she hollered, looking at me with dagger eyes. "You fiendish harlot!"

Angie had told me not to talk to her, no matter what she said. It was hard to ignore her calling me a harlot and a demon. Still, I worried about Aunt Ida. I told Angie, "Her arthritis is bad. She won't be able to free herself without help. She'll die up here alone."

Angie scowled at the back of Aunt Ida's head but more in the way you'd scowl at a flat tire or a busted water main. "How else are we gonna keep her down?"

"She can't put up much of a chase. And you've already cut the phone line."

All the while, Aunt Ida was screaming and crying in rage. "You foul devil! You ungrateful whore! I'll not have you in my house after this!"

"Get me a rag," Angie said. "She's fraying my nerves."

I handed her a dishcloth off the counter. She held the old lady's head tight and whispered in her ear, "OK, Sister Ida. Spit 'em out." She meant the dentures, and that gave me an idea.

Aunt Ida hollered, "Let go of my head, Satan. Stay thee behind me!"

"I said spit 'em out," Angie repeated, gritting her teeth. "I'm liable to snap your neck, the way you keep on."

Aunt Ida froze up, and her eyes welled with tears. She slowly worked her teeth loose and gently spit them into my hand. She sure gave me a spiteful look, though.

"She can't talk at all without her teeth in," I said while Angie stuffed the rag in Ida's mouth.

"Get me that duct tape you keep in your tool drawer yonder."

I got the tape and handed it to her, but I appealed to Angie as she taped over the cloth. "So if we undo the straps and let her loose, she ain't got no way to call for help, not for a while. No phone, bad knees and joints. Even when she reaches somebody, she won't be able to talk. Nobody understands a word she says when she don't have her teeth in. And she can't write a word with her hands the way they are. Well, she can, but it takes forever."

Angie took off her belt and wrapped it around Aunt Ida's chest and buckled it tight in back of the chair. "Watch her," she said, and ran into Aunt Ida's bedroom.

Aunt Ida's eyes bulged as the realization came to her what Angie was in there doing. She tried to shout, but the cloth and tape stifled her, and she began to cough and choke against her rage. She struggled against her binds with such fury as I wondered that God hadn't miraculously cured her of arthritis. "Hurry!" I shouted, careful not to call Angie by name.

"Let's go," she said at last as she breezed into the kitchen. "Get the car started."

So that's why we took her teeth. Not out of meanness like everybody on the news has been making out. We weren't evil, just desperate. We took pity on the old lady and left her untied, though she seemed wore out by the time we had packed her Cadillac with our belongings and her money. I daresay it was hours before she made her way to a neighbor's house, and by the time she made any sense, I'd surmise we had already ditched the Cadillac and picked up that Honda we found in a Wal-Mart parking lot. I doubt anybody knew Angie had a thing to do with it before we crossed the state line into Kentucky and caught a bus to Chicago. They know now, though. We saw it in a national newspaper this morning. That's why we're lighting out of here today, Canada-bound. Angie says that's where we'll find some peace, and I guess I believe her.

Cop Out

Rosalind Christine Lloyd

Troi was into picking up women at straight clubs. Tonight her destination was Butter, a hip-hop club in TriBeCa.

An ex-marine and former college hoop all-star, Troi was now a New York City police detective; her preoccupation with combat and competition defined a quiet but powerfully aggressive demeanor. She kept her five-foot-ten, 160-pound body buffed to masculine perfection with rigorous daily workouts that included pumping iron with the muscle queens at a gay gym in Chelsea where she matched their workout regiment to achieve similar macho results. Every inch of her was solid, sinuous, rippling muscle.

Her skin was a deep brown like dark fudge, rich and even in tone like a sinfully delicious chocolate cake. When she laughed, a mouth full of perfectly spaced teeth framed by thin silky lips accentuated a smile that ignited the light in her unusually light brown eyes. Her hands were massive, designed to palm basketballs, handle heavy artillery, and apprehend "suspects."

Tonight Troi opted for a pair of soft brown leather pants and a suede camel-color shirt. She had an eye for fashion when choosing loose-fitting clothes that enabled her to neutralize any semblance of femininity. Her breasts were almost always held hostage, bound tightly around her upper torso, released only when necessary. She selected one of her larger dildos, named Shaft, along with her new leather travel harness. Shaft was handmade, designed precisely to her specifications to include, among other things, a skin tone to match her complexion. The startling replica even came equipped with a fake foreskin membrane that made it feel that much more authentic. It had set her back quite a bit, but she quickly discovered it was worth every cent and more. She finished her outfit with her favorite Kenneth Cole square-toe boots (men's, of course), splashed on Versace cologne for men, and dared to accessorize with a fat ruby in her left ear and a matching pinky ring.

When passing, in order to throw people off her trail, she'd flash her police badge while cruising clubs, which also provided some bonuses: She avoided being carded and was admitted at no charge. This particular evening, it was obvious that Butter was rigorously implementing its ID policy—throngs of underage kids were hanging out behind the ropes trying to get in.

Hip-hop clubs were perfect venues for Troi's obsession, since they were dark and crowded enough for her to move around freely without inciting suspicion. The carnival feeling of these social gatherings reminded Troi of her freaknik college days. Most of the men were typical in their bad-ass attitudes, adhering to the negative stereotypes of male posturing and taking the pessimistic connotations of the music way too seriously. This all worked to Troi's advantage as she offered an alternative: Her meticulous, classy, cash-money look attracted attention from the ladies every time. The only problem she ever encountered was undercover bisexual switch-hitter boys who correctly picked up on her gaydar—but incorrectly as well, assuming she was a gay man. Troi found these occasions amusing and quite off-putting. Using the rest rooms, any rest room, was strictly out of the question.

Scanning the club, she easily found her mark: a tall redbone with two long French braids that went down her back, tickling a fat, juicy ass squeezed into a cheap, tight, Lycra hoochie dress. The slinky fabric stretched and strained against milk-fed curves of breeder hips. Her calves, sprung from svelte golden thighs, were incredibly sculpted in a pair of chic platform ankle boots that had a sci-fi look as the entire boot, including the heel, was encased in stretched black leather. Long and wispy eyelashes, like the fringe on a gypsy's shawl, draped huge eyes. Wearing too much jewelry, she was wrapped in "bling bling." Her nails were long, decorated in startling designs and funky neon colors that could be best described as outrageous; but her tits, piled into a push-up bra, were voluptuously for real. Ms. Thing was ghetto fabulous in all its original, bona fide glory.

Troi watched as the girl stood at the bar as if waiting for a bus. At least three men asked Braids to dance. She declined all of their offers. Braids was waiting for Mr. Right. She was waiting for Troi.

Troi sent her a glass of champagne with a shot of Hennessy poured on top (thug's gold) and waited for the young lady's reaction. Initially, Braids hesitated with suspicion, refusing the cocktail. But when the bartender pointed at Troi, she stared for a moment with those eyes, accessing her admirer before smiling seductively, mouthing "Thank you" with her luscious burgundy-coated lips. She then proceeded to sip from her glass as if digesting something very precious. Troi would not allow the woman much time to think before she turned up the charm.

Their eyes remained locked while Troi slowly walked to the end of the bar like a pimp strolling along a catwalk. Troi couldn't read anything from those eyes. Instead she relied on her feminine intuition, feeling adrenaline surge through her. It was the same feeling she got before making the winning layup or the feeling she had during a stakeout, or the feeling of victory while in enemy territory. Flexing her muscles, she walked right up to Braids, feeling an aura of heat emitting from the girl's body that startled her for a moment. As if reading Troi's mind, Braids took another sip of champagne. Taking a deep breath, Troi leaned in toward the woman, telling herself not to inhale her whole.

"I can see you appreciate the finer things in life," Troi whispered in her ear, sniffing her neck for a trace of her scent. She approved of the light French perfume.

"That's original. I like your idea of an introduction, sending over champagne and everything. What's your name? Mr. Got-All-the-Right-Moves?" Those eyes turned into magnets, drawing Troi in.

"I'm Troi, and what do they call you? Ms. Got-All-the-Right-Moves?"

"If you're nasty."

"Oh, I'm plenty nasty."

"I bet you are. My name is Staci." She sipped from her glass again, her eyes lowering, her comfort level improving.

The dance floor was a virtual free-for-all. No respect was given, and every liberty was taken with the feminine gender. The brothers practically mauled the girls alive, and the girls *appeared* to enjoy the attention, but whether this was really the case was another matter altogether. This kind of behavior played in Troi's favor as she gently removed the glass from Staci's hands before leading her onto the crowded dance floor.

It was so hot in the club it seemed everyone was simulating sex. Staci wrapped her arms around Troi's neck, rubbing herself against Troi's thigh like a puppy in heat. Something was on this girl's mind. Troi was enamored by the overture and didn't waste any time stroking Staci's back provocatively before grabbing her ass, positioning Staci so that she was gyrating on the head of Troi's dildo.

"You a big boy, Troi. You can hurt a girl," she purred in Troi's ear.

When Staci stuck her hot, wet tongue into that same ear, Troi wanted to sink her cock right in what she imagined would be Staci's juicy, hot pussy, but she settled for plunging her fingers through Staci's lacy thongs, in between her meaty lips.

Staci felt so good riding Troi's dong and fingers, her soft breasts crushed against Troi's bound, puckered nipples. Troi felt Staci's muscles clench in the palm of her hands. Staci found Troi's lips with her own, forcing them into a kiss so provocative it made Troi's head spin. Sucking tongues and lips like sucking on the world's best-tasting treat, each of them settled into some serious dry-humping, riding the crest of the maniacal vibrations of their quivering horniness. Before Troi realized it, the front of Staci's dress was hiked up against her hips and Staci began stroking Shaft through Troi's leather pants: a great big no-no.

Troi reached behind her belt, retrieved her handcuffs, and placed them on Staci.

"Am I under arrest, officer?" Staci was unfazed.

"Yeah, I'm taking you into custody." Troi made only a small spectacle leading Staci out of the club in handcuffs. Security and other patrons looked on as Troi flashed the badge attached to her belt. Staci loved every minute of the crude public display.

Troi's truck was strategically parked on a secluded side street. Listening to the sounds of their heels clicking against the slick cobblestone street, Troi continued to guide her handcuffed "assailant." Her eyes were locked on Staci from behind, while Staci enhanced the view by shifting her ever ripening ass while she walked, her calves casting a spell over Troi's mind. They stopped once they reached Troi's jet-black Toyota Pathfinder.

"I like your big, black truck," Staci whispered over her shoulder.

"I like you," Troi whispered back, gently pressing Staci up against the hood of the truck, the girl's hips and thighs shivering alongside the cold fiberglass frame.

Staci giggled nervously, spreading her legs apart obediently. Troi pushed herself against the lean girl, built like a gazelle, tall and graceful with limbs so delicate and fine they seemed breakable. If only Troi could feel those long, thin hands wrapped around her

Shaft, it would be a sensual nirvana. If only Troi could feel those burgundy lips wrapped tightly around her Shaft, Troi's strong hips pumping like a piston, she knew she could fall in love. Instead she would have to settle for the ass, which she exposed to the cool November air. Super-tight, lacy tiger-print thongs encased two fleshy mounds of delight.

"The cool air couldn't cool this ass off." Troi was kneeling now, her eyes layering the vision that stood before her.

"But I bet you can." Staci's tiny voice grew up in a second, morphed into a mature growl.

Troi sank her teeth gently into the flesh of Staci's right cheek, pretending to gnaw while allowing her hand to reach into Staci's bush, which was now moist, her pussy feeling like a hot piece of fruit left out in the sun too long, mushy and sticky, oozing sweet nectar along her fingertips. Staci wiggled around, her breathing getting heavier as she whispered, "That's it, baby. Come on. I'm ready for you. You'd better take this pussy now!"

If this girl said anything else to Troi, she knew it was entirely possible that she could come right there, just by the sound of Staci's voice and the scent of this girl sticky on her fingers and thick in the air. Troi reluctantly refrained from any more finger and oral play. Safe sex between two women was so unnatural to her, but she couldn't have sex any other way with any woman—straight, gay, or otherwise.

Standing back up, she reached for a condom from her back pocket, ripping the packet open with her teeth.

"What you got for me, Big Daddy?" Staci was writhing now, the handcuffs both restricting and exciting her. As Troi readied herself for the ceremony, steadying them both by shoving a leathered thigh along the slick backside of this hot, young thing, Staci began to moan, as if she'd seen one too many instructional porn videos.

Young, "straight" girls especially loved Troi's handcuffs.

Anything considered freaky and kinky was cool. But the handcuffs served a much more important purpose. Troi slid the rubber along the sheath of Shaft, lubricating the tip with a little of her own saliva before ramming into Staci's young, hot pussy with a sharp thrust of her hips. Staci went flailing against the hood of the truck while Troi skillfully guided herself deep into Staci's life. They moved together, Troi going in deeper after every thrust while Staci gyrated against every push, ensuring an easy, slippery fit full of friction. Her hips swayed and bounced, pushed and pulled, bumped and grinded to some mad truncated rhythm in her head and in Troi's pelvis. Troi could have pumped inside Staci until the break of dawn, but after the third multiple orgasm racked Troi's body with dizzying episodes of heart-stopping mini seizures, sweat popping from what felt like everywhere, she had to disengage herself from the girl who resigned herself to Troi in total submission. Troi had to ignore the girl's desperate pleas for more (they always wanted more)—a precautionary measure, as she could never give too much away.

The drive to Staci's home in Brooklyn was quiet. These were awkward moments for Troi because nothing would ever come from these encounters. This was just how she liked it, how she planned things. There was always the mystery of whether any of these women knew the real deal. That was part of the allure. Sometimes in the heat of passion, Troi could testify that it didn't really matter, because she knew she had skills, amazing skills. She drove the girls insane with her shit.

With Staci, she had half a mind to put the handcuffs back on her, because Staci was all over her.

"I can't believe you're still hard!" she kept squealing whenever Troi couldn't keep her out of her lap.

Actually, Troi had half a mind to bend her over the backseat and slip her another heavy dose of Shaft, but Staci was way too into it.

In front of Staci's brownstone, Troi wrote down her phone number.

"Can I get yours?" she inquired.

"No. That isn't a good idea," Troi replied, deliberately not looking at her. It was all part of the routine.

"Why not?"

"It's not important. Maybe I'll see you again at Butter."

"Damn, it's like that?"

"Girl, if you only knew, you could never handle it."

"Don't be so sure," Staci smirked, crumpling up her phone number and tossing it into Troi's lap before climbing out of the truck. Troi followed those long sculpted legs up the brownstone stair with her own pretty, seductive, huntress eyes before pulling off in her beautiful black truck into the cool November night.

Rest Stop
Dawn Milton

When I wake up it feels like I haven't slept at all. I blink against the desert sunshine, squint at the road. My eyes already burn from last night's fighting and the too early exit this morning. God, this is going to be a long drive.

Joey looks tired too, but she confronts the road with her typical steady gaze. She sucks at the straw of her Coke, and as she slides the cup back in the plastic holder, I admire her hands again. Next to her expressive sky-blue eyes, I love Jo's hands most of all. Small, strong, and honest, deeply lined and capable, they're the most unself-conscious part of her, the only part that seems to stay unguarded.

The bony shoulders of treeless mountains loom over the highway on the left side of the car. I wonder how anything but scorpions can survive heat like this. Outside my window, nothing but miles of dust and brush. Las Vegas is still almost two hours away. With barely any cash between us after the long weekend, there's no way the haul home to Colorado is going to be as much fun as the trip out to California.

"Did you sleep?" Jo glances over at me.

"Not much. I tried. How are you doing?"

"Tired," she says, her voice flat. "Last sign said eighty-five miles."

"Jesus."

I take a sip from the Coke. It's two hours old and watery. I try to think of something to talk about, but Jo seems cranky enough already. Maybe she's still sore about the wedding. I'm still surprised she felt neglected. I was so proud to have her with me at Josh's wedding; I loved introducing her to everyone. It was the first time I'd had an available girlfriend to be with in the presence of practically everyone connected to my family. With her there I didn't have to feel shadowed by the collective affirmation of my straight brother. But on the way back she told me she'd felt a little left out anyway, and instead of just listening, I got surprised and defensive and, of course, we had to fight about it in my parents' kitchen after too much cabernet. So the night ended unsettled, and we left early in the morning to make it back to Denver for work. The smog had hung heavy over L.A. on the way out, stagnant as the feeling between us.

The rented gray Elantra coasts quietly over a long hill. As we rise over the other side, I catch a glimpse of something twinkling far ahead.

Apparently it's not a mirage. "What the hell is that?" Joey wonders aloud. "That can't be the outskirts of Vegas, can it?"

"I doubt it. Not if it's supposed to be eighty miles out still."

But it looks something like Vegas. It's hard to tell with the July sunshine rendering everything, even rocks, into a hot, shimmery puddle. Still, there seem to be lights and buildings and some sort of glimmering bridge that stretches all the way across the highway. Jo speeds up to eighty-five to catch a better look.

The closer we get, the weirder it is: some kind of mini Las Vegas smack in the middle of nowhere, with hotels clumped on either side of the highway. The whole thing's knit together by a tramway that arches across the four-lane road, carrying passengers from casinos and outlet stores on one side to more gambling and restaurants on the other. Snaking in and out of one of the hotels is a huge yellow roller coaster called The Tumbleweed.

Jo slows down as we near the exit and looks at me with her wide baby-blue eyes. I know what that look means.

"Do you want to check it out?" I offer, smiling a little. "Maybe we can stay here and just start early in the morning."

"God, yes," Jo exhales. "I gotta get out of this car."

The vehicles in the parking lot glisten like hard candy on the verge of melting. The asphalt's so hot it warms our flip-flops as we slap across the lot to the entrance of a sprawling gambling complex on the mountain side of the highway. From a giant sign above us, a grizzly looking neon cowboy lassoes us into Whiskey Pete's Hotel & Casino.

Inside, the air's smoky cool and ringing with slot machine bells. Glazed patrons yank at the handles, glance blankly at their spinning apples and grapes and dollar signs. The reservation desk is camouflaged between mirrored pillars and busy gold-and-maroon carpeted walls. The fifty-something gal behind the counter is pleasant as can be.

"What can I do for you ladies today?" She smiles behind her rose-frosted glasses.

"How much does a room cost?" Jo asks.

"Well, let me see what I can do... We have a little special going on. Let me check if I can get you ladies an upgrade. We just might have one. You look like you've been on the road awhile."

"You got that right," Jo snickers. She loves to banter with strangers.

"Well, how's about a queen suite for thirty-five dollars? Y'all just staying one night?"

"Hold on—thirty-five dollars for the *room*?" Jo asks. We look at each other, almost laughing at the deal. We thought sixty-five for a room at the Holiday Inn on the Strip on the way out was a good price. "Can we use the pool too?"

" 'Course you can. You just go right through these doors at the end of the counter, down the hallway a tad, and out another set of doors and you're there. You ladies think you're gonna stay? It's a real nice pool."

"Most definitely. God, who knew there were places like this in the middle of the desert," Jo muses, laying her hand across mine on the counter. Rosy Glasses smiles like she knows.

"Well, we call this Little Las Vegas. And you know, we get some pretty big acts at the concert hall out here. Willie Nelson, Clint Black, and, what's her name…Pat Benatar, and the like. Y'all should come back sometime, when you've got a few days to spend, and go over to the stores on the other side. Just wait a sec while I run your card. Now, we also have a great steak house right over there, if you girls like steak."

Joey is brightening. She's a gourmet chef trying to start her own restaurant, but she loves heartland steak houses for their great cuts of beef. And she digs hotels, even if they're cheap and random like this one. I wander a few yards over to a slot machine and slip a quarter in. Three cherries and five bucks. "Hey, Jo," I smirk as she signs the credit card slip. "Check it out. I just won breakfast."

Our "upgraded queen suite," a generic room at one end of the L-shaped six-story building, smells vaguely stale. But the view across the desert (and over the parking lot) is gorgeous. It's four in the afternoon, and the dust kicks up a hazy gold light. The sky's a perfect purple-blue. If I press my forehead against the hot window, I can see the patio of the pool down below.

Cheap reprints of circus clown faces hang over the slightly bowed bed. Creepy. I pluck them off the wall and toss them on the faux oak desk. Jo sprawls herself on the bed and rubs her belly.

"You wanna check out that steak house later?"

"Yeah," I say, "we have to check this whole place out." I straddle over her, bouncing her around on the bed, then snuggle into her neck. She smells salty and warm. We giggle at the gaudy decor.

"Let's go down to the pool!" she yelps, jumping up, and digs around for her bathing suit.

The pool is like an LSD-induced dream. Shaped like a figure eight, it's flanked at the deep end by a rust-brown cement "mountain" nearly two stories high, with a plastic blue water slide curling out of a "cavern" in the center. Every few seconds a shrieking child shoots out across the water on her butt. A handful of parents and teenagers bob around on plastic floats. The patio is lined with lounge chairs, several of which are occupied by pasty, haggard-looking truckers in undershirts snoozing beneath their caps.

We spread out our towels on a couple of lounge chairs, jump in the cool water, and swim straight for the slide. I watch Jo's strong shoulders disappear down the slippery tunnel as she lets out a long howl. I climb up, sit down, and the next thing I know I'm plummeting into the water, practically landing on her head. We're cracking up, choking on chlorine.

Several spins down the cavern later, we collapse on our chairs and let the water evaporate off us in the still-searing heat. The light, however, is slowly mellowing. The tips of our fingers touch as we're lying there, and Jo suggests a nap. I'm suddenly very glad we did this.

I never know what I'm going to get with Joey.

She seems like she's about to pass out from exhaustion in the elevator, but as soon as we're back in the room she peels off her bathing suit and pushes me onto the bed, pressing my mouth open with her tongue. Her full breasts and soft but muscular belly are cool against my skin, her nipples are erect, and I'm wet in a second. It's all I can do to get my bottoms off and the scratchy comforter yanked away from us before her fingers are pushing into me. I arch back and submit, welcoming the intensity of her energy, the conviction in her touch. We're rolling around like ferrets on the bed until she fixes me across her horizontally so she can slip her fingers back and forth inside me, holding the rest of my body in place with her other arm. She fucks me hard and deep while she watches my face. I press into her hand, and every part of me is focused on that sexy, sexy part of her. I come in gushing spasms of relief.

A few panting breaths and I disengage from her and, sliding chest-to-chest against her, I kiss and lick her lips, teasing her with my tongue. We're both salivating; our spit tastes sweet. My heart pounds at the sound of her panting. I flip her onto her stomach and press my left palm between her shoulder blades. She's breathing hard and her legs drift open, asking for me. I know what she wants, but I give it to her slowly, first opening her wider, then getting her on her knees. She's swollen, presenting. I lean my head in and slide my tongue slowly, starting at the tip of her clit and running to the edge of her ass, pausing long enough to breathe hot air against her slippery pussy. I can taste hints of pool, sweat, heat. I lap at her, but lightly. What she wants is my fingers inside her, and after some gentle teasing, I oblige.

I'm always amazed at her slickness and the way the walls of her vagina tighten against my fingers. This time she clearly wants deep penetration. My rhythm is steady and firm, rolling like whitecaps in a windy ocean. She opens and opens, clenches and groans. I'm full of tenderness for her—how she is revealed in the softness of her skin, the warmth inside her, her concentrated press for pleasure. My hand is covered with her, and with my other hand I stroke her back and ass. She lifts up into me farther, heaving and sighing, and then she comes in wave after wave, her wetness gushing out over my wrist.

Once she gets going she can stay in it for a long time. She rolls onto her back and asks me for more. I'm still inside her, but now I can put my lips against her warm, swollen mound of Venus. I stay soft and gentle on her—she's tender after coming—but gradually tug at her clitoris from the base so that I'm slipping all of it in and out of my mouth like a summer cherry. In and out over her, never losing contact, my face becomes damp with her wetness, her light, sweet scent. She moans and opens her legs wider, laces her fingers through my hair and pulls gently. I'm hugely wet and she's trying to thrust harder, but I have control. I coax her to the edge as slowly as I can, sucking deeply now and watching the pleasure in her face as she clenches her hips and presses farther into my mouth and against my hand and then, finally, explodes again and again with new moans of relief.

We fall asleep sprawled across each other under the sheets.

When I wake up it feels like I've been gone for hours. For a second I wonder if it's morning. It's dark and Joey is in the bathroom. The air is still and quiet. I feel more well-rested and alert than I have in days.

The bathroom door opens. Jo walks into the dark room and turns on the light on the nightstand beside me. I suck in my breath and prop myself up on my elbows. She's wearing her black rayon mini-dress—I've never seen her wear it—and makeup to beat the band. She's smiling like the proverbial canary-eating cat.

"Oh, my God, Jo. What are you doing?" Jo isn't the type to wear a lot of makeup. The most she'll do is a little mascara on her blond lashes, and lipstick when she's going out. But right now she looks like a full-blown Mall Girl, complete with blue eye shadow, rouge and dark lipstick, and fluffed-up hair. She flips up her dress for a split second to show me she's not wearing underwear (she never does). She has transformed her Jodie Foster tomboy look into a sassy feminine alter ego, but she's still cute as hell standing there grinning at me.

"Get up," she commands. "Take a shower. We're going out on the town, dressed up like ladies."

"Town?" I say, hauling my ass out of bed, "Are we in a 'town'?"

"Whatever. We're going out there. We're going out for a night at good ol' Whiskey Pete's!"

"All right, girlie. Watch out then. Here I go."

I emerge from the bathroom in my black platform sandals, black miniskirt, and this tiny, flowered Ann Taylor sleeveless, button-up top I'd brought to California in case we went out after being at the beach. Fluffing up my curly hair isn't much of a problem given how much of it there is, and I've helped myself to generous portions of the makeup Jo left on the counter. (Where did she get that stuff anyway?)

She lets out a long whistle as I make my appearance. She's cross-legged on the bed, with the TV on. "*Now* we're talkin'."

"You ready, darlin'?" I say, winking like a stripper.

"I got my credit card in my little black backpack," she grins, and we both laugh because she's talking about the bag with the broken zipper she's been carrying around for the last year.

"Let's go then." I slip my arm in hers and we're out the door.

Downstairs in the casino, Whiskey Pete's looks like it's had a caffeine infusion while we were asleep. People have obviously gone back for their naps, changed into new sets of polyester, and bought fresh packs of Winstons and Virginia Slims. It's hard to locate a face that's our age or younger. I get the impression that middle-aged, middle-class couples have been brought in by the busload. The women make clicking noises against the slot machines with their gaudy jewelry as they play, their husbands fixed at their own stations nearby. Periodically someone hits a jackpot, and coins clank into the trough to be scooped up by bloated hands that don't seem remotely relieved to be winning. To me, gambling parlors have a sickening sticky energy like being stuck in the funhouse at the fairgrounds, but Joey is a warm, sweet thing at my side and we feel devious and foreign, giggly in our disguises.

Of course, the first thing we want to do is ride the tram that arches over the highway, carrying people back and forth. While we're waiting for it to come gliding over the lighted tracks, we give each other personas. Jo is Carmen. I'm Sheila.

Carmen starts telling stories.

"Sheila, remember that time we met those guys at the Egyptian?"

"Oh, God, Carmen, why you gotta bring that up now?"

"Ah, come on, Sheila. You know we had a good time. Those guys were fun. And you were with, what was his name? Claude? You two went skinny-dipping until security found you, as I recall."

"Oh, Jesus. Yeah, Claude. More like 'Clod.' And being dragged out naked by that guard, remember that? But what about you and that dark-haired guy? You coulda made a flying carpet out of the hair on that guy's chest."

We're camping it up, talking loud. An entire family waits on the platform with us; a group of seniors next to them. Carmen smiles at everybody. They avoid eye contact.

"Well, we're gonna get ourselves some good stuff tonight, if you know what I mean," she goes on. Who knew my girlfriend was an actress? She's loving it.

"Definitely. Where there's a will, there's a way."

The tram arrives and the doors open. The passengers spilling out are as generic and robotic-looking as the guests we're leaving at Whiskey Pete's. We step on and keep bantering as we slide out over the highway. A steady stream of cars and eighteen-wheelers passes in the dark below. Jo reaches so far up on the steadying pole that her dress rides almost high enough to reveal her nakedness. She keeps a straight face, but I'm cracking up.

We exit into another large gambling parlor. This one has an

underwater motif: blue-and-gold carpet, mermaids and conch shells on the wallpaper, and tiny twinkling lights everywhere. I'm arm in arm with "Carmen," who struts like she knows where she's heading. Truckers, uncles, and husbands eyeball us idly as we pass, and I'm sure they think we're hookers.

Farther inside, the parlor opens into a cavernous circus arena where glamorous acrobats (more mermaids and mermen) swing on trapezes over safety netting adorned with spongy seahorses and starfish. The performers dance and tumble earnestly to loud flute music, but the clumps of spectators on the balconies seem unfazed at best. This is, indeed, a very strange Vegas.

Jo keeps us moving past the circus area, through a casino called the Treasure Chest and up a gleaming escalator beneath a monstrous chandelier.

"Carmen, you sure you know where you're going?" I call behind her.

"Trust me, girly girl. I know this place like the back of my hand," and oddly, it seems like she does. There's an intermittent rumbling overhead, and I'm wondering if somehow they tucked a giant wave pool into this unending complex of casinos, shops, and restaurants. Carmen leads me straight to the entrance to ride the Tumbleweed roller coaster. This is the only place I've seen a crowd under thirty.

"Oh, no you don't!" I protest, feeling butterflies in my stomach. Even from across the highway I could tell this was a huge roller coaster, steep as hell and probably way too fast. My stomach's growling anyway from not having eaten since lunch.

"C'mon, Sheila," she says loud enough for the people in line to hear. "You know we've done this a million times. Don't tell me you suddenly got cold feet, girl?" And she buys two tickets from a scraggly senior in a ticket booth.

"Jo-e-e-ey…" I try to whine in her ear, but Carmen won't relinquish my girlfriend.

"Nope. Can't get out of this one, sister," she smiles.

So we stand in line, and luckily, it's not too long, or I'd surely bolt. We're sandwiched between sweatshirt-and-denim-wearing tourists and Latino couples dressed up in shiny outfits, the men in Wranglers, their girlfriends in Lycra and gold chains. It's an odd party, and suddenly I'm craving bourbon. I clench Jo's arm when it's our turn to climb into the train. She's grinning at me as we pull down the safety bars, and I'm convinced I'm going to vomit. I put my hand on her smooth thigh and slide it up under her dress as we start climbing the terrifying first ascent. I squeeze my eyes shut but realize halfway up the hill that we're outside now in the ninety-something desert heat.

The Tumbleweed is a roller coaster I will not forget. It carries me, heart pounding, high over the sparkling buildings and glowing swimming pools. The highway below is a distant candy cane of red-and-white lines, and beyond all of it, the desert is engulfed in a velvety blackness. Jo whoops and hollers beside me, and with my breath caught in my throat, we suddenly plunge, twist, climb, hurtle—in and out of a building, looping in the heat, tearing up and down giant hills. At one point I look over and Jo's dress is whipping up around her waist and her laughing face makes no sound I can hear and she is beautiful and naked and open. Our hands are squeezed tightly together, and I want her beside me always.

When the train finally brakes back into the hotel, our faces are fixed in the laughing position by the shocking heat. It feels like God held a giant blow-dryer up to our mouths, and I have to lick my lips to get them back to normal. Jo is out and halfway down the escalator before I catch up with her. "OK, that's all I really wanted. You wanna go back to Whiskey Pete's for some steak?" she asks.

We ride the train back, windblown and rosy-cheeked. We stay

Carmen and Sheila, making up stories about Las Vegas parties and drugs and sports cars, entertaining ourselves mostly but occasionally catching the attention of a passenger.

Back at Pete's we head straight for the steak house and are nearly turned away by a stuffy maître d' who tells us that, because I'm wearing a "tank top," we don't meet the restaurant's dress code, though the place doesn't look more than a cut above Sizzler. Jo gets in his face a little, offended at the innuendo, and apparently not wanting to risk a conflict, he appeases us: "Seeing that it's a Sunday and we don't have our typical crowd…" It's not a bad wine list, though, so we order a nice pinot noir, steak, and potatoes. Jo's eyes twinkle at me across the table. We talk about the things we're going to do when we return: her restaurant plans, my teaching, trips we'd like to take this winter. The meal is tasty and simple. After, our feet flirt under the table.

"Let's gamble a little," I suggest when we exit the restaurant. "I've still got twenty bucks."

At the slots, we split the twenty. Jo takes her ten dollars and goes off looking for cigarettes. She figures if she's going to smoke (which she rarely does), this is the place to do it.

I change my money into quarters and sit in front of a machine. Three quarters in and I win ten more bucks. Jo comes back over, and I stay until the streak runs out. I win twenty-five dollars, then lose twenty. We decide to quit while we're ahead.

"I'm getting tired," she says. "Let's go back to the room."

We're on the elevator with a very tall, handsome older black man and his petite Asian wife. "How y'all doing?" he asks.

"Pretty well," Jo answers. "Are you folks having a nice evening?"

"We sure are," he says. "This is our anniversary."

"Well, happy anniversary, then! Hope you enjoy yourselves."

We all get off the elevator and the anniversary couple heads down the hall to the left. Our room is to the right. We're kind of bleary now, stopping to gaze at the sentimental portraits of old-time Western barroom characters on the walls. There's a lady with piled-up curls in a Victorian dress, with one gartered leg resting on a beer barrel, and down the hall, a skinny old drunk in a torn hat and dungarees. We name them "Luellen" and "Clyde" and so forth, as we make our way to the door of our room which, as we get closer, we realize we accidentally left open a crack. For a second I panic, but, pushing it open, I can't help laughing. Two matching red suitcases sit neatly opened on their stands. This is not our room.

"Jo…"

"What?" Jo says behind me. "Is our stuff still there?"

"This isn't our room. What floor did we get off on?"

Now we look at the number on the door. We're on the sixth floor. Our room is directly below. But it's my turn now. I grab her wrist as she's turning back toward the elevator.

"Not so fast, sweetheart."

"What are you doing?" She looks at me with her wide baby-blue eyes.

"Get in here," I say, pulling her into the room and locking the door in one motion.

She protests.

"Shh," I say, and with my arms around her waist, I back us straight into the closet, pushing two men's shirts and a silky dress to one side. "Don't move."

I slide the doors closed and it's pitch-black. She wants to wriggle free, but I have both arms around her now, and besides, she's softening. We're both sweating and nervous in the stuffy darkness, but my palms are sliding up the sides of her hips and around her thighs fast, and she's shaking a little and holding me by the shoulders. We're kissing hard, and I move her so her back is up against the wall. I press her there with one hand and move the other down between her legs, where she's quickly becoming hot and damp. I keep my mouth on hers while I rub my fingers against her in circles, sometimes spanking her gently, sometimes teasing the wet opening of her pussy. She brings her resistance down slowly, and I take her, bit by bit, teasing and fucking, caressing her full breasts, kissing her mouth and neck the whole time quietly in the dark, until she begs and heaves and shudders her orgasm in my ear.

I wipe my hand on one of the men's shirts on the way out.

The next morning I awake to light peeking dimly between the heavy curtains. It's six A.M.—time to get on the road. My lover is curled tight against me, sleeping.

"Honey," I whisper, "it's time to get up."

We stretch noisily, massage sleepy eyes open, stuff suitcases closed, hang pictures back on the walls. We are two rested girl-friends trundling down a fluorescent hallway on our way home. In the lobby, the same smoke-scented gamblers concentrate on their slots as we glide out of Whiskey Pete's into the already simmering desert morning. Joey smiles at me, squinting into the sunshine.

"Thanks for stopping," she says. "I needed that."

The car feels cool and new. We swing into a drive-through on the way out and grab a cheap, salty breakfast. Joey leans over and kisses my neck as I pull onto the highway. The flat horizon grins at us as we leave California behind.

Private Lessons
Lesléa Newman

> *Woman*
> *the round sound*
> *in my mouth of you*
> *resounds like clouds*
> *around the moon...*

She was my teacher. I knew being at the hot tubs with her
would be considered inappropriate at best, but I didn't care, and
obviously, neither did she. She taught at a nontraditional East
Coast college like Goddard or Bennington, though it was neither
of those, and I was a nontraditional student, older, though hardly
wiser than the others in my class. Yet despite this, we were doing
something that couldn't be more traditional: We were embarking
on a student-teacher affair.

I had never been with a woman before, and she knew this. I
suppose it was something she decided to teach me about, much the
same as she was teaching me how to write poetry. She already had
a lover, a blond, buxom woman twice our age (she was only four
years older than me), also a teacher at the college, over in the art
department. She was away that semester, in Italy on sabbatical.
And while the cat's away...

Her name was Cat. Catherine to the public, as that was the
name she published under, but Cat to everyone else, including me.
And she *was* catlike, with those gold-green eyes, that skullcap of
black hair, those long limbs, that muscular, sinewy back. Her body
was the most amazing thing I'd ever seen as it wavered in the tub

under the water, shimmering like the lilies in a Monet painting. She had taught me the power of comparison, of using *like* or *as* to describe something by way of simile, the irony that anything could be seen more clearly when presented as something other than itself.

I thought this over as I sat fully clothed on a wooden bench off to one side, my eyes fixed upon Cat. She was naked, relaxed, her body submerged, her head leaning back, her arms outstretched along the tub's rim, her dangling hands making wet, splashy sounds as she lifted them in and out of the water and let cool, jeweled drops drip from her fingertips. We'd been lucky enough to get the one tub that was up on the roof; there was nothing above us but a mile-high sky full of a thousand glittering stars and a glowing, full-to-bursting moon. Cat loved the moon, had insisted we wait until it was full so that everything would be perfect. Now she raised her face to it as if she were tanning. Cat's most famous work, her signature piece that had garnered all those awards, was a series of twenty-eight poems, each describing a different phase of the moon.

> *Praised be the moon*
> *as she rises tonight*
> *a round white pearl*
> *in the velvet earlobe*
> *of the world...*

The moment was pure magic; Cat, the moon, an owl hooting nearby, the cool night air brushing my cheek. If she would have said something, anything—"Come on in, the water's fine," for example—the spell would have been broken. She knew this, of course. Hadn't she told us in class over and over that what *wasn't* said in a poem was just as important as what was? Hadn't she told us the week that she taught haiku to pay attention to the white space on the page—there was even a Japanese word for it, *yohaku*—and to the emptiness surrounding the poem, the distance between each line? Everything became crystal clear that night as I watched her, as she allowed me to watch her, taking as much time and space as I needed to absorb her chiseled beauty with my eyes.

I knew she wanted me to join her in the water, but I was hesitant, and this surprised me. Wasn't this the moment I'd been waiting for, the moment we'd been building toward all semester? The poets whose work Cat had suggested I read—Adrienne Rich, Audre Lorde, Marilyn Hacker, Chrystos—were all women I had never heard of, women who obviously took other women as lovers. I had wondered if she'd suggested the same poems to other students, and I burned at the thought. I wanted to be special to her. Her favorite. Her pet. And tonight, at long last, I knew I was.

> *The moon, half full*
> *And I half-drunk*
> *At the sight of you*
> *Shimmering beneath it…*

Finally, I started to undress. But first I moved to where she could see me, as I knew she wanted me to. I'd often caught her staring at me in class, her eyes lingering just a second too long at my nipples, which she could clearly make out underneath my sweaters—soft, low-cut cashmere pullovers I began to wear for her torment and her pleasure. I knew I was driving her crazy; she could barely keep her mind on the day's lesson, and this pleased me enormously as I sat in the front row and watched her watching me, my breasts beckoning to her as I sat straight and still in my chair. Her clothes were loose, billowy; it was impossible to know what her body looked like beneath those windy skirts and dresses, which, after a while, became as torturous to me as I hoped my tight, bright sweaters were to her.

She smiled now, leaning her head back against the tub's edge, as if she were about to enjoy a show. I began by loosening my auburn hair from its woven braid and removing my tortoiseshell glasses. Everything became softer, fuzzier; everything lost its edge. Somehow that made it all easier. Cat grew blurry, watery, less definite, less sure. I hadn't expected to be so shy, yet it made sense. Wasn't I about to cross the line, enter new terrain, embark upon an exciting yet terrifying adventure from which I could never return? I didn't remember feeling like this the first time I'd made love to a boy. I was seventeen and eager to get on with it, get it over with, as I was the only one of my friends who had yet to complete the task. I thought I'd feel differently afterward and be a brand-new person, a woman instead of a teenager or a girl. But I'd felt nothing. Unlike now, when I was shivering, even though I was fully clothed, my heart racing, my face flushed, my palms sweaty, and Cat still halfway across the room.

I stepped out of my flats, removed my socks, stared at my feet, thought about Cat's. Her feet were the one part of her body I knew well, for she wore sandals every day, and her feet were lovely. Pale, delicate toes. High, elegant arches. I found myself staring at them in class, much to her amusement. She could say so much without uttering a thing. She'd see me staring at her feet and lift her eyes to catch mine briefly, and silently ask: *Do you like what you see?* She knew the power of silence, of watching and waiting, of delaying and postponing, until the yearning was so exquisite, you almost didn't want it to come to an end. But everything does come to an end, which is another thing Cat had taught us. She explained a principle of Japanese poetry known as *wabi:* the moment something begins it is already ending. Nothing is permanent, which is what makes everything so sorrowful and beautiful, so precious and rare.

Black cat in the night
Invisible save her two eyes
Glowing like two moons
In the dark…

Each moment came and went that night, moments I couldn't hold on to, moments I couldn't bear to let go. I locked eyes with Cat as I unbuttoned my sweater and slipped the sleeves down my arms. She tried not to gasp, but her breath quickened at the sight of my torso, exposed to her at last. I took my time, folded my sweater neatly, and placed it on the bench before stepping out of my jeans and allowing her to behold me in my plain cotton underwear. I had never thought of myself as particularly attractive; I was too soft and round everywhere, and envied the tight, lean bodies of women like Cat, but now, for the first time, standing under the spotlight of the moon and feeling Cat's unbridled admiration, I felt truly and utterly exquisite. The feeling was intoxicating, like the peach juice and champagne we had drunk at dinner earlier. At that moment I would have gladly done anything for her, anything at all.

Cat let me stand there—for how long, minutes? hours?—before she gave me the signal I was waiting for. She lifted one arm and held out her hand, white and pale against the darkness. I climbed out of my underwear and slipped into the water. It was hotter than I'd expected, or perhaps it was the juxtaposition of the steamy water against the chilly night air, a delicious combination that made me shudder. I kept my back to Cat and felt rather than saw her glide across the water to me like a swan.

Bits of moonlight on the water
Like diamonds around your neck
Ice cold and delicious…

Without a word, Cat lifted my long, thick hair off the nape of my neck and licked the delicate, soft skin she found there. I swooned, melted, fell back against her, surrendered to her strong embrace at last. The feeling of Cat's body against mine was exciting and comforting, it was home and a place I'd never been to before. She floated me across the tub until she was sitting back on her bench and I was sitting on her lap. I listened to her breath in my ear, felt her fingertips against my skin, heard myself mewling like a kitten as she taught me the wonders of my own bones and flesh. We sank, we floated, we melded into each other, we let the water part around us, enter us, keep us afloat, wrap us in its warmth. And all the while the moon watched over us, pulled at us, called us, bathed us in its white, wondrous light.

> *Moonglow in the sky*
> *Afterglow on your face...*

Lifetimes later there was a knock at the door. "We're closing," a male voice informed us. It felt strange to hear words, as neither Cat nor I had spoken all evening. We continued our silence as we emerged from the tub, our bodies soft and glowing, our fingers as wrinkled as slept-in clothes. Cat dried me off tenderly, from head to toe, and then saw to herself as I got dressed. Back in our clothes, I felt distant from her, but then she embraced me again, and as her lips found mine, everything between us fell swiftly away.

> *The moon slips*
> *Behind a cloud*
> *Like your pale arm*
> *Inside a velvet sleeve...*

Without asking, Cat knew I would come home with her. We drove through darkened streets in silence, her hand on my thigh, our wet hair streaming. Once inside Cat's house, it was only a matter of minutes before we were undressed again. Her bed was covered in white, and through a skylight above I saw a smattering of stars and the lovely translucent moon.

This time Cat let me touch her. I was surprised at the sound she made, something between a sigh and a grunt, as I explored her with my fingers and tongue. I couldn't believe how soft she was; I was unspeakably moved by the gift she was giving me, how completely vulnerable she allowed herself to be. I licked the beauty mark on her belly with my tongue; I placed my hand inside her warm, wet sweetness; I kissed the hinge where her hip met her thigh. Finally, we were filled with each other, the moon disappeared, and we slept, curled together like the two *s*'s at the end of a long, tender kiss.

The morning light was bright and harsh as I opened my gritty eyes. Cat stood beside the bed holding open a kimono, and I rose to step toward her and slip my arms through the long, silky sleeves.

> *You stood behind me*
> *lifting a kimono to my shoulders*
> *And I was the sky*
> *A full moon rising*
> *From my feet...*

She made a pot of green tea, toast with blueberry jam, and small talk: the weather, the class she had to teach later, a film that had just opened in town. I listened to her chatter, mute with the wonder of it all. Cat was now my lover, and she acted like it was perfectly natural for me to be sitting at her table, drinking tea from her mug, eating toast off her plate, watching her move about her kitchen with ease, as she got me a cloth napkin, put another slice of bread into the toaster, opened a window to let in the morning air. It was all very strange and new to me, but I didn't let my confusion show, or if I did, Cat didn't seem to notice.

As Cat poured me a second cup of tea, there was a knock at the door. She excused herself, and I remained at the table, not knowing what else to do. It wasn't her lover, home from Europe for a surprise visit. That would have been too contrived, too melodramatic. It was a friend, another teacher from the English department, returning some books she had borrowed and asking Cat if she could loan her a particular volume of poetry. "Wait here," I heard Cat say, but as she moved into her study, the woman stepped into the living room, peeked through the doorway, and saw me sitting at Cat's kitchen table, wrapped in the kimono, my hair unkempt, my face wearing a mixture of embarrassment, defiance, and pride.

"Uh, Cat, I'll see you later," the woman called, backing out the door.

Cat returned to the kitchen, poetry book in hand, but something had been interrupted, lost, the spell had been broken. I was already on my feet, heading for the bedroom, for the safety of my clothes, eager to put a wall between us.

"I'd better get going," I mumbled, trying to ignore the hurt and bewildered look on Cat's face as I struggled into my jeans.

"Wait," she said as I reached for the door. "Don't go," she implored as I turned the handle. "I love you," she whispered as I opened the door and stepped through it, her hand on my arm unable to stop me.

"I have to run," I stammered, not bothering to shut the door behind me. And I did begin to run and then kept running, without once looking back. I never went back to her class, I never returned her phone calls, the letters she wrote me, the notes she tacked to my door.

Moonless night
Like my bed
Without you in it...

I dropped out of school and moved clear across the state without saying goodbye. What was I running so hard from? I couldn't explain it to her because I didn't understand it myself. All I knew was that I couldn't bear to face her. Sure, I identified as bisexual, but that didn't mean anything. Everybody did; after all, it was a nontraditional school. But embracing a label was very different than embracing an experience. And that's what Cat was to me, just an experience, an experiment, a litmus test, wasn't she? Or was she?

Cat had her own theories about my disappearing act. Perhaps it was because she was my teacher. ("Don't be ridiculous," she said in a letter. "We're practically the same age and it won't matter once the semester is over.") Or perhaps it was because she already had a lover. (Cat informed me in another letter that they had an "understanding," and besides, they were on the verge of splitting up.) Was I afraid that we had gotten carried away by the moon, the champagne, the water, and that her feelings for me weren't real? (She assured me they were.) How could I tell Cat when I couldn't even tell myself I wasn't afraid it was those things, I was afraid it *wasn't* those things. I was afraid that whatever was between us was real, too real, as real as the ache in my heart every time I thought of her. I kept running from the questions that plagued me, running from the answers I didn't want to hear. But there was one thing I couldn't run away from and that was the moon.

Moonlight spilling through my window
Filling my empty teacup
Stroking my sleeping cheek
As I reach through my dreams
For someone who is not there...

Every night the damn moon rose high in the sky, making it impossible for me to forget what had happened with Cat. There it was, just a sliver, like a disembodied smile. Then, it was half full or half empty, depending on your point of view. Next, it grew fat and bulging, almost as if it were pregnant with itself. Finally, it was full, a silver coin, an incandescent opal, Cat's smooth white cheek glowing in the sky. Then all at once the moon disappeared completely, giving me a night of peace, only to return again just as suddenly, forcing me out of my denial. It took months for me to realize I wasn't running from Cat; I was running from what Cat had taken a great risk to teach me: that I was just like her; that I needed the warmth, the comfort, the thrill of another woman beside me. It hit me sudden and hard, without warning, like turning the corner and coming upon a golden harvest moon bigger than a house in the sky. How powerful and peaceful, how tremendous and true. And so a year later I gathered my courage and went back to find Cat, to thank her, to apologize, to beg for forgiveness, to explain.

> *Twelve full moons*
> *Have risen and set*
> *Since you have been away.*
> *An old woman greets you*
> *At your young lover's door.*

Sharp Objects
Gina Ranalli

On the eve of my thirtieth birthday, I went insane.

Not completely, mind you. But enough. Enough to be able to call it that and not have it be an exaggeration. Enough to have turned my life upside down and inside out and have it twist off in a direction I'd never imagined, spinning through the universe like a renegade satellite.

Some of what happened was planned, but the big thing, the dangerous thing, was not. It was stupid and crazy and fucked-up, and I'd do it again in a second if I could. Because it was such a rush. It was stepping up to the edge of the cliff, knowing you don't have wings and knowing that you're sure as shit not about to sprout any either. It was looking down at jagged rocks a mile below you, looking down at one death or another. And then, without a thought in your head, you jump…

I arrived at Jen's place a little after nine P.M. lugging a case of Coors and sweating my ass off in the August heat. Even in denim cutoffs and a ribbed red tank top, I was dripping. I was a big salty puddle, ready to evaporate into the cast-iron sky where stars sizzled like white-hot sparks and threatened to leave scars on my retinas. A little river rushed through my cleavage, forming a sticky little lake that was slowly, but *too* slowly, being absorbed into my bra. It felt pretty fucking gross.

As I climbed the stairs to Jen's apartment, stomping in my mammoth boots, I could already hear the stereo cranking out the latest Patti Smith CD, a selection I knew she'd put on solely for my benefit. Her new girlfriend, Brenda, was strictly an Indigo-Ferrick-Etheridge kind of chick, so that's what I had to listen to every time I came over lately, but apparently tonight Jen was making an exception. I smiled a little as I rapped out "shave-and-a-hair-cut, two-bits" on her front door, knowing Jen was probably catching some shit for playing my goddess Patti so loudly.

I stood there for a while and was just about to knock again when the door whipped open and Brenda shot out of it, nearly slamming into me. "Oh, hi, Kit," she said, stopping short. "Did you ring the bell?"

"I knocked," I replied, giving her my best simulation of a friendly smile.

She nodded. "Well, the cunt is inside waiting for you, so you may as well get in there." That said, she tromped off down the stairs, her nose high in the air, as usual.

"Okey dokey," I mumbled to her back and turned, entering the apartment. "Yo, cunt!" I yelled over the music as I kicked the door closed. "I'm here!"

Jen came out of the bedroom in blue jeans and a black sports bra. Her feet were bare. "What the fuck did you just call me?" she asked.

"Hey, don't bitch at me." I shrugged and made my way to her tiny kitchen so I could finally put the beer down. It was getting pretty goddamn heavy. "What's wrong with what's-her-name this time?" I called over my shoulder.

"Who the fuck knows," Jen said, entering the kitchen behind me. She helped herself to a beer, snapped the pop-top, and said, "Happy fucking birthday, bitch."

I laughed. "Thanks, douche bag." Then I unloaded the case into the fridge, and Jen went out into the living room to turn the stereo down.

"I got some weed," she told me when I joined her on the sofa.

"Excellent."

"And some chips. Are you hungry?"

"Nah." I shook my head and cracked open my own beer.

Jen sighed. "Some party, huh?"

"My favorite kind," I grinned. And it was true. Jen was basically my only friend and had been for almost seven years. But it wasn't like I couldn't make friends; I had plenty of offers for friendship. It's just that, in a nutshell, I pretty much hate people. Or most people, anyway. And in all honesty, a lot of people find me kind of hard to take. They call me things like "abrasive" and "moody" and "hostile." Claims that may or may not be true. In return, I call them narrow-minded, judgmental hypocrites, which I'm pretty damn sure *is* true.

OK, so maybe I am a bit hostile. I'm woman enough to give them that one.

Jen, on the other hand, is indisputably antisocial. She can't even fake it for a good cause, like meeting the parents of a girlfriend or something. She's lost about eight jobs and half a dozen women on account of her refusal to kiss ass, to play the games so many women have been forced to play: the nice game, the stupid game, the straight game. She flat-out, positively will not do it. I've always admired her for that.

"So, you're sure you wanna go through with this tonight?"

"Hell yeah," I replied. "If not tonight, who knows when I'll get up the courage again."

Jen took a long gulp of beer. "When do you go back to work?"

"Not for a week. Plenty of time to get used to it."

"Yeah, and plenty of time to stock up on a dozen different colored bandannas too."

I chewed my lower lip and listened to Patti wail. "You don't wear bandannas," I said finally.

"No," Jen agreed, and ran a hand over what was left of her sleek black hair. "But I've been wearing a buzz forever. I couldn't grow it out now if I wanted to. When it starts to touch my ears I have a panic attack. Drives me crazy."

My own reddish-brown hair was long compared to Jen's, hanging down an inch past my shoulders. But I was turning thirty now and it was time for a change. I'd always wanted to shave my head but had constantly come up with an excuse for not doing so: My boss would complain, my parents would freak, I would then be an "obvious" dyke. All the regular bullshit.

Now, however, I'd finally decided to say fuck you to all of them, give the whole of conservative society a good long look at my short-nailed, chubby middle finger. And I couldn't have been more excited about it.

"I'm psyched," I told Jen. "It's long overdue."

She held up her beer. "Then here's to your new look."

"And my new attitude."

We clinked our cans together and took long, greedy swallows. We talked about regular shit for a while then. Work, women, families. Small talk, mostly, catching up on all the crap we missed since the last time we'd talked, which was only four days ago. While we chatted, we drank and passed a joint back and forth, each of us pausing the conversation momentarily to hold harsh clouds of smoke deep within our poor abused lungs for as long as possible.

Three beers and a CD later, Jen asked if I was ready.

I grinned, pleasantly high. "Yesss."

She grabbed a straight-back chair out of the kitchen and told me to take a seat. As I sat in the center of the living room with my drink, Jen disappeared down the hall in the direction of her bathroom. I listened happily to Grace Slick and her boys doing one of their eerie tunes, perfect stoner music, and felt a little surreal. Was I really about to go through with this? Was I really about to cross over from cute boy-lez to empowered, invincible, back-the-fuck-off-'cause-I-don't give-a-fuck *DYKE*?

I couldn't help smiling as I thought about it.

When Jen returned, she was carrying electric hair clippers and a pair of scissors, which she placed neatly on the coffee table.

"OK," she said, and held up the scissors for my inspection. "Whack whack."

The scissors weren't haircutting scissors. I guess they were sewing scissors or something, the big fat kind, thick and bulky, gleaming stainless steel I could see my reflection in, my crazy spaced-out grin.

Jen stepped behind me and gathered most of my hair to the back of my head, as if she were intending to put it in a ponytail. Then I heard a single snip and knew there was no turning back. I'd stepped onto the path, and now I had no choice but to follow it to the very end.

"Here," she said, dangling the chopped ponytail in my face. "You want it?"

I shook my head, gulped down more Coors, and began tapping my foot in time with Jefferson Airplane.

She dropped the hacked-off hair onto the table and began cutting recklessly, not caring where she snipped or how much. "If you want, I can shave you too. Brenda has a bunch of razors in the bathroom."

"That's cool," I replied, hoping I sounded like I really didn't give a shit one way or another. "Whatever."

Jen said nothing, apparently engrossed in what she was doing. I tried to remain still, but it gradually became more and more difficult as my excitement grew. I became antsy, like I do sometimes. Whenever I'm anxious for something to be finished, whether it be a workday or a movie I'm hating or who knows what else, I get horny. I have no idea why. I only know that when I need something to be over, need to be released from whatever it is, a tension starts to build between my legs. My belly twists in on itself and my hands tremble; I feel like I'm being shot up with electricity, tiny volts that cause my muscles to spasm, coil and uncoil. It's a nerve-racking state of mind, and for some reason I always feel like the only thing that will end it is a good hard come.

I shifted in the chair and killed the beer in my hand, but still my tongue stayed glued to the roof of my mouth, parched as the surface of the moon. The heat in the apartment was suddenly unbearable, though it had seemed a good ten degrees cooler than outside when I'd first entered it less than two hours before.

Get a grip, I told myself. *Jesus Christ, Kit!*

Noticing that my breathing had increased even before I did, Jen asked, "You doing OK there, ho-bag?"

"Uh-huh," I blurted, too quickly.

The scissors paused for an almost unnoticeable instant, then went on clipping as if they'd never stopped, but I caught that instant and wondered if Jen knew. Actually, I didn't have to wonder much. We'd been friends forever, and sometimes I think the woman knows me better than I know myself, a fact I find disconcerting at best, downright creepy at worst.

I swallowed hard and hoped *she* wasn't getting creeped out.

Barely five seconds later I discovered that she wasn't creeped out. Not in the least. She suddenly stopped cutting my hair and drew the sharp points of the open scissors slowly down the back of my neck. I jerked involuntarily.

"What are you doing?" I asked, my voice squeaky.

"Nothing," she said, dragging the scissors over my shoulder and down my upper arm. "Nothing at all."

Looking down at my arm, I saw the twin scratches the scissors were leaving in their wake, like smoke trails from a jet slashing across the sky. Not deep scratches but shallow ones, not even breaking the skin. I shivered.

Jen brought the scissors back up to my shoulder, increasing the pressure ever so slightly, and slid a chilly blade beneath the straps of both my tank top and my bra, snipping them apart. "Oops," she whispered, barely audible. "Hope those weren't expensive."

I started to turn in the chair, intending to ask again just what the fuck was she doing, but she hissed, "Don't move," and I froze. "This is very delicate work."

Unsure how I should react, I remained still as she destroyed the straps over my left shoulder. She slipped the scissors under the fabric at my side, just behind my right armpit. I became marble, bronze, a work of art while she carefully cut my tank in half, the cool blade grazing my rib cage. I wondered vaguely what my head looked like, assumed I probably didn't want to know just yet.

When Jen finished cutting, she leaned over me and, with the hand that still held the scissors, peeled away the destroyed top, exposing my full, sweaty breasts. With a twinge of embarrassment, I saw how erect my nipples were, puckered and eager and betraying.

Behind me, I heard Jen emit a low growl of satisfaction. "Easy," she said. "Be very careful."

I had no idea if she was talking to me or to herself, and I didn't care. There was nothing in my head now that wasn't directly linked to my aching clit. I had no thoughts of her lover or our potentially ruined friendship or any guilt whatsoever. All I wanted now was to be fucked and fucked hard.

But Jen was cruel; intentionally, I think.

Still refusing to allow me to move, she placed one hand on my shoulder and traced the circle of my nipple with the point of the scissors, occasionally rubbing the blades along the underside of my breast only to return to the nipple with an added fierceness. I sucked in my breath as I saw the scissors open and then close around the tip of my nipple.

"*Fuck*," I gasped. "Jen, I—"

"Shhh…" Jen gave my nipple a gentle tug with the scissors. "Relax."

A trickle of sweat traveled down my neck as I released my breath through clenched teeth. I watched the tip of my nipple change from nutmeg-brown to an angry, raw crimson and couldn't watch anymore. I closed my eyes.

"This has been a long time coming, hasn't it, Kit?" Jen asked softly. "You and me."

It felt like she was *sawing* my nipple with the scissors, simultaneously sawing and pulling, and the sensation caused me to groan aloud.

"You like it, don't you?" Jen removed her free hand from my shoulder, and I heard the muted sound of a zipper behind me, *her* zipper. "I always knew it would end up this way, you know," she said, her tone almost conversational. "Right from the very beginning, I knew. I never thought it would take as long as it did, but…" She trailed off, and I sensed that her hand had reached its desired destination. An instant later she confirmed my belief by making a thick, guttural sound and murmuring, "Fuck, I'm drenched…"

It took every ounce of willpower I possessed to not turn around and yank her to the floor then. My own pussy was sopping; I didn't know how much longer I could stay still. "Jen," I started. "I need—"

"Get up," she demanded, abruptly removing the scissors from my tit. "Come on, hurry."

I quickly opened my eyes, stood and whirled to face her, and by that time she was already on me, roughly grabbing and kissing me with bruising intensity. Our tongues met, rabid and thrashing as my hands found her hair, her hips, her breasts. I wanted them everywhere at once.

I hadn't even been aware that her own hands were at my waist until I felt the familiar steel slither between my waistband and my skin. I jumped and took a step back. "No," I said, grasping her wrist and forcing the scissors away from my body. Instantly I began unbuttoning my shorts, pulling them down the old-fashioned way while Jen stood staring at me, her face flushed and amused, the scissors poised and gleaming with beauty and menace.

She only let me get the cutoffs to my knees, and then she lost her patience. Tackling me to the floor, she pulled off my boots and carelessly threw them across the room, where they collided loudly with an end table. Wrenching my shorts from my body, she tossed them aside as well, immediately positioning herself between my legs.

Forcing my knees apart, she raked her long fingers through my pubic hair, mumbling, "This is too long." She looked up, offered me a mischievous smile, and then the scissors were back, flashing brightly. "I have just the thing."

My eyes widened even as my hips jerked forward, my legs spreading completely. I was no longer in the mood for games and reached down to stroke my throbbing clit only to have my knuckles rapped with the heavy scissors. I whined like a wounded animal, bit my lip, and removed my hand.

Jen grinned like the evil fucking jackal she was and gave my pubes a few indifferent snips before teasing my slit with the closed blades. I thrust my pelvis up, afraid but begging for it just the same. She glided the scissors up and down my aching pussy, endlessly it seemed, until she carefully dipped the point into my cunt. I cried out desperately, not in pain but in frustration, as she quickly withdrew it again. I stared at her, pleading, as I watched her tongue snake out and slowly, seductively lick the pearly drops from the tip of the blades.

I wanted to scream. I wanted to cry. But more than anything I wanted to come; I wanted it more than I'd ever wanted it before, and I guess Jen saw it in my face because she stopped smiling then, stopped smiling and became utterly still and serious for what could have been forever. Time stopped when her smile stopped, and we were faced with only each other and no games, old friends and new lovers, meeting and assessing and wanting.

Then the moment was over, and she plunged into me, tongue and fingers and sharp, biting steel and then I *did* scream, almost instantly, my entire body shuddering violently while my mind shrieked, *Don't stab me. Jesus, don't stab me!*

Somewhere in another world, I heard Jen crying out, registered that she was getting off somehow, and I was vaguely glad, but mostly, all I could concentrate on was my own cunt, pounding around that dangerous inanimate object, and that I was being fucked by my best friend with a potential murder weapon.

Closing my eyes, I rode the wave down, rode it for all it was worth, trying hard not to think about the weirdness of the situation, this fucked-up thing we'd done to ourselves, to our friendship. And even after the spasms stopped, the come done, I kept my eyes closed, maybe because I was already feeling sort of embarrassed.

Jen slid the scissors out of me and crawled up the length of my body, positioned herself over me. "Open your eyes."

I hesitated but eventually opened one, peeking up at her, wondering if she would still look the same to me, still my one and only bud, still Jen. She did. And again she was wearing her sordid grin, beaming down at me with the pure wickedness of her black, black heart.

"You look like someone ran over your head with a fucking lawn mower," she told me.

Frowning, I knocked her over and sat up. "Shut the fuck up, you goddamn cretin."

That got her laughing, and it was either cuff her upside her flaky head or put my clothes back on, and although the first choice was tempting, I chose the second. As I dressed, Jen eventually got all the snickering out of her system and left to fetch us both fresh beers while I went and helped myself to an old Nirvana T-shirt out of her dresser, since she'd so completely destroyed my top. Before heading back, I made a pit stop in the bathroom to survey the wreckage of my hair. It was pretty bad. Monster corkscrews sprouting up in all directions, while in other places patches of stark white scalp showed through the brown like demonic crop circles.

"Jesus," I whispered. Then I giggled a little until I looked down and saw all the shit on the counter beside the sink. Hairspray and lotions and *makeup,* for chrissake. All kinds of *Brenda* shit. How the hell could I have forgotten, even for an instant, *Brenda,* Jen's current flavor of the month?

Standing there, gazing down at all her crap, I finally admitted to myself that I didn't like the bitch. In fact, I finally admitted that I'd *never* liked *any* of Jen's floozies, starting way back with that little rich bitch she'd been dating when we'd first met. I stood, wondering why that was, and then I looked up at my reflection, sighed, and said, "Figure it out, Einstein."

Back in the living room, Jen was on the couch, her bare feet propped against the coffee table, sealing the end of a new joint with the tip of her tongue.

"Am I fixing this or are you?" I asked, tugging a wayward tendril of hair.

Jen looked up and laughed. "What? You don't like the chemo-punk look?"

I shook my head, feigning disgust. "You know, you really are a twat."

"Yeah, yeah, yeah," she said, rising from her seat and walking back to the kitchen chair in the center of the room. "C'mon, sit down. I'll buzz you."

I sat and she buzzed and it didn't even take five minutes but it felt like a lifetime. I wanted to ask her so many things in that brief span of time. What did it mean, if anything? Was it just one of those things, one of those for-shits-and-giggles things that just happen sometimes? Would it ever happen again? Would she even want it to?

But the whole time, Jen was so cool, so goddamn fucking cool, like nothing was out of whack, like nothing had happened at all, and so I just choked. I kept my questions to myself and played it cool right along with her. I figured I can play the game too. No biggie? Fine. Business as usual? Perfect. Sport fucking? Hell yes, I can deal with it. What-the-fuck-*ever*.

When Jen finished buzzing me and brushing all the hair off my shoulders, I took another trip into the bathroom to check out the new 'do. I stared at myself for a long time, the new me, the new badass me. I looked like a different person, like a stranger. A tough stranger I wouldn't want to fuck with but someone I might want to fuck.

I stood up straighter, puffed my chest out, and grinned.

Jen entered the bathroom behind me, peering at me in the mirror. "What do you think?"

Running a hand over the short stubble, still smiling, I said, "I love it."

She nodded and took a pull from her Coors. "So do I."

Our eyes met in the mirror then, for a long, lingering moment, and though neither of us spoke, neither of us had to. We were good. We were cool. We'd known each other a long time, and now we would know each other in a different way, a better way. We'd crossed over, as we probably always knew we would, eventually.

I stayed for another beer, just shooting the shit like a thousand times before, while Patti Smith rolled around again, scorching the air with her righteous anger.

Sometime after one A.M., I finally decided to get going, and Jen walked me out. Back in the sultry night, I was clomping down her stairs just as good old Brenda was climbing up. We exchanged nods, and I noticed her eyeing Jen's shirt on my body, but she didn't say a word, and when I reached the sidewalk I looked back just in time to see her push past Jen, who didn't even glance at her. Jen's eyes were on me. I smiled and called up, "Hey, thanks for the buzz, cunt."

She grinned down at me. "Happy birthday, ya fucking pinhead."

Instead of waving, we flipped each other off, and I got into my car trying to determine how it felt to finally be the dreaded 3-0. Catching a glimpse of myself in the rearview mirror, I decided one thing for sure: It doesn't suck.

On the eve of my thirtieth birthday, I went insane.

Not completely, mind you, but enough. Enough to be able to approach the edge of that cliff and do what needed to be done, despite the fear, despite gravity. When they say the fall will kill you, they lie. It's the fall that frees you, frees you and possesses you with more courage and power than you ever thought you owned. You can look straight at all those sharp, deadly rocks screaming toward your face, filling up your vision, and you can say, "Back the fuck off 'cause I don't give a fuck."

You can soar.

The Problem
Ruthann Robson

With most women, you get them into bed minus a major article of clothing, under the covers so that the flat sheet slides across their skin, and you can pretty well predict what the next hour will hold. Not every little detail (how boring would that be?) but the major outlines. Although with Beth you could never tell.

Or at least I couldn't.

She could be kissing and writhing one second, and say in the next "My body just isn't into it right now." She often talked about her body as if it were some third person, some object, some recalcitrant pet. A dog that wouldn't roll over, sit, stay, or come.

At times it could be kind of exciting. It could keep me on edge and far away from that deadly center of complacency. Some women say they like comfort, but I'm not one of them. I thrive on ardor.

You might say it's what keeps me alive.

It's also what makes me a virulent serial monogamist. Well, not always monogamist. Before abandoning someone's bed because of boredom, it's best to check that she's the one who is the problem, don't you think? I mean, it could be me who has fallen into a rut. So far, it hasn't been.

Yet Beth is also annoying. Sometimes I feel as if I'm in one of those experiments in which the scientists shock the rats at random intervals. They—the rats—go really crazy. Crazier than the rats who endure predictable though more intense electricity circuiting through their little nervous systems. They—the scientists—postulate that this explains an important aspect of human psychology.

Don't you think it's a problem that we make generalizations about human nature from observing a few rodents?

Scientists are now making claims that lesbianism is natural because it occurs in animals. Not rats, as far as I know, but other little furry creatures, such as chipmunks and marmots. Bigger animals as well. Giraffes (my favorite animals as a child). Seals. And peach-faced lovebirds.

I wonder if any of these animals acts like Beth. Forget the details of clothes and bed but recall the reversal of the erotic trajectory. The Beth-like peach-faced lovebird suddenly stops the mutual preening to make sounds like *sip-sip-lik-lik* or whatever means I've changed my little bird brain. And what does the other peach-faced lovebird do?

Maybe something close to what I'm doing. Getting up, taking off my boots, putting on my sandals, and flying away.

"Where are you going?" the Beth-bird twirps. She sounds petulant and vulnerable.

"The bar," I answer, hoping she gets the message that I'm not going to walk three blocks for a peach daiquiri or a microbrew. Actually, I've never been fond of alcohol, as Beth knows. And I certainly can't drink it now.

The bar is populated with the usual suspects, one of whom I seem to be becoming since I've become lovers with Beth. I'm not someone who takes note of my lover's former flings, but by my second club soda (with a twist, as always), I start thinking that maybe Beth's proclivities aren't a secret. Or maybe I think this because Desirée—you know the type: too fluffy hair and pointy boots— sidles up to me to say, "You leave Beth alone at home trying to decide which way is up?"

I try to stare levelly at Desirée, though this is a little difficult since she's eight inches shorter than I am, even with her boots. So it probably seems to her as if I'm staring into space.

Desirée finds this sexy, I guess, because she puts her hand on my ass.

I'll admit to considering which article of her clothing I would like to remove first, when—as you could probably predict, but I didn't—Beth walks toward me.

I hadn't even seen her arrive, but then I guess I'd been busy.

"Hey, stranger." I stare levelly. We are the same height, give or take a centimeter.

"Hello. And hello, Desirée."

From Beth's screechy tone, I think that there might be a catfight over me. I don't like to believe I'm the kind of person who would find this exciting—I'm more a fighter than the girl fought over—but my ego's been pretty scratched up these days. A little uncontrollable passion with me as its object might be fun.

Disappointingly, Desirée points her boots toward the bathroom and departs without the desperate backward glance I hoped Beth would see.

"You know what your problem is?" Beth hisses.

Here, I had thought that *she* was the one with the problem. For a while I thought I had it figured out. You know how that goes. Lots of intimacy and trust issues. But when I asked her (being both sensitive and direct, as I'd read in some feminist self-help tracts), she denied being an incest survivor.

"Do you want a drink?" I answer her with a question of my own.

"That's your problem! Precisely!"

"What? That I'm considerate enough to ask the woman who is supposed to be my girlfriend if she's thirsty?"

"No. That you avoid *real* interaction."

"I'm not the one who avoids *interaction*," I say, putting the stress elsewhere.

"It's always *that*, isn't it?"

"Hey, babe," I say, trying to sound conciliatory. "Let's not argue. A drink sounds better than a litany of our problems."

(Don't you just love that word *litany*? It's got just the right tinge of the religious to sound serious but not psychotic.)

"I'll have what you're having," she relents. Yes, *litany* is a fine word.

We settle with our club sodas (her glass has a lime and a bit of Beefeater's) at one of those too small, round-and-rickety tables.

Now what?

I can feel the argument gathering in her chest. I've never understood why everyone thinks the mind resides in the head. I think it's spread out between the breasts. The center of it is that hard bony place on the sternum, a bedrock surrounded by soft hills, that I just love to kiss. That's the third eye, I'm convinced, equidistant between the unblinking nipples. Forget the forehead, which is childish and not a very sexy landscape.

"Sex. Sex. Sex," Beth is saying.

I can feel myself smiling, but I notice she isn't.

"What about affection?" Beth continues. "It doesn't always have to be raunchy, down and dirty, does it? What about some sweetness?"

"You're making me sound like I'm some insensitive lout of a husband."

"I'm not saying that. All I'm saying is that it doesn't have to be fireworks every time."

"Why not?"

"Because that isn't always fun."

"And kissing you on the forehead is fun?" Luckily, I don't really say that. Or maybe I do, but I don't mean it to be insulting. I mean it as a serious question, but since she isn't answering, I ask something else: "So you want more foreplay?" Now I really sound like an oafish husband circa 1957, or at least before *The Myth of the Vaginal Orgasm*.

"How about just affection? We could kiss and that would be enough."

Making out, as it was once called, hasn't been enough since I called it that, probably when I was fourteen. But now is not the time to discuss my adolescent adventures.

"Is that why you freeze?" I ask. It's time to shift the focus back to the real source of the problem.

"Maybe. Maybe not. It's just that you make me feel like my body is just an object sometimes."

"Are you sure there's no incest?"

"No incest. I've told you before. Why do you always ask me that?"

"Well, I guess it would explain a lot."

Beth is chewing on her lime rind. I think this can't be good for a person, but once when I commented, she told me that the pith of limes was a very good liver tonic. I can't see the how or why of this, but I wasn't about to press her. I don't like to discuss internal organs.

"Were you?" she asks when she finally swallows the lime.

"Of course not," I feel mildly insulted, but I'm not sure why. "What the hell would that explain?"

"This isn't working."

"An eye for the obvious. I like that in a woman." She doesn't laugh, but I think I see the slightest smile. I offer to get her another drink, a double. Maybe if I ply her with liquor.

Instead she suggests we go back home.

It's half hour from last call. If I leave, I won't be able to come back.

Where did that Desirée go?

"I need another drink," I declare.

"There's club soda in the refrigerator."

"I was going to have a Coke."

"Coke too."

"Caffeine-free?" It feels good to be difficult.

"We can get some."

She is leading me out the door before I quite realize it. Outside, my breath escapes in little clouds and my sandals crunch on glass and crusted snow.

"You should have worn boots. Or at least shoes," Beth says needlessly, maternally.

"Probably," I agree. But instead of saying that I hadn't noticed the cold on the way here because I'd been too hot in various ways, I try for something more cordial. "But don't you think sandals are incredibly sexy?"

If it were you, you'd agree, wouldn't you? On the facts and just to be amiable. But Beth snaps back: "Then why don't you wear them to bed instead of boots?"

The world is too white for me to answer. The street lamps and the bar's security lights are too many little moons reflecting the ice-blue ground. Even the dirty mounds made by the snow plows glitter with iridescent purity.

"It's like a pastel fairy tale." I lean over to kiss Beth's forehead, as if she is a princess.

"It's fucking freezing out here," she scolds.

"You know what your problem is?" I don't wait for an answer. "You have no ability for fantasy. I can't believe you call yourself a poet. You're more like a goddamn accountant."

"Let's not talk occupations."

"What's that supposed to mean?" I'm honestly not sure how I'm being insulted, though I have my suspicions. I have a nice secure job with the government, which is what allowed me to even move here in the first place. And I have good benefits. Meaning good health insurance. Some people don't understand that. Don't need to.

"Your job doesn't mean anything. It's not the job. The problem with you is…"

"Fuck you," I interrupt.

"You wish."

"I used to. Until I figured out the problem is that you can't even do that."

Things have deteriorated, haven't they? I thought Beth and I were on the road to saving the night, if not the relationship, but when it gets to implying that your lover is deficient in bed, it seems as if a corner has been turned. And not just the corner toward home but a corner toward something irrevocable. A corner you'll think about later, when you're mulling over the straw that broke the rat's back. The corner you'll try to forget about, deciding it was all awful from the very beginning. You should have known. How could you have been so stupid? Only an idiot would not have seen the signs. And your new lover (Desirée?) will agree.

"Are you saying we've never had good sex? That you haven't liked it even once?" Beth's words come out moist and hot, like her breath, in little puffs.

I'd like this moment to be frozen instead of my toes.

"Babe." I elongate this into a moan, hoping to melt her.

Have you ever made love in the snow? It's not as cold as you'd think, though afterward it's kind of scary how soggy you are. And your whole body temperature is lowered, I'd guess. There is probably a risk of hypothermia just from the dried sweat. Not to mention being arrested for public sex. Though we were away from the streetlights and on a little patch of private property, between two rows of privets, actually, though these were mostly thin branches that seemed to cover some birds that were trying to survive the night there. I think we were on a walkway into the house, though it was circular and hadn't been shoveled.

To say that we fucked like dogs wouldn't be wrong, but I'm not going to say it and ruin the mood. So I'm glad when Beth does. Although she doesn't seem as thrilled by it as I am. In fact, her tone borders disgust.

"I don't know what got into me," she says.

A million sarcastic comebacks flit through my mind, but I resist. Instead I suggest that we get home. I'm afraid my feet will turn blue, then black, with frostbite.

That was over much too fast, don't you think?

You read, at least in part, for the sex scenes, don't you?

Don't be embarrassed. I mean, I do it too. The backs of cereal boxes, advertisements, the inserts of my boots: I'm reading with the bone desire for the words to assemble themselves into a text of lesbian passion. So far I haven't been lucky. But when you commit yourself to something that starts off with two women in bed, I think you have the right to expect a little explicitness for your devotion. Which is what I usually think when it comes to Beth, but you've probably already made that connection.

So let me try to describe it. Remember that it's cold so I will not have to keep repeating that. There is enough repetition as it is. Tongue. Wet. Hand. Breath. Arch.

Arch of her back. Arch of my sandaled foot.

Her wet tongue. My wet hand.

Inside her pants.

My tongue under her shirt seeking her breast.

Her shoulder curves. Protectively. Excludingly.

I wait.

I'm waiting for her, but what greets me is some small epiphany, some release of anxiety. I'm freezing out here in the middle of the night, stretched on the street as if it were a bed, but I'm no longer worried that Beth will freeze. The dawn will be pink, no matter what, extending its rosy fingers toward the body of the earth even if Beth should push my own cold-reddened fingers away. Haven't you always loved that refrain in Homer? Not Beth or the earth-body but the rosy fingers of dawn. It's always sounded so sexy to me. Maybe I was the only one in whatever class that was who saw Homer as a great lesbian writer. The teacher was busy trying to leave us impressionable students with the impression that Achilles and Patroclus were friends ("Friendship was very different for the ancient Greeks") and some guy behind me kept sniggering "Greeks!" but no one seemed very worried about the obvious lesbian implications.

Yes, dawn will be rosy, no matter what happens. No matter if we consummate whatever it is we are doing on the cold ground or not. No matter if Beth decides she'd best jump up this moment and go write some doggerel she envisions as the next Iliad. Dawn will be pink.

Except if it's not. I don't mean cloud cover; I mean no dawn for me. I mean mortality, the big *M*, which is separated by the big *O* for orgasm by a little *n:* nothing.

It's called *le petit mort,* the little death. In Italian or French or one of those Romance languages, though it doesn't seem very romantic to me.

I hope you are not the kind who thinks that dying is romantic. Life isn't a made-for-TV movie or a nineteenth-century novel, at least my life isn't. And I don't want it to be. I don't want to be the heroine who makes other people's eyes shine with tears. I want to be the one who can turn off the set or close the book and get back to the small satisfactions of life, like finding some good sex.

I left Memphis because everyone I knew had heard. How could they not? The first treatments made me look like I was at death's doorway. I lied and said I'd developed a heroin habit, but no one believed me. Then I got honest and told people I had a rare disease that was not contagious. No one believed me. Not even about the "rare" part.

Though I don't know what difference the rarity makes. Except that I have research scientists working on my case. I intrigue them. They suck my blood and use it in their experiments on rats. They correctly predicted the treatments would make me sick and be unsuccessful. But they said they were worth a shot. A bad shot, as it turned out. Though now that I've stopped the treating the disease, I'm not feeling too terrible, at least for a time bomb.

Probably no one believed the "not contagious" part either. Why else would people suddenly stop sleeping with me? Not even the former nurse–turned–sex educator was interested, and she would go to bed with almost anyone. She took me aside and told me a story about a woman who had a terminal something-or-other but had survived for ten years with "large doses of pussy juice." A little crude, but that's how she always talked. I guess she thinks it's a way of "connecting." Or maybe she's just numb.

Though I guess I decided to follow her advice.

Which was part of the reason I moved away.

Pity is so unsexy.

So I'm here. On the ground with Beth, who is not only cooperating but reciprocating. The snow is melting under us. Beth is pulling me down and farther down.

It's always like falling, which is why it's so often confused with falling in love. If you're lashed securely to life, then the landing is soft: Your images are feathers, floating, clouds. If you're dying, it looks like the abyss of death and there's no white light at the end of it. Believe me, I've looked.

Sometimes as I'm crashing down that dark tunnel, voices assault me. My own voice. Protesting.

No.

That's all I say and I say it now: no.

"It's all right," Beth soothes, continuing to move her body hard against mine.

Sometimes entire enigmatic sentences pronounce themselves. I hope they stay inside my skin, where they belong. I hope Beth can't hear that they are banging against the cement that is rising under the melting snow to greet my head. Because they make no sense. Because I can't explain them. Because I share them with you only because I don't know who you are and if we ever meet you will be too polite to repeat them to me.

rage is a useless medicine
hopeless because the soul is nothing but a trope
murder of the bones is harshest
pussy juice is the poison of choice

You can see why I'm uncomfortable. Maybe sex is the rehearsal for death after all, but I still can't believe that. Sex is affection. Fun. A romp. I have never been self-destructive. Did I mention I don't even like to drink?

Here's what I still think: Sex is the life force. The connection to something greater than our cramped selves. If I can come, I'm still alive. Isn't there a phrase for that? *Ergo* something? Do you know how to say "fuck" in Latin?

"Fuck," Beth is saying, in English. Over and over. And not in a sexy, stimulating kind of way. But in a panicky and hyperventilating sort of way.

"Babe, babe," I whisper into her hair. Little pieces of ice dangle from the ends. This is not a good sign. It's time for us to go, but I can't get Beth off the ground.

At the bottom of Beth's particular abyss is a trampoline, or at least that's how I picture it. Beth falls and then it propels her back up with a force that defies any mental or bodily notions of gravity. Only to descend again. And ricochet back up. It makes her nauseous, this thrilling problem of multiple orgasms. At times she actually vomits.

This is one of those times.

Her soda-and-limes splatter on the snow.

Suddenly we are both cold.

Luckily, the walk home isn't long.

Beth once said my sexuality was capacious. I once had a dog with a capacious nose and a *pot-cassé* bark. These are the hallmarks of the breed and I thought my dog a fine specimen. He had black boots of fur on his white fur legs and a long tongue. I adored that dog, and I believe he adored me, so much so that lovers would be jealous. I'd say unduly jealous, but really they were justified. He could replace any of them, except for the sex, and I wasn't much interested in sex then. As unbelievable as Beth would find that.

Rapacious.

Beth meant rapacious, not capacious.

For a poet, she is often careless with words.

My dog died of a rare disease and I had him cremated.

The first thing I asked the doctors was whether I could have the same thing that had killed my dog several years ago. They said it was impossible. But I insisted they check. I even brought his veterinary records to them. They told me it was a completely different disease. Do you believe them? That they even checked?

Beth and I are warm now. Back home, back in bed, I've got on my boots (over woolen socks) and dry jeans (except for a spot in the crotch) and a shirt that scratches against my nipples in a pleasingly brusque way. Beth is under the covers, *sans* one major article of clothing. I'm waiting for her to become disassociated from her body. I won't really mind if she does. Meanwhile, I kiss her sternum, the really flat part between her breasts.

"I wish you could tell me what the real problem is."

That's Beth. Whispering.

Should I tell her? Tell her I would like to get another pet. Maybe a pair of dyke peach-faced lovebirds. Giraffes, I know, are out of the question. Birds, however, seem possible. But I'm afraid.

Not afraid of the birds. Though I once dated a woman who was afraid of birds.

But afraid what will happen to them.

After.

"There's no problem, babe."

If I were the melodramatic sort, I'd tell her that somewhere there are little rodents being injected with my genes so that their reactions can be monitored and a cure can be found. But I am not the histrionic sort. I've always disapproved of drama queens. Especially when they are dykes.

I think I've told you that the least sexy thing in the world is pity.

The dawn is pink. Somewhere the parrots flit-flit. The rats in their cages die. Why do you think I'm not afraid of frostbite? Why do you think I like to be on top? If you saw through your shirt, the one I've slipped off your shoulders as sexily as I knew how and looked through the third eye in your chest, you'd see that I'm dying.

We are all dying, you say.

Which is why I don't want to say anything else.

You, like Beth, like Desirée, like every woman I fuck or don't, like everyone I know, don't have a fucking clue what it's like.

Or maybe you do.

Heat Vents

Lana Gail Taylor

Last night I called to Estela through the heat vents.

"Estela! Come down!"

"I'll come down," she responded, sounding as if her mouth were close to the vent.

"Estela!" I called up again. "Gotta sweet tooth right now?" I was below the vent in my bedroom, waiting for her voice like the heat turned on.

"Always in the mood for a sweet!" tunneled through the pipes to warm me.

"I'm a terrible cook, you know. Make us something?" Chuckle. "Please?"

"I'll make you something!" she shouted back before giggles echoed around the ducts and trickled out the steel grate. I listened to footsteps above me. She was pulling on jeans, brushing her hair maybe, moving away from the vent to the door.

Downstairs in my apartment, Sugar Ray was on. Estela tried singing the words. Then she asked, "Any Alanis Morissette? Fiona Apple?" She was carrying a box of tapioca mix.

"I have Limp Bizkit," I told her, smiling.

"Testosterone rock," she retorted before playfully shoving past me to get to the kitchen. She pulled a bowl out of a cupboard, located a mixing spoon, found the milk in the fridge.

"I think my testosterone level is high right now," I quipped.

"Why do you say that?" Estela's dark eyes caught the light from the stove.

"I can't stand wearing skirts anymore."

"That's it?" Estela's smile was teasing. "If you're going for a dyke fantasy, Patty, I have a pair of leather pants you can wear." Estela leaned over the stove, stirring the milk and the mix together. "Leather would suit you, I think, and boots." She glanced at me under her lashes then dipped a finger into the pan, plugging it into her lips, slow as if she were enjoying it. I watched her tongue flicking. Pudding dribbled down her chin. She swiped at it, licked, smiled. "Milk scalds easy," she told me.

"You think it's a fantasy?" I went around the stove, stood close to her side, didn't wait for an answer. I dipped my finger into the pudding, burned myself and barked "Shit!" while Estela giggled. I blew at what was left on my finger before I touched it to her lips. I traced the shape of them first, like a bow, leaving a shine before probing just inside; warm, pappy flesh and then past her teeth to her wet tongue wrapping around my knuckle, licking and sucking before she pulled her mouth away.

"Patty, I think it's a fantasy."

"Maybe you could call me Pat."

Estela returned to stirring. Sweet heat filled the air. "Have you ever fucked a woman, Pat?"

I paused. She added, "With a cock?"

My hip leaned into the side of the stove. "No." Then after a minute, "Not yet."

Estela blew on the pudding and then stuck her finger in again. She gave it a slow tongue bath.

I watched, enraptured before I inched close enough to catch my reflection in her pupils. I think I was blushing. *Damn.* She blew tapioca breath on me.

"It's ready?" I guessed.

Estela nodded. "But we need to talk about your music."

When I woke the next morning I had tapioca in my taste

buds. Pudding lingered in the pores of my hands and wrists. I inhaled sugar and milk while pushing yards of hair out of my face, mouth, ears. God, I hated all of this hair. I grabbed a tie off the headboard, bunched it all back in a bun. Estela wasn't in the apartment. She had left about an hour after we finished the pudding, straight from the pan with spoons, then our fingers scooping. Much of it splattered the front of our clothes, the stove. We enjoyed the mess. Estela removed her shirt, then mine, before tossing them in the sink.

"Have you ever fucked anyone with a cock?" I turned it on her suddenly; drunk, I think, on sugar. My gaze drifted down the smooth, white cleavage spilling out of her black lace bra. Black as her hair and eyes, her eyelashes. I stared at the swells of skin beneath the lingerie; the way she breathed as she ran water over the shirts.

"Maybe I could throw these into the wash?" She wasn't looking at me.

I nodded, eyes trailing her as she carried the balled-up shirts to the mini-sized washer and dryer stacked in a hallway closet, holding them away from her, trailing water all the way.

When she came back, she told me, "No, I haven't. But I'd like to get fucked, maybe, sometime..." Estela folded her arms across her chest and I thought, *No, don't do that.* She looked at me. "Think I could pick the next CD?" She dropped her arms to her sides, and my eyes went right back to her tits, the slight blush rising on her skin between them. I didn't say no.

Estela selected No Doubt. While she shimmied around the kitchen, singing in a silly voice, I sat on the counter, licking the last spoon and admiring the way Estela's eyes glowed as she danced and the way her boobs bounced. The song changed, slowed down, and Estela's eyelashes fluttered. She lifted her hands to tangle them in her thick hair. Her body moved in a circle.

"Dance with me?" she asked.

I wiped my palms on my jeans before I positioned myself in front of her. I felt kind of clumsy taking her in my arms, holding her waist. It took a second before I established a pace—languid and steady. I felt her warm, soft curves pressed against mine. I inhaled sugary heat off her hair. A few of my fingers brushed a bra strap, her skin. I enjoyed the way her lace scratched against my simple cotton cups, how our nipples stood up and then touched through the lingerie, and the way the waistband of our blue jeans met perfectly, bumping as we swayed. Estela sighed. Her head nestled into my shoulder. I felt my clit thumping inside the crotch of my pants before I imagined it growing as big as a dick, fucking her with it.

This is my chance, I thought, and then the song ended. Estela's lips pushed through my hair to skim my ear. She pulled away. I tried making eye contact. She joked about throwing out my Kid Rock CDs.

"He fucks lots of women," I shot back, and Estela shook her head, black sheen tumbling around white shoulders, lace straps, her smile.

I lifted an ear off the pillow to listen. Most mornings, Estela's off-key voice drifted down the heat vents, serenading my shower; my tongue burning itself on coffee, or my impatient hands ripping open manila envelopes, jotting down messages from the answering machine before flicking on the computer to return E-mail and start plugging in new files. I lay under the blanket and sheets, scratching myself, watching the heat vent and thinking I heard her. But she wasn't singing. Mornings were usually Sheryl Crow.

"*Estela!*" I wanted to shout. "Sing for me! I gotta get up!"

I scooted out of bed, and the scent of slept-in flannel sheets mixed with my own morning breath floated in the air near my head. I needed to wash my mouth out with coffee—Colombian roast, strong and acidic. I needed a shower, but first I posed in front of the full-length mirror tacked to the closet door. Lately I was wearing men's underclothes to bed. I thought I looked pretty damn good in them. I lifted the sleeveless T-shirt to inspect my tits. Round, firm flesh still warm from sleep held my eyes in the mirror. The nipples awoke; light to dark pink and standing up like two morning erections. Make that three. Behind the thick cotton fly of the red briefs my clit was thumping again. My pubic hair looked shiny in a streak of sunlight when I took off the briefs.

I squeezed my thighs together, enjoyed the zing, the way my eyes flickered, and then turned slowly in the mirror. Lately I'd been working out. Estela had a club membership and invited me to join as her guest. I liked pumping iron best. I didn't want to bulge. I wanted tone. I could see it already in my biceps, thighs, and ass. Even my calves appeared tighter, sleek. Would she like it? Estela told me she found it sexy to hold my feet while I did sit-ups. So I did four sets of twenty-five, zeroing out the burn by focusing on the curve of Estela's throat, the way she smiled as she counted: "Twenty-three, twenty-four, twenty-five! God, that's great, Patty!" she said, her eyes gleaming.

I went into the bathroom, crouching over the toilet. I remembered reading that men's morning erections were full of piss. I wondered what my erections were full of as I released my bladder. When I wiped, my clit thumped a little harder. I considered masturbating with my vibe on the bed; the one called the Tongue. I imagined the intense, steady massage against my burning clit until the moan-shudder took over and I shouted an effective expletive like "Fuck!" Maybe I'd wait. For what, I wasn't sure, but I'd wait for as long as I could.

I went back to the mirror; practiced curling my lip. In high school, my best friend Sammy was infatuated with the punk rocker Billy Idol. She taped his pictures to mirrors and then applied makeup with Billy and me watching. I'm not sure about him, but I was transfixed. Eyeliner to begin with, brownish-black, maybe blue, and smudged with a fingertip. Then eye shadow, always shimmery, like frosting. Mascara next—combed through her lashes, making them luscious-looking, curling. Then Sammy put on the blush: names like Coral Kiss and Crimson Sheets. She powdered her cheekbones while making the fish face and then smiling. Finally she took out the lipstick. Her mouth became hot-pink or violet-purple, glossy and sticky-looking, bright, and then she blotted with a tissue, showing me the perfect mouth mark. Sammy confided in me. "I'd like to leave a mark like this on Billy Idol's dick."

Her confession propelled me forward, posing behind her, mimicking the rocker's sneer.

Sammy laughed, delighted. "That's convincing," she said.

Around the same time, two boys in Sammy's and my geology class asked which I liked best: bananas or peaches. When I replied "Peaches," they snickered and whacked each other on the back. "We knew it!" they hooted. "Peaches!"

Sammy stayed quiet. I think she was blushing. I overdosed on peaches after that. Stole them from the supermarket—under my T-shirt like a couple of extra breasts. Sometimes I scaled the fence around the orchard near my house, stomped through rows of trees until I found one that was ready. I jiggled the fruit off the vine with a stick so it landed at my feet or straight into my hands. I sat near the trunk, cool in the shade, hidden, while my tongue flicked at the fuzzy skin before my lips sucked out the flesh, juice that smeared my chin, sticky, sugary, sweet. Sometimes tears welled in my eyes; the experience was that good.

When the same two boys teased Tina Laudry about liking peaches, I grabbed a set of balls and spat, "You're worried about your banana. Right? That's your problem!"

Sammy told me I shouldn't have done that. I tried harder. I dated Mark Johnson. Grew my hair like Lady Godiva's. Wore tiny banana earrings.

But it was peaches mingling with my morning breath this morning. I leaned into the mirror. Blurry sunlight illuminated the shine in my cheeks, the freckles. I dug the vague lines around my eyes. I was thirty, after all. But the real bonus was no zits. Maybe the Ortho Tri-Cyclen was working. Six months ago my gynecologist talked me into trying the pill for my skin, although I hadn't fucked a guy in two years. I remembered telling Dr. Wendell that I thought the trade-off for impending wrinkles was not getting zits. She told me she was forty-six and still got zits. And laid too, which was more than I could say lately.

"No boyfriend?" she quizzed me.

I shook my head.

"You had one when you started seeing me five years ago. What happened to him?"

What happened was that my relationships with men always evolved into fights over my unwillingness to commit to them. When my last boyfriend proposed moving in, I told him I had cheated on him. Of course, he assumed that I meant with a man. What I meant was the party two months before when I met Brenda Gonzales. Her hot, moist palm held onto my knee while we chatted about hip-huggers, brands of zinfandels, Spanish lessons, and videos on MTV. Her brown skin and short, spiky hair did something for me. One of her eyes was brown. The other was green.

"That's really sexy," I told her, and she smiled on one side of her mouth. Then she licked her lips, jerked her head for me to follow. I did. Before long, Brenda had located a closet. We tumbled through thick, scratchy coats and rattling metal hangers. I closed the door. Brenda positioned herself against the wall, yanked down her fly. Her voice turned gravelly. "Get down on your knees," she said. "Suck me off."

I fell against her instantly, kissing her swollen nipples through her tank top before I kneeled in front of her opened fly, licking pubic hair and then the clit jutting out at my tongue, swollen, erect.

She told me, "Yeah, pretty girl. Suck me like you wish I could fuck you with it."

Fuck me with it? Small sounds, maybe whimpers, escaped my throat. It was hard to tell, muffled by all those coats. And I could hardly see her through the dark. But I felt her body beside me— tight and toned. Her hands gripped my head, sometimes pulling my hair. Brenda whispered through her teeth at me while I clung to her by the ass through her jeans, digging in my nails and sucking her like a peach. When she came, shoving her cunt in my face, peeing juice, and swearing, I came too, clit jerking under my skirt, inside my panties.

It wasn't Brenda that turned me on so much as the idea that I could become her.

I was in the middle of a long dry spell when Estela started calling to me through the vents.

"Hey there!" Her playful tone echoed, spun around warm in the air. "Got any good books I could borrow? How about CDs?"

Estela hated my CD collection, and I didn't dig hers all that much either, but when she brought me an anthology of erotica including stories by Carol Queen and Serena Moloch I thought we had discovered something in common. I especially liked stories about butch lesbians fucking their femmes.

This morning in front of the mirror, I pushed my hands through my coppery-brown bun, unraveling it so it was down to my waist—healthy enough but heavy. Hair stuck to my neck, itched sometimes, was always tangled. What if I cut it all off? I could ask Estela to cut it. Cutting it was a commitment.

"Estela!" I yelled at the vent. "Estela, you hear me?"

"I hear you!" she yelled back.

"Come down! Bring your scissors!"

I wriggled back into the T-shirt and briefs, wondered if she would like me in them. Estela was wearing a silk blouse over underwear (yellow, I think), nothing else. *Jesus,* I thought, and dropped into a chair at the kitchen table. Estela located a towel and wrapped it around my shoulders. She grinned at my briefs, let her fingers slip under the elastic waistband, snapping it.

"What've ya got under there?"

I squirmed.

Estela tipped her head to one side, smiling in a way that was familiar. "I don't see any bulge." She laughed before her finger pulled on the band again—pulled it out farther so her finger could slip inside to stroke the skin above my mound. I shivered, wondered if she noticed.

"Are briefs a part of your fantasy, Pat?" Her voice was coy, breathless.

"Yeah."

The way she stood in front of me put her breasts just above eye level. The front of her blouse was unbuttoned, revealing her breasts, a glimpse of dusky nipples. The tingle behind my fly was becoming unbearable. I stuck my hand inside the blouse, held a cup of flesh, squeezing until she moaned. I painted one nipple in languid circles with saliva on my fingertip. Estela moaned again.

"Pat, what're we doing?" She pulled back but stayed close. The scissors were poised in her hand. "Trim?"

I shook my head. "All off. Short."

Estela's dark eyes widened. "Off?" she repeated, and then she stroked a handful of strands. "Those rock star dudes you like so much—they sport long hair and bad skin. You'll never fit in." She laughed.

I let a hand rest on her waist. "Short hair, most of them, but do they really have bad skin?"

Estela massaged my scalp. "Hmm, I guess I don't pay attention." She massaged harder, my neck and my shoulders. I let my head slump forward. My forehead pressed her belly. I inhaled nutmeg-cinnamon-mint. Only Estela would smell like that.

"Going all the way with your fantasy?" I heard her ask.

"Feels good," I murmured before my thoughts wandered back to a night Estela invited me upstairs to watch a movie. Gina Gershon starred as an incredibly sexy dyke. Jennifer Tilly played her voluptuous lipstick lover. I remember the charge I got when they kissed. My body curled against the end of the couch, shivering.

"Cold?" Estela asked.

"No," I almost said, and then, "I guess so," and she tucked a wooly blanket under my bare toes, under my ass, around my shoulders, and close to my chin. She touched my cheek. "Anything else?"

I liked the way she cared for me. I shook my head and imagined a scene of mutual masturbation, both of us under blankets, hands creating movement, reappearing lumps beneath the thick wool until I was so close I ordered Estela to put her head under my blanket. "Suck me," I ordered her in the fantasy.

Estela lifted my head now, staring into my eyes. "You sure about this?" Meaning the haircut. When I nodded, her practiced eye inspected my head from every angle. She studied my face, directed my chin up, down, sideways, and then nodded. "You could definitely pull short hair off."

I heard the scissors slicing, felt Estela's hands against my head, watched chunks of brownish-red hair drop to the floor near my feet.

Snip, cut, drop: more and more hair, piles of it, but Estela never hesitated. I never flinched. She kept cutting, checking, cutting some more. My arms and scalp tickled. Pretty soon I felt air on the back of my neck and Estela's fingers touching me there. Estela removed the towel, stepped back to examine her work. Her eyes were sharp, pensive. I motioned her closer until we were eye level, inches apart, and I gazed deep into her pupils, saw my reflection. "I like it," I said.

Estela stood up, smiling shyly. "Want a mirror?"

"After a shower."

Beneath the spray of hot water, the lingering scent of cinnamon-nutmeg-mint mixed with my own musky cunt smell, drove me nuts. My clit was thumping fervently. I grabbed the shampoo bottle and fondled it, thought about sliding its plastic, smooth surface over labia lips, back and forth, slow and sticking; back and forth, fast; spreading my cunt open, hitting my clit with a plastic phallus, which felt cool at first but then matched the temperature of the water, the heat between my legs. And then I thought about getting behind Estela, fucking her with a big one that felt and looked like a real dick, and it was pink, no purple, and it was lubed up with spit pooling in her mouth before she licked the rubber skin. Her eyes stared up at me, smoldering. And her cunt was as beautiful as the rest of her. Mother of God... I rinsed my head off, amazed by the sensation of short, slick hairs beneath my wet hands, the lack of weight hanging over my shoulders.

"What were ya doin' in there?" Estela teased down the heat vent ten minutes later. "You used all the hot water."

"Have not."

"How's it look?"

"Still wet, but I think good."

"Told you."

"Yeah."

I remembered Sammy again: inseparable our junior year. In November, Sammy's mother, Maggie, had to drive to Dallas for a funeral. She invited us to join her, if we wanted. We did. But not for the funeral: for the *road trip*. Maggie hunched over the steering wheel, glaring through her glasses at the dark road, window rolled down to let her cigarette smoke out, the moonlight in, a bit of wind, and the sound of the cassette tapes Sammy and I requested: Berlin, Depeche Mode, Duran Duran. Sammy and I shared a blanket between us across the backseat. Our legs intermingled. We held hands. In whispers we revealed plans; shared secrets we told no one else. I whispered "I wish I was a man," which was easier than admitting that I wanted to be with her the rest of my life, no matter what sex we were.

Sammy whispered back, "Me too."

In her bedroom, in front of the world's longest mirror, Sammy curled my hair, feathered it around my face, combed it neatly down the nape of my neck, shoulders, and then down my back. Sammy loved to do me up. I loved the way the pores in my skin opened up with nerve endings, aching, whenever she touched me. It was winter outside. Ice frosted the windows and chilly fingertips poked at us until the heat kicked on and hot air blasted through the grill near my feet. When Sammy held up a mirror I didn't look a thing like Billy Idol, but she looked as beautiful as any of his girlfriends, so I said, "Looks great," and she answered, "Told you" while my toes curled beside the heat vent. I started to sweat.

The snow had disappeared, exposing gnarled and naked tree limbs, yards flat and thin and the color of piss, when Samantha's mother confronted me, unexpected, beneath the awning of the porch. She wouldn't let me into the house. She spat at me: "You know what people are saying? They can say it about *you* all they want, but not about Samantha." *Samantha* instead of Sammy, my pet name for her.

Sammy called once after that. I pictured her hunkered inside a closet or something. "I miss you," she said. She never called again. I never called her.

Today, I was calling to Estela through the heat vent. "Still there?"

"I'm here." Her voice floated down.

I paused, didn't exactly know what to say. "Feels fantastic! My hair! Thanks!"

"It's very sexy!" she shouted back.

My hands toyed with the short strands starting to dry, feeling silky and straight, and standing up all over. I traced my bare neck. I yelled up again. "It really feels fantastic!" Silence. I gnawed at my lips, stared at the vent. "Estela?"

"Yeah?"

My mouth moved and nothing came out. I imagined Estela on her back, me directing her there while I leaned over her sleek white body sprawled across my bed, writhing beneath me, and my hands tugging her panties away, a wisp of silk beside us. Then I'd push her thighs apart, and my chin would slide down the mound of black hairs, curling and coarse. I imagined her labia lips, ripe and soft, clit hardening to a seed beneath my tongue. I imagined her back arching, her hips undulating against me, lifting it all closer to me; right there, all of it, right off the tree, for me. I saw her red mouth open with a moan, her cunt open with wanting me, and my tongue licking her all over before the tip stabbed through her wet slit—thrusting, rolling, fucking her deep to the nutmeg and mint. And then I mounted her body. She took me into her arms. Our fervor forced all the blankets back off the bed, and I told her in a gravelly voice: "Estela…wanna…gonna…fuck you, fuck you, pretty girl."

"I want that," she told me, and her hand guided my cock in. I released a long moan. My strap-on sunk all the way inside her. The pressure against my clit was intense, steady as my hips thrust and rocked. I exploded. Estela screamed, "Goddamn it! Coming! All over the place!"

Her body went limp and satiated. Both of us breathed hard, embracing, smiling in that way at last. This wasn't a fantasy anymore.

"Estela!" I yelled at the vent. "Jesus! You gotta come down!"

"Right here." And her warm breath blew down my neck.

Personal Savior
Sheila Traviss

Outside, the snow sifted down like confectioner's sugar in the hands of a God turned drunkard; generous, reckless, not knowing when to stop. Inside, the heat of the radiator pacified me along with the rest of the algebra class into a herd of nodding cattle. I looked out the window and caught the image of white, closed my eyes, turned back to the classroom, and carried the color inside.

Mr. Aceto caught the movement of my head and bellowed, "Miss Taylor, what are you up to now?"

"Just thinking."

"That's new. Why don't you share it with the class?"

"I'd rather not."

"No, I insist." He waited to pounce.

I tried imitating the voice of Mush Mouth from Fat Albert, and it came out a little louder, actually a lot louder, than I had expected. I shouted, "I bud abd-lying mad-a-matics."

The silver chrome of his head burst and mercury hit the fluorescent. "Get out. Now! Out."

I knew where to go: the vice principal's office. Mrs. Countryman and I had been seeing a lot of each other. She was systematically destroying my senior year of high school. She had me kicked off the debate team for saying the word "fuck" and stripped me of my cheerleader skirt for drinking peppermint schnapps.

I arrived at her office, sat down, and waited for the attack. She calmly pulled out her chair, stood up to her full height of six feet, and pulled out my file.

"You're a real comedienne, aren't you?" She waited for an answer. "Aren't you?"

I wanted to cry, but I laughed. "It was just a joke."

"Oh, it always is. I don't know about you, but I think it's funny when I see a young lady wasting her life. I suppose I'll laugh too, in a couple of years, when I see you sacking my groceries."

I bit the inside of my cheek until it bled to keep myself from laughing. But I wanted to cry.

"How do I get through to you? What's it going to take to wise you up?"

"I don't know." I really didn't.

"Why don't you think about it for the rest of the week? You're out! And that's it. This is your third strike. Once more, and you're not coming back."

I had never needed safe refuge more than in my senior year of high school, a place to get away from my mother's obsession with diet pills that made her thin and neurotic. Each night, as I tried to reanimate her burnt offerings with ketchup, she transfigured herself with dietary supplements. Quarter-inch squares that gave "fudge" a bad name. As quick as she lost the weight, she gained a temper.

Mom would receive "the call" before I'd be able to make it home. Even though I dreaded Dad's tears more than Mom's wrath, I wouldn't go home until he was there. Dad would cry whether I was beaten or not, but Mom wouldn't hit if he was home.

A blizzard raged outside; it was twenty below and falling. Snow cut into my face, and my throat burned with sorrow. I slid behind the wheel of my Duster and waited for the engine to tremble toward warmth. I couldn't find a roach big enough to smoke, so I lit a cigarette.

I put the car in reverse, and that's when I saw her. For the first time she was by herself and not crowded by the type of girls who didn't go to beer blasts. Karen Johnson. What a beautiful name. She walked out of the school with her hands stuffed into parka pockets, head up and forward as the wind played behind her.

I rolled down the window and shouted, "Hey, Johnson, want a ride?"

Her smile broadened, and when she moved it was for more than just travel. She glided into the car and said, "Praise the Lord. I've been wanting to talk to you for such a long time."

Karen was liquid marble, the type of girl you shouldn't touch without purpose. She was a Stradivarius, while I was a tambourine used to being banged about.

"What about?" I asked.

"I've been praying for you every day since you streaked the assembly."

It had been a dare. My best friend, Joyce, also an ex-cheerleader, had just had an abortion, and I wanted to cheer her up. "Oh, I just did it for fun."

"I said to the Lord that he could use a girl like you. Someone with your kind of courage." She stroked my cheek with her hand and widened her smile.

I rolled down my window, threw out my cigarette, and said, "Sorry."

She talked all the way to her house. Giving me directions where to turn and the blow-by-blows of recent conversions. When we got to her house she asked me in, and I went.

Her house was blue-collar-Iowa poor. Throw rugs failed in their attempt to cover up waves of warped linoleum. Fried eggs and bacon grease clung to the radiated heat of the air. Half a pan of brownies sat on the kitchen table. There was nobody home.

I was a stranger in a new land. Never had I seen food sitting out without a Saran Wrap cover. My mother's house always smelled of either Glade Pine Forest Fresh or Flowering Spring. And my mother was always home shifting food from one Tupperware container to another or cleaning up ketchup bottle lids.

Karen reached past the brownies, grabbed a couple of apples, and took me up to her room. Macramé planters hung heavy with ivy. Hundreds of sprouts shot fuzzy blind prods through the room. It was her little Eden. We sat next to each other on the bed. She opened her mouth and out sprung honeyed promises of a love that would never die: "I have prayed for you every night. I have a love for you that can only be explained because of Jesus," she confessed.

She took my hand and got down on her knees and prayed. The force of her passion coursed through her body and leaped into the pulse of my soul.

"You just have to believe in Him, Mary."

I wanted her to say my name again.

"Mary, accept Jesus Christ as your personal lord and savior. "

And then she cried. Something I was only able to do after chugging a quart.

"Jesus loves you. And so do I."

My organs flipped from the in to the out. Struck by the light, night from the day, empty now full, I heard myself say, "OK." A word as small as a split atom with twice as much punch.

She wrapped herself around me, "Oh, Mary, I love you so much."

"Me too." And we kissed open-mouthed. That quick, and then back to the path.

I believed I was new, and as you believe, so shall it be. I certainly felt different, and for the next three hours I fell into the words that Karen dug beneath me. Sinking, falling, knowing I didn't want to climb out. Her dad knocked on the bedroom door to say hi.

Karen proudly pronounced, "Dad, Mary will now be joining us in the rapture." He threw back his white-man Afro and lifted his arms. "I pray to Jesus that it will be soon."

I gave Karen my number, twice, before I left her house. In my car I went to light a cigarette but threw it out when I remembered I was born again. I prayed for forgiveness as I dumped the full ashtray along Interstate 5.

When I got home I found that Jesus had taken care of my parents. They had worn themselves out fighting over whose fault I was. Dad's face was streaked with blotchy tears and Mom's teeth ground down to nubs. I went up to my room and called Karen. She told me of the other girls she had led to the Lord, but none had seen the sins I had seen. She assured me that I was special and not just another notch on her spiritual belt of conversion.

The next night, I went to Karen's house for dinner. Her parents couldn't think of a sin that I hadn't committed—except for maybe murder—and of that they weren't so sure. Drinking and driving! Oh, my! As they passed around the mashed potatoes, I titillated them with my transgressions.

I told the stories horror-style. All that was missing was a campfire. "Well, I started smoking marijuana in ninth grade." A carny by the name of Dusty had turned me on. He ran the tilt-a-whirl at the state fair and was missing a thumb. They praised God that I had been saved from the likes of Dusty. I soaked up their attention like white bread in water.

"Mary, do you still have your virginity to give as a gift?"

"Mom!" Karen protested.

I wasn't even sure that my own mother knew I used tampons.

I answered, "No. The first boy I slept with was…"

Mr. Johnson pushed away from the table and said, "To the one you love, it will always be a gift."

Mrs. Johnson cooed, "Oh, Mary, did you know it is harder for a rich girl to get into heaven than for a camel to get through a needle?" All I knew was that I was glad I wasn't high, because sober, I couldn't understand a word that she said. But then she asked, "Why, you didn't know what love was until Jesus, did you?"

I looked at Karen and said, "No." I also didn't know I was rich.

They praised God for bringing me to Karen. They encouraged me to sleep over, and they put my mother on their prayer list. My ignorance, which they called innocence, was a constant source of entertainment to them. They got such a kick out of me when I said, "I think my Bible has a misprint. Matthew, Mark, and Luke all say the same thing."

They fell into conniptions. "Misprint! Oh, that's funny. You should be a Christian comic." They turned to each other at this stroke of brilliance. They would suggest it as a ministry to their Wednesday-night Bible study.

My mother found nothing funny nor good about my conversion. When I tried to talk to her about the Lord, her nails would drive deep into the arms of her chair. "Lord! What do you know about the Lord? You wouldn't know Jesus if He came up and bit you on the ass." She missed the appearance of my popular friends and didn't trust Karen's mother.

Evelyn was Iowa's most popular host on the Christian radio station, KROS. Her show, *Cross Talk,* played daily, and her topics concerned a woman's walk with the Lord. Evelyn had a mouth that looked able to swallow a face up whole, slow-motion eyelids that whisked you in with each sweep, breasts worthy of pagan devotion. I once told Evelyn, "You look just like Sophia Loren." She gasped, blotted the liner from around her eyes, and brought me into the cult of her body.

When I returned to school after my week of suspension, my friends winked and waited to hear the punch line about "the conversion." I said, "No, really, I believe." Mrs. Countryman rolled her eyes and said, "Whatever it takes." A prophet is never greeted in her own lunchroom.

Karen believed that I needed the fellowship of Christian friends, so she invited me to a taping down at KROS. Her mother was hosting a special, *Can Christian Women Be Rock and Roll Stars?* All the great Christian women of rock were going to be there: Annie from Second Chapter of Acts, Lil' Evie, Kim from Peace of Soul, and Julie of John 3:16. The radio station wasn't far from Karen's house, so we walked. I wanted to tell her about the time I hid in an ambulance to get in free to a Neil Sedaka concert.

We were late getting to the station, and the rock stars and Evelyn had already been seated. The room was no bigger than a one-car garage. Photographs of Christian celebrities hung on the walls. I recognized Dino, who had been a protégé of Liberace, and Jerry Falwell, Phyllis Schlafly, and, of course, Jesus.

Annie opened up the show with "Not Dead," her most requested song.

"Hear the bells clinging / They're ringing that you don't have to be dead / The angels dance on the tombstones…" Annie's albino-blond hair had been dedicated to the Lord. She hadn't cut it since the day she accepted Jesus into her heart. Her pink eyes swelled as she sang, and Kim from Peace of Soul quietly wept.

Karen eased herself next to Kim and gave comfort by rubbing circles into the small of her back. Circles that I had been praying to Jesus for. At night, during our sleepovers, Karen read from the Psalms as I tickle-rubbed her back, arms, and stomach. On the previous night my fingers brushed over her cotton briefs. I felt the soft down of her pubic hair as I waved my fingers gently back and forth, praying she would beg me to slip my fingers inside her. Just when I was about to cross the elastic barrier Karen rolled over and said, "Isn't it a blessing that Jesus always watches over us?"

Kim laid her head on Karen's shoulder and accepted the stroking calm of her hand. I was developing a lump of jealousy in my throat when Julie of John 3:16 stood up, leaned into me, and whispered, "Don't you love her voice?" She wrapped her arm around my shoulder and slowly breathed into my ear as she awaited my answer. I couldn't speak, struck mute by words so expertly slipped into my ear. Ricocheting desire careened through my vessel with no means of release. I heard bells. It was the ringing end of the "Not Dead" song.

Evelyn spoke into the microphone. "That was an inspiration. Annie, why do you call your rock group the Second Chapter of Acts?"

Annie nodded an *Oh, I've heard this question* reply and lisped, "The second chapter speaks of Pentecost and the gift of tongues."

Julie sat me down in her chair and wriggled herself between the V of my legs. Two bodies, one heat. Her lips butterflied around my ears as she quoted, "Acts, second chapter, twenty-eighth verse: *Thou hast made known to me the ways of life; Thou wilt make me full of gladness with thy presence.*" And then she winked. Full of wet guilt, I looked over at Karen, turned into a pillar of salt, and crumbled at Julie's feet.

Evelyn announced that after the commercial break the next voice heard would be that of Julie Freel of John 3:16. Julie stood, removed herself from between my legs, and left my throb to just one hand clapping. Karen came over and introduced herself to Julie and asked if she would like to join us for dinner that night. Julie looked straight at me, put out her hand, brushed the bangs out of my eyes, and answered, "Would love it." She turned to Karen and asked, "You brought this girl to the Lord, didn't you?" Karen gave an "aw shucks" smile. Julie picked up her guitar, turned toward the soundstage, looked back at me, and said, "I wish it had been me."

Karen sat down next to me and groaned that she wished the Lord had given her the gift of song. "It's such a powerful tool of conversion. Think of the souls that will be saved today."

I thought of nothing but dinner that night. We would be going to La Pizza House. They have booths there. I was plotting the certainty of Julie on one side and Karen on the other. I wondered where Julie was staying while in town. She could have stayed at my house if my mother was dead.

Julie strapped on her guitar and put her fingers into motion. Her voice was chestnut-colored and ran maple syrup–slow into the microphone. "I'd like to thank Jesus for shedding his blood for me, because if he hadn't I wouldn't be here. And if I were not here today, I would not have met a girl who I believe is going to be a very special lady for the Lord." She placed two fingers to her lips and blew a kiss to me.

When the taping was finished, we walked out of the studio and into the light of day. I carried one of Julie's guitars and put it into the trunk of her powder-blue Karmann Ghia. She called the car Puff. I said, "What a great name for a car." Then, as I had prayed for, Julie asked, "Would you mind riding with me?"

Karen was busy listening to Lil' Evie's cure for asthma. With each suck on the inhaler, she croaked out, "Praise Jesus." I said to Karen, sweet as marzipan, "Save me a seat." She nodded her head up once and averted her focus to Kim from Peace of Soul.

Julie patted the seat beside her, and I hesitated before slowly sinking in. I waited for Karen to say, "No, Mary, stay with me. Mary, I love you." But she and Kim were holding hands and praying over Lil' Evie's flooded Chevy Nova.

Legs horizontal, inches between us, Julie drove in the right direction, never making the destination. She said, "This may be rude, but I'm going back to Iowa City tonight, and I would really like to get to know you. Do you mind if we just take a ride? Maybe pick up a couple of Big Macs, go to the country, and praise the Lord there?"

I prayed for forgiveness to God when I thought that I had heard this same line from boys who had already begun to unbuckle their belts. But this time I meant it when I said, "That would be great."

With fish filet and fries on my breath I spoke to Julie about how she sounded just like Joni Mitchell.

Julie pushed in an eight-track with the palm of her hand and sang full-throttle along with Joni, "Court and Spark." The car bumped down a cow path I had discovered while tripping on acid before finding Jesus.

Out of fear of implosion, I leaped from the car when it came to a halt. Wordlessly we walked, listening to the voices of nature. The magnetic pull brought our hands together. I started to think of Karen but forced myself to stop as we walked past fearless rabbits thumping soft pelt upon pelt. Julie spread out a down-filled sleeping bag on the hard pack of snow. Our legs unfastened beneath us. We lay on our backs and Julie started singing "Both Sides Now."

And then silence. A light breeze gently entwined our hair. I closed my eyes and readied myself for what I prayed was coming. I leaned up on my elbow and looked down at Julie staring up at me.

"You're shaking," she said.

"Cold," I lied.

Julie reached up and brought my head down to hers. Her eyes opened and then closed with the parting of her mouth upon mine. Cool tongue firmly tracing the space of my lips. With one inhalation I breathed in new life. One hand under a peasant top, another tugging at buttons.

When she lay on top of me, I closed my eyes and saw Karen. Desire betrayed my heart. But if it was Julie and not Karen whom the Lord meant for me, then I would accept and be grateful, for it too was good.

Now naked Julie quoted from Song of Solomon. "The curves of your hips are like jewels. Your navel like a round goblet." We pushed hand against hand. Julie smiled a devilish grin and said, "You're good."

Incredibly high water bills had made me a thoughtful lover.

"Thanks. So are you," I said, taking her hand and putting it back between my legs.

"Was Karen your first?" Julie asked while wiggling her thumb up my ass.

"No, you are."

Julie removed herself from me and sat upright. "No?"

"No. Never." Oh, I had in the privacy of my mind, thousands if not millions of times. Karen, and Raquel Welch after seeing the movie *Kansas City Bomber,* and others.

"Oh, really," she said, sounding more frightened than doubtful.

"You're my first." And I took this gift from the Lord with wide-open arms. I wanted to give back by taking Julie to Dead Baby Bridge and showing her where to stand to hear the baby cry; taking her to the train track where you could hop on a car and go to Dubuque for the day; playing her Frank Zappa on my eight-track.

Julie started to dress, held my face with her hands, and said, "If you say anything, I'm going to have to deny it."

Peter! You didn't even wait for the first cock to crow.

I prayed that I would laugh rather than cry when Julie asked, "When do I get to see you again?"

"When will you be back?" I answered.

Julie kissed me on the nose, rolled on top of me, and then into the snow. This time she stroked me with her tongue as my body thrashed out a snow angel. She dropped me off at Karen's house, where I had left my car. Karen was waiting and ran out as soon as we pulled into the drive.

"Her mom would feed us to the lions." Julie squeezed my crotch before Karen reached the car.

"I'm not going to say anything." I was more fearful that if Karen knew, I would never get to make love to her.

"Hey, where'd you guys go?" Karen opened my door.

"Flat tire and then an axle problem." Julie was quick.

"Want some hot chocolate?" Karen asked.

"No, I've got to get back to Iowa City. Hey, Mary, give me your address so I can send you the money," Julie said.

"What money?"

"For the tire, you goof." She wrapped her arms around me and kissed me hard on the forehead.

"Oh, yeah." I gave her my address and phone number, and Julie drove off.

"It sure took you guys a long time to get the tire fixed." Karen took my gloved hand in hers and led me inside.

"Oh, and then we went to IHOP and talked, and Julie got sick." I am a terrible liar.

"I don't mean to gossip, but Kim told me that Julie has been backsliding for a while. She even believes in the ERA. If Mom knew Julie believed in killing babies, she wouldn't have had her on the show."

"I thought about you all day today," I said.

"Isn't that funny? Me too. I think you would really like Kim. She's really sweet," Karen said.

"Really? I think you would really like Julie. She's really nice."

Karen poured us both a cup of hot chocolate, and then we ran up the stairs to her room.

"Do you think your mom will let you spend the night?" Karen asked, knowing the answer.

It wasn't until we climbed into bed that I noticed I still carried Julie's scent on my fingers. I cupped them around my face and levitated at least a foot off the bed.

"Do you like tickle rubs?" Karen asked.

"Give me your arm," I answered.

"No, do you like them?" she asked.

"Yeah," I answered.

"Give me your arm."

"Eww, I've got to go pee." I jumped from the bed and into the bathroom. I was so swollen I had to tickle my labia to make myself pee. And then I washed Julie from me and prepared myself for Karen. God was so good, God was so good. I jumped back into the bed and held out my arms. Karen's hand was too heavy to make the tickle rub truly a tickle. It was more of a rub.

I reached one hand below me and checked out what was going on between my legs. I could have gotten a Chevy Impala inside me. The excitement got me a little carried away.

"Karen, I love you." And I turned to look her in the eyes.

"I love you too," she answered with a hug.

I pulled slightly away and said, "I *love* love you."

"I know. And I hope we get to die with each other," she answered.

And then I kissed her. Our lips were warm and tender. Her open mouth was so trusting and dear. I cupped her breasts in my hands and pulled off her panties with my foot. She pressed herself against my leg and gently rode it until she quivered. I trembled and cried.

Karen opened her eyes, rubbed her face as if in a dream, jumped off the bed, and said, "You've got to go."

My lips moved, but a swarm of locusts devoured the words from my mouth. My tears fouled waters. The sea parted between us.

"What's wrong?" I went to touch her hand, but she pulled away. She yanked on her clothes and then a robe.

"Are you kidding?" She crossed her arms across her stomach and bent at the waist.

"Karen, everything is OK," I said.

"That's the devil talking. Mary, I will pray for your soul every night that I live. Only Jesus can save us. Let's pray. Let's pray that Jesus will forgive us." And she dropped to her knees.

"Pray for what?" I really didn't know.

"Forgiveness. You know this is wrong. It's all over the Bible how wrong this is." She was crying, and I was getting scared that her parents would be getting home soon. I wasn't certain what they would do to me.

"I don't remember reading anything about it," I said, not quite sure what it was. I had never really thought about *it* other than I wanted *it*.

"I will never do that again. Ever. I swear to God." Karen clasped her hands together and held them up to God.

"Karen, do you want some water?" I asked.

"I don't even believe that you're saved. Let's pray." She kept spiraling outward.

"Karen, it's you that I pray for." I meant it as a compliment.

"Oh, my God! Get out! You've been posing as Satan. That's what this is. Even the Lord's shiniest angels had to be thrown into hell. If God couldn't tell the difference, how was I supposed to know?" She kept talking, but I couldn't make out her words.

Karen ran past me and into the bathroom, where I could hear the lock of the door. I dressed and then knocked. She didn't answer, and then I heard the shower turn on.

"I'll call you when I get home," I yelled.

I stopped at the Git 'n' Go and bought a pack of Marlboros from a guy I'd gone to school with since kindergarten.

"I thought you was a Christian," he said.

"So what?" I answered.

"Want a shorty?" He popped the lid off a miniature beer.

I took the long way home and drove past the church where Karen's parents' car was still parked. Past the Latin King, where over half a dozen of my friends were playing pool inside. Past the water tower I had sworn I would paint my name on, and then home.

Dad was watching the news and Mom was doing her nails. The house smelled like canned cedar.

"I'm home," I said as I kicked off my shoes.

"About time," Mom said.

"How's my sugar?" Dad asked.

"OK." And I went up to my room, closed the door, and called Karen. I dialed over thirty times, but it was always busy. I changed into my pajamas, crawled into bed, picked up my Bible, and looked in the concordance for the word *queer*. It wasn't there. I called Karen again, but her mother answered.

"Hi, Mrs. Johnson. Can I talk to Karen?"

"No, you may not." Her voice was rigid, and I heard her hand cover the speaker.

"OK. I just wanted to—" I was cut off.

"We know very well what you want, and that desire will take you straight to hell."

"What?" I couldn't believe Karen would have told her parents. That was gross. Disgusting.

"It won't stop us from loving you and praying for you, but you are not welcome in this house. Good night." And then, *click.*

I picked up the phone and tried to decide who I could call. I could call Julie and ask her how she had her feelings and still followed the Lord. But then I knew the answer to that. Joyce, my ex–best friend, wouldn't be home, and what could I say to her: "I like screwing girls more than guys"? I was scared.

So I called Karen again. Her mother picked up, and all I could think of to say was "Fuck you." And then I hung up.

The Girl in 8G

Yolanda Wallace

The girl in 8G has only one breast. She lost the left one to cancer when she was eighteen. That was seven years ago. Her right breast is perfect: more than a mouthful, not quite a handful; firm without being too taut, a nice, comfortable weight. There's a tattoo where the left one used to be. The tattoo looks like something off a mechanic's pinup calendar: a gorgeous big-breasted woman in a halter top and cutoffs straddling an oversize Craftsman wrench.

The girl in 8G marches with her shirt off in gay pride parades, a pink ribbon tied around her arm in honor of breast cancer awareness.

The girl in 8G has a shaved head. Not because it makes her look like a cancer patient but because it makes her look tough. Like Joan Jett as Columbia in *The Rocky Horror Show* on Broadway. Or Joan Jett as Joan Jett every day of her life.

The girl in 8G has a twin sister. They don't look much like twins anymore. As a matter of fact, they don't look much like sisters. The twin is one of those girls in power suits at lunch who rises meteorically within the company she works for until she smashes her head against the glass ceiling. With long legs, full lips, and flowing chestnut hair, she looks like Cindy Crawford without the mole. When she heard about her sister's diagnosis, the twin had a preventive double mastectomy followed by reconstructive surgery.

The girl in 8G works in a vintage clothing store in the Village. Underscored by a propulsive soundtrack of rave, dance, and goth music, she sells broken-in jeans, old concert shirts, and leftover wardrobe from cinematic costume dramas at outrageous prices. She jacks up the price even more for those who can afford it. For the ones who can't, she turns a blind eye while they steal whatever they want.

The girl in 8G is in a band. She plays lead guitar—sometimes topless, sometimes not—for a group of protopunkers called Piss and Vinegar. They aren't very good, but it doesn't seem to matter. They look like they're having fun, and the members of the audience are usually too drunk to ask for their money back.

The girl in 8G has a dog, a terrier that looks like Moose, the dog that plays Eddie on *Frasier*. I see them in the park a lot playing catch with a Frisbee or just lounging in the sun on slow summer Sundays.

The girl in 8G was the star of her cross-country team in high school. She was state champion three times. On her fourth try she was well ahead of the field when she turned back to help a runner who had tripped over a root and injured her ankle. She knew she'd be disqualified for it, but she did it anyway.

The girl in 8G is from Oregon. Most people who live in New York City weren't born here. We all came from somewhere we didn't fit in to call someplace that doesn't care "home."

The girl in 8G wears a Portland Trail Blazers jersey to Knicks games just to piss off the Madison Square Garden crowd. Works every time, though her Michael Jordan Bulls jersey works even better.

The girl in 8G broke up with her boyfriend last week. Though she identifies as bi, he was the first man in her life in four years. They lasted three months. Where does that leave me? The same place I've always been: on the outside looking in.

The girl in 8G lives across the street from me in a rent-controlled building called the Georgian. Her apartment is directly opposite from mine. I'd love to move into her building because the rent's more affordable and the interiors are retro-cool, but the waiting list is so long that my best shot at getting an apartment there is by inheriting it from a dead relative. Unfortunately, all of my relatives—living and dead—are in North Carolina.

The girl in 8G is a Rolling Stones fan. She has all of their releases on CD, cassette, and the original vinyl. The framed jackets of the albums line her apartment walls like works of art. The one for *Tattoo You* even bears Mick Jagger's autograph. Ron Wood signed *Voodoo Lounge;* Charlie Watts, *Sticky Fingers.*

The girl in 8G is having a dinner party. I received my invitation yesterday, though I think it's a mistake. We've never officially met, and when we've passed each other on the street I haven't merited a second glance. I show up five minutes early, carrying the invitation in one hand in case a mistake has been made, and a bottle of wine in the other in case one hasn't.

The girl in 8G answers the door. When she sees me, she smiles and says, "You came." OK, so my invitation wasn't a mistake. Sweet. "We've been watching each other through our apartment windows long enough. I think it's time we met, don't you?"

The girl in 8G hasn't invited anyone else to dinner. Just me. "Not much of a party, huh?" I tell her I guess that depends on how well this works out.

The girl in 8G says, "I'll keep my fingers crossed," then she asks me if I like spaghetti. Pasta is the one thing I could eat every day. I ask if she needs me to do anything. She says I can keep her company while she finishes the sauce. She was in the middle of chopping vegetables when I rang the bell.

The girl in 8G drops diced bell peppers, onions, and mushrooms into the simmering pot on the stove. As she wipes her hands on a towel, she asks me what I do. While I tell her about my job, I do something my father hates: I sit on the counter. It's my favorite place to talk when I'm in the kitchen and someone's cooking. My father says you shouldn't put your ass where you prepare your food, but it's not like it's my bare ass, so what's the big deal?

The girl in 8G tells me she's been getting information about me from mutual friends. I didn't know we had mutual friends. I got my information about her the old-fashioned way: through careful, near-constant observation. I'm not a stalker, though. Just a huge fan of hers.

The girl in 8G stirs the sauce and searches for a smaller spoon. She finds a teaspoon, dips it into the sauce, and blows on it. "Taste this." She dips the tip of her left middle finger into the sauce and offers it to me. "Too spicy, not spicy enough, or just right?"

The girl in 8G has small pads of hardened skin on her fingertips, little calluses from gripping her guitar strings. Holding her wrist, I draw her finger over my lips and into my mouth. The sauce is an afterthought; I lick it off right away. Then I go down on her finger like Madonna with a bottle of mineral water. Stroke down. Up. Down. A little more suction. A little less. Then a little tongue. Her eyes remain locked on mine the entire time. I slowly pull her finger out of my mouth and kiss the wet tip. I tell her it tastes just right.

The girl in 8G pushes my knees apart and steps between them. She presses her cheek to mine, and my breasts long for the touch of her hands. "That squishing sound you hear? That's me," she says.

I know the feeling. "How am I supposed to make small talk after that?" I ask. I stroke her forearms. The tiny brown hairs are standing on end.

The girl in 8G pulls away. I miss her immediately. "What's left to talk about?" She leans forward again and kisses me. "What you want me to make you for breakfast in the morning, which side of the bed you prefer, and how many times we do it before we call it a night." Bagels and coffee; the left; and as many times as possible.

The girl in 8G is wearing a form-fitting Lycra T-shirt. I pull at it, wanting to get to that tattoo. "It's a bodysuit," she says. I hate these things. The snap closures are always such a pain to deal with. They never want to cooperate when you're in a hurry to get someone's clothes off.

The girl in 8G unbuckles her worn black leather belt and unzips her jeans. Then she takes my hand and directs it to her crotch. The bodysuit comes with snaps. I love these things. I caress her mound in the palm of my right hand before I flick my fingers and undo the snaps. I pull the bodysuit over her head and hold it in my left hand to keep from dropping it on the floor. I put my right hand over the tattoo.

The girl in 8G reaches over and turns off the burner under the spaghetti sauce. Then she pulls me off the counter. "Come down here," she says. "I want to feel you." As she grinds her hips against mine, I put my mouth where her left breast should be. The erectile tissue has been cut away, but she gasps as if it's still there.

The girl in 8G takes my hand and directs it back inside her jeans. I caress her mound with the palm of my right hand. Then I slip the tip of my middle finger inside her underwear to tease her clit. Warm and wet, it's already hard.

The girl in 8G asks, "What are you into?"

I say her.

"No," she says, "I mean what do you like?"

I say her.

"So no toys?"

Indicating what I'm holding in my right hand, I tell her I have more than enough to play with right here. Pushing her jeans and Jockeys down around her ankles, I kneel in front of her and bury my face in her cunt.

The girl in 8G moans and leans against the counter for support as I wet her with my tongue, then suck her dry. I part her lips with my tongue and thrust it inside her. I cup her ass in my hands as her hips rock back and forth against my mouth. Her movements take my tongue deeper and deeper inside her.

The girl in 8G, her knees buckling, says she can't do this standing up. I crawl with her, my tongue flicking in and out like a snake's, as she duck-walks to the table. She's too close to make it to the bedroom.

The girl in 8G lies on top of the kitchen table, the one with the green Formica top and the spindly metal legs. After I finish undressing her, I pull up a chair to continue my meal. It's silly and whimsical, but it fits. She did invite me to dinner, after all, though I doubt either of us thought she'd end up being the main course.

The girl in 8G is a screamer. When she comes, she sounds like Jamie Lee Curtis in *Prom Night*. Mmm, that's a pretty appetizing thought too.

The girl in 8G reaches around me to undo the thin ties that secure my handkerchief top. "You owe me dinner," she says.

"Surely you don't expect me to cook," I say. "I'm the take-out queen of New York."

"You don't have to cook," she says, taking my hands. "Just come with me."

I follow her to her bedroom, my pleather pants creaking with each step. That squishing sound you hear? That's me.

The girl in 8G lays me across the futon in her bedroom. "Sing me a song," I tell her.

"Which one?" she asks.

"Surprise me," I reply, lifting my hips so she can pull my pants off.

"Well," she says, running her hands with its callused fingertips over my body, "there's no way I can sing '(I Can't Get No) Satisfaction' and mean it, so how about 'Emotional Rescue' instead?"

As her lips explore the terrain of my body, she sings to me between kisses. "Gimme Shelter" has always been my favorite Stones song, but she may be about to change my mind.

The girl in 8G has incredible hands. She plays me like an Eddie Van Halen guitar solo. Wrong group. OK, Keith Richards then.

The girl in 8G is looking down at me. "I hope you're hungry," she says.

I tell her I'm full but I may have room for dessert.

The girl in 8G grins and comes back for more. "Spaghetti sauce is always better the second day anyway."

Yonsei
Leslie Kimiko Ward

Her grandparents lived in the relocation camps during World War II. She learned about them in college history class, along with everyone else. Growing up in the suburbs of Maryland, she was only vaguely aware of her almost almond eyes and quick-tanning skin. Oh, sure, there had been hints: sushi and turkey on Thanksgiving, Grandpa Yamaguchi's naturopathic cold remedies, even the occasional summer Obon festival; but these were only glimpses into a world that was, until recently, unfamiliar to her and, ironically, foreign.

"What are you?" was the childhood question she most despised. "Human," she'd spit defiantly. "A girl." In time, she became used to the stares of strangers as they contemplated her unique assortment of features and strained to put her into proper context.

"Where are you from?" is the marginally tactful question she receives in adulthood, and while the venom has faded from evasive childhood responses, inquisitors rarely fare better with this approach. In fact, this particular inquiry often sparks dialogue resembling an old Abbott and Costello routine.

"So, where are you from?" asks a curious stranger.

"Annapolis," she replies, flatly.

"No, where are your parents from?"

"Which, my mother or my father?"

"Your mother?"

"Oregon."

(A frustrated sigh.) "Your father, then?"

"South Carolina," she teases with a smirk. She never simply

offers the information being sought after so awkwardly. Truth be told, she is *hapa*, of Japanese and Irish descent, and *yonsei*, fourth generation in the United States. Her mother is Japanese. Linda Jean. Like her mother, most *sansei*, or third generation, bear American first names. Assimilation was rapid after the war. Many *nisei* parents bestowed American names upon their *sansei* children to help accelerate the process. Linda Jean went to school with a whole slew of Kathy Saitos and Dave Hamadas; their cut-and-paste appellations broadcasting this hasty blend of cultures. In keeping with the quickened pace of assimilation, most *sansei* married inter-racially, as her mother had done, thereby creating a whole new gen-eration of biracial, or *hapa*, Japanese-Americans.

Her family frequently makes jokes about the arrangement. A yellowed photo in her grandmother's hallway depicts her Japanese relatives and alongside them her father, a lanky, pale Southerner. Whenever the picture is shown off to a new guest, it's laughingly referred to as the "guess who married into the family" portrait.

There are other running jests as well. She and her sister share very few features in common; each seems to possess the opposite combination of inherited genetic material. Her cousins, who are also *hapa*, likewise have their own unique genetic prints, and for this reason, she jokes that they are all the products of a true Darwinian grab bag.

The mood is light, her extended family is close, and no one dis-plays any indication of lingering racial tensions. Still, she never truly felt connected with her Japanese heritage aside from a few faint genetic footprints and a whisper of culinary influences.

She moved here to the Northwest after college, hoping to explore the region's strong Japanese-American community. She had plans to uncover the stories of her older Japanese relatives while they were still alive to tell them. She bought several sushi cook-books. She let her dyed blond hair grow back natural and dark. It was here that she began a workshop in the Japanese art of *taiko* drumming and in that workshop where I finally caught up with her again.

***

"I'm almost ready, Sam," I shout from my bedroom. It comes out more condescending than convincing. "Just chill out, we don't have to be there until six."

Sam stops pacing long enough to stand in my doorway. "You know I wanted to get there early. C'mon, Sydney," she whines. "What's taking you so long?"

"I can't find my other shoe," I say, my voice muffled as I dig around in the pile under my bed.

"You know, you wouldn't have that problem if your room wasn't such a sty."

"Thanks, Mom," I retort. "You can lecture, or you can help. Only one is going to get us there on time."

Sam sighs and wades into the mess. After some shuffling, she finds my shoe wedged under the closet door and tosses it to me.

"Now, put it on and let's get out of here," she says. "I'll drive. I know where we're going."

She knows exactly where we're going because she drove there in a test run last week as soon as she found out the address. I gave her a hard time about it. She already knew the area and the cross streets, but she said she wanted to be sure there was plenty of parking. Good ol' Sam. Organized and reliable in true anal-retentive Capricorn fashion. I tell her it's because of that darned Virgo rising; she says she doesn't believe in that stuff, and I say, "Of course you don't. That's because you're a Capricorn."

Fact is, she needs me. I'm here to remind her that a little chaos can lead to Grand Adventure. In turn, Sam helps motivate me to finish a project now and then. It's our differences that hold us together, and even when our friendship seems completely out of whack, I take a brief moment to recall how much the teeter-totter sucked on the playground all alone and figure life pretty much follows suit.

Sam and I met when I showed up for a temp job at her office. She's a Web developer for an E-business. Internet companies and coffeehouses account for about ninety-seven percent of Seattle's booming new economy. Within the leftover three percent are people like me, eking out an existence in the wonderful world of temping while trying to pursue a monetarily challenged, artistic career. I call myself a dancer, even though I spend most of my time busting my butt to make room in my work schedule for a few classes and a measly amount of rehearsals. It can be rough, but it's my passion, and I wouldn't trade it for anything, not even health insurance.

Sam, on the other hand, is completely content to spend copious amounts of time behind her desk. She was my supervisor for the week I was assigned to her office. I attempted—quite successfully, I might add—to spice up the long hours of data entry by flirting with her shamelessly. Eventually we realized that her reticence and my spontaneity made for better buddies than bedfellows, and we've gotten along famously ever since.

So Sam drives, and we get there early, in spite of my sneaker snafu back at the house. A few people are milling around on the concrete steps outside the teeny, well-worn building. A faded wooden sign reads NISEI MEMORIAL HALL. I walk closer to get a better look at a peeling laminated pamphlet tacked beneath. It talks a little about the history of the hall: when it was built, how the funds were secured, what programs it hoped to house. A small brass plaque next to the pamphlet dedicates the building to the "proud memory of *nisei* veterans who served our country during World War II." I find that whole situation difficult to digest. Japanese-Americans proving their devotion to a country that had just robbed them of their basic freedoms, demonstrating loyalty to thankless Americans by taking up arms against the land of their mothers and grandmothers.

I settle my inner tirade long enough to look over at Sam, practically chomping at the bit outside the double doors. As much as I am looking forward to our class, I have to admit it is nice to spend some time outside on this beautiful late-summer afternoon. The air is clear and warm, and people seem content in a way only twelve hours of sunshine could account for. I take a few relaxed breaths and slowly pan our surroundings. Across the narrow street, I see a small, brightly painted Japanese fruit market. A few young children horse around on a rickety metal cart, climbing inside and pushing each other around the parking lot before an elderly Japanese woman shuffles out of the store to reprimand them, chattering loudly and ushering them inside.

The market doors swing shut and the street falls quiet. A summer breeze gathers momentum. I half close my eyes and let the warm air caress my cheeks and eyelashes. Through my hazy focus, I can barely make out the figure of a woman striding up the fractured sidewalk, heading straight for our gathered group. Her narrow hips swing heavily from side to side, exaggerated by wide, steady footfalls, each precisely in line with the last. Shoulder-length black hair billows behind her with each step, brushing sexy shoulders that are bare but for the thin straps of a bright red cami top. I recognize her long before her features come into view. I'd know that tantalizing gait anywhere. I followed it around incessantly in college, inhaling every moving nuance of her in a ballet class we shared years ago.

Lily-Nariko. Her name epitomizes the wild contradictions of her demeanor. Soft and graceful, skin smooth like a delicate flower. In situations calling for subtlety, Lily finessed like a princess. But this serenity is as thin as rice paper. Underneath the satin veneer pulses the voracious blood of a tigress and the raw, unleashed power bestowed upon her by her middle name, Nariko, Japanese for "thunder peal."

I heard she moved to Seattle after graduation. I finished college a year earlier and set out for the bright lights of the Big Apple to pursue my dancing dream. What I found fell far short of the kinesthetic romance I had hoped for. I fought every day to carve out my jagged niche in New York and finally left, exhausted from overstimulus, half drowned from trying desperately to stay afloat. I moved as far away as possible and snuggled in tight to the Pacific Northwest, cozy among the trees, tucked safely between glistening waters and cascading mountaintops.

I tried to look Lily up when I first moved here but quit after a few fruitless attempts. I figured she had either moved away or changed her name. I heard a rumor that she found some man and gotten married, whispered venomously by scorned ex-lovers in darkened nightclubs back in Ohio. I didn't know how much stock to put in the gossip, but when I couldn't reach her, I figured there might be some truth to the rumor and stopped trying to locate her.

But here she was, sauntering right to me. I forget all about rumors and gossip and heterosexual love affairs and instead give in to the breathtaking feelings of longing and desire that had been lying dormant all these years.

It's a funny dynamic in a dance institution. On the one hand, there is an increased sense of physical intimacy between colleagues, simply because we spend hours scantily clad, moving close, breathing hard and sweating together. Dancers comfortably crawl all over one another, often with no more sexual implications than if they were merely shaking hands. And therein lies the rub, for in order to maintain that delicate balance between physical and sexual contact, most of us were hesitant to blur the line further by sleeping with our classmates.

There was no denying my attraction for Lily, however. She was part of what got me out of bed on cold, dark Columbus mornings to don layers of warm clothes for the long trek to our early technique class. I'd stand at a ballet barre across the room so I could watch her as she stretched. When it came time to perform the longer combinations, I made sure we were in separate groups to secure maximum viewing ability. I loved watching her move, sinuous and strong, with delicate hands and feet, and no signs of strained effort on her gorgeous face.

God, I'd missed her. I had forgotten how much so until she was standing right before me.

"Sydney?" she exclaims, breathy and beaming, once she realizes it's me. "What the hell are you doing in Seattle?"

"I came to find you, sweetness," I tease. "No, seriously, I moved here last summer. New York was just too harsh."

"Tell me about it," she empathizes. "I'm forever counseling friends there ready to end it all with one flying grand jeté from the Empire State Building. Welcome to Washington, anyway. Give me a hug already."

She reaches her arms out and I fold her into a tight embrace. Inhaling deeply, I bury my face into her thick, dark hair. Her scent, a warm, spicy musk, fills my nostrils and tightens up in my chest, sending electrical currents through my veins. I want to devour her on the spot and catch myself just before I start planting hot kisses on her neck and shoulders.

She must have sensed it too, because we hold onto each other moments longer than manners require, parting slowly, fingers lingering around waists, cheeks brushing not so casually against one another, backs arching and bellies aching to remain pressed together. When we finally separate enough to look into each other's eyes, glazed expressions give way to the joint recognition of our mutual desire. This delicious moment is followed almost immediately by Lily's awkward withdrawal, a sobering acknowledgment of the inappropriateness of these feelings, on this sidewalk, surrounded by a group of strangers. It's too bad. I could have lived in that moment forever, feeding off the stares of our future classmates, smiling at the dropped jaw of oh-so-responsible Sam, imagining the fruit market woman shuffling out of the store yet again, frantically this time, to cover the eyes of gawking children stunned by our ardent display.

But for now my ego has swelled large enough to respect her choice to pull away, temporarily sated with the mere knowledge of our shared fervor. Somehow, I resist the urge to grab her by the sweatshirt and yank her back, smothering her lips with mine. We remain in passion's limbo indefinitely, too drawn to each other to break the spell, too wary of everyone else to fall completely under.

Sam finally steps in to fetch us back to reality.

"Hey, Sydney," she interrupts, "they're letting us in." She nods at Lily, "Who's your friend?"

"Oh," I stutter, shaking off the reverie, "Sam, this is Lily-Nariko; Lily, this is my friend, Sam." Did I just put as much emphasis on the word "friend" as I think? "Lily and I used to go to school together."

"Are you a dancer as well?" Sam asks, tossing me a little wink in acknowledgment of the dissipating heat between Lily and myself.

"Um, yeah," Lily stammers, "I mean yes, I dance, and did, in college, with Sydney." She's so adorable when she blushes.

"Fascinating," Sam smiles knowingly. "Well, we'd better get inside before they start without us."

We follow Sam up the steps into the hall, trudging like obedient schoolchildren in from recess, feet obeying the call inside, minds lingering out on the playground, savoring still-fresh moments of exuberant bliss.

***

There's a registration table just inside the big wooden doors. Our name tags are already lying out along with some handouts for the workshop. We shuffle to find our names, happily participating in scrambled introductions as tags and packets are passed through the group.

"Hey, Sydney," shouts Sam, hunting for the perfect place to set her water bottle. "Grab mine, will you?"

"No problem," I shout back. I find her packet and mine, and begin to work my way out of the huddled mass. I'm almost clear when I trip and stumble headlong into Lily.

"Whoa there," she laughs, struggling to hold me upright. "How long has it been since you took a ballet class?"

"Too long," I whine. "They just aren't the same without you." I'm hardly joking.

"I know what you mean," she says with a wink, sending my knees buckling a second time.

When I finally make it over to Sam with our packets, she is still laughing at my physical faux pas.

"Smooth moves, Baryshnikov," she jokes. "I thought you guys were supposed to be graceful."

"Shut up," I mumble, half smiling. "I'm saving my coordination for class, OK?"

"Whatever, Grace. I'd tap into it soon if I were you. You were pretty lucky that time," she says, "but I wouldn't make a habit of it. You might bruise the poor girl."

Thankfully, the rest of her chastising is interrupted as our instructor calls us into the hall to begin.

"Welcome, everyone, to the Pacific Northwest Taiko Summer Workshop." Obviously excited, the class bursts into a round of applause. Our instructor, a small, slight Japanese man in his early fifties, smiles as he puts up his hand to quiet us. "My name is Tom Takahashi," he says. "I'll be leading the workshop. Before we begin, why don't we take a second and go around the room with some introductions."

Turns out we are quite a diverse group. There are roughly twenty of us, in all shapes, sizes, and colors, ranging in age from about fifteen to sixty-five. The oldest and youngest are a father and teenage son. The son is *hapa*, like Lily. Only a few participants have any prior experience with *taiko*.

Our first task is to unload the drums. Not so difficult, I think, until I actually see the drums, some of which are more than three feet in diameter. Most require two people to carry. Each is stored in a soft case with handles, a minor convenience when considering the daunting chore ahead. Sam and I team up on one of the medium-size drums, which Tom calls a *jozuke*. I'm feeling pretty buff lugging our heavy drum up the steps from the storage closet. Once upstairs, we set the drum down in the big empty hall and begin to unpack it.

"Hey, Sydney," whispers Sam. "Check it out. Your girlfriend's a brute."

I look toward the stairs where Sam is pointing to see Lily and Chris, the teenager, hoisting a huge drum up to the landing. It makes ours look like a kiddie toy. Lily's face is pink and her muscles are straining, chiseled and gorgeous on her bare arms.

"Jesus, that thing's huge," I whisper back to Sam. "I'd better go see if I can help."

"Just don't knock her down the stairs, Casanova."

I leave Sam to finish unpacking our drum and head over toward Lily and the boy.

"Can I give you guys a hand?" I ask once I reach them.

"Thanks, Syd," Lily grunts, "I think we've got it. We could use some help setting up though, once we make it to the hall."

"Happy to oblige, ma'am." Note to self: Never, ever utter another word in that ridiculous Southern accent again.

Tom comes over to assemble the stand for this whopper of a drum. Two connected crossbars on either side will support the drum at about head height.

"Ready?" asks Lily. "All right. On my count: One... Two...THREE." The three of us hoist the drum up to the stand while Tom helps guide it into the correct position.

"This is the *Odaiko*," says Tom. "It's the name given to every group's largest drum. It's also the way we complain after lifting it: *Oh, daiko!*"

"No kidding," Lily mumbles, massaging her reddened palms.

"By all means, allow me," I offer, grasping Lily's small fingers. She smiles and rests the backs of her hands inside mine. Folding my thumbs over, I begin to make small, gentle circles in the center of each delicate palm. Her skin is so incredibly soft, as I always imagined it would be. With her eyes on me, I lift my chin, inhaling sharply when we catch focus. My stomach turns backflips. Her hungry eyes send a river rushing down the leg of my sweatpants. I give her hands a tight squeeze, and my cunt contracts in empathy, or jealousy, it's hard to tell which.

"We should really help set up," she breathes. To me it sounds more like "We should really make mad, passionate love—right here, right now." I agree, of course, and we stand there for another minute or two, entertaining both possibilities.

Once again, it is Sam who steps in to diffuse our mounting sexual tension.

"Hey, twinkle toes," she interrupts. "Before you two begin your little X-rated pas de deux over here, you might want to grab a couple *bachi* and join us for warm-ups." She winks at me. "As if you need warming up, Romeo."

"Not funny," I warn her under my breath. "And besides, what's a *bachi*?"

"Drumsticks, Einstein," she replies, holding up two thick wooden dowels. "They're in a bucket in the corner. Go grab some. I'll save you a spot in the circle."

"Thanks, Sam," I reply, trying hard not to sound disappointed.

"No problem," she smiles. "Just don't get stuck over there. I don't want to have to peel you girls off each other, or clean up any misused *bachi,* for that matter."

Lily laughs nervously and starts over to the bucket. I grab Sam's arm just before she heads to the circle. "Are we really that obvious?" I whisper.

"Only to me," she replies. "Now hurry up. I think they're about to start."

Lily's already on her way back from the corner when I finish whispering with Sam. She hands me a pair of *bachi,* squeezes my hand, and seductively mouths the word "later." Ohmigod. Could I be more turned-on? I stagger over to the circle and flop down between them.

***

Warm-ups are a blur. I can't concentrate on anything save my rediscovered feelings for Lily. Our relationship has progressed further in the last half hour than in the past seven years. Needless to say, the sudden change has me reeling.

I try to participate in the stretching exercises Tom demonstrates. Fortunately, my muscles are loose and limber thanks to a Lily-induced adrenaline rush. Unfortunately, every act of physicality at this point only increases my excitement and decreases my ability to focus. Twinges of pain from stretching muscles translate to sensuous aches duplicated in my crotch, driving me to complete distraction. Glancing beside me, I realize I'm not the only one getting off by warming up. Lily looks euphoric. And gorgeous. And incredibly sexy. And, shit, I'm totally spacing out again. Focus, Syd. Focus.

Tom starts to walk around the circle, stopping to give pointers on some basics of stance and form. I manage to peel my eyes off

Lily and transfer them to Sam, who is hard at work perfecting her *taiko* technique.

"Hey, Sam," I whisper. "What are we doing exactly? I, um, wasn't really paying attention."

"Oh, but you were," she says, "just not to Tom. Look, I don't blame you, Syd. She's definitely a hottie. But hurry up and learn this so you don't look like a dork when he gets over here."

Good ol' Sam. She knows just how to motivate me. The thought of flailing in front of Lily solves my focus problem immediately. I shift into high gear without so much as a hiccup, copying Sam's movements, integrating Tom's corrections to the other students. I'm determined to become a *taiko* virtuoso in the next three minutes, wowing Lily with my incredible skill.

"Not bad, Sydney," comments Tom, once he reaches us. "Not bad at all." I knew it. I'm a natural. Lily, I hope you're paying attention. "You need more wrist, though. And less follow-through when you raise your right arm. And you might want to loosen your grip on your *bachi*, or you'll kill the sound when it hits the drum." Crap. Maybe Lily wasn't watching. I hope she wasn't watching.

I glance over. Of course she was watching. She winks at me again. "Later," she reminds me, letting the word drip off her perfect ruby lips. Jesus Mary. Close your mouth, Syd.

***

After a few more drills and a successful air-drum of our first song, it's finally time to approach the *taiko*. I take a wide lunge in front of my *jozuke*. Sam is next to me on a drum about the same size. Lily and Chris share opposite sides of the *odaiko* they carried up the steps. I can feel the strain of my leg muscles holding the new stance while Tom walks around the circle, making last-minute adjustments and corrections. Satisfied, he takes his place at the *shime-daiko,* a smaller, higher-pitched drum on an upright stand.

"*Yo!*" Tom shouts. On this cue, we all raise our *bachi* over the stretched skin of the drumhead.

"*So-ré!*" We draw our *bachi* back on a high diagonal, ready to play.

"*Ichi, ni, san, shi,*" Tom counts to set the tempo.

Then we strike.

"*DON…DON…DON…DON*" go the drums in a deafening chorus. The sound is so huge and so round, I feel it fill the hall and resonate down to my bones.

Holding the thick wooden *bachi* heavy in my hands, I strike the drum with all the power and tenderness of a stormy lover. I'm rewarded by the *taiko's* tempestuous response: a resounding echo that sends waves of sound rippling up through my body and vibrating out into the cosmos.

Occasionally, I allow myself to look over at Lily, and feel layers of desire wash over me. I'm swept up in billowing, sweet clouds of nostalgia from ballet classes past. Our earliest communication was in that wordless language, difficult if not impossible to misrepresent. Naked and thrown open in front of each other's eyes, we surrendered to our love of the music and the movement. We played innocently within the confines of the studio, revealing breath, body, and soul through a vocabulary entirely physical. Now I drown in the possibility of erasing those old, imposed boundaries and exploring every inch of physicality together with this vibrant woman.

She attacks the *taiko* with all the strength and vigor I remember, yet not a single lash ruffles on her beautiful eyelids. The pools of her eyes remain lucid and serene, even as her arms slice swiftly through the sound. She focuses directly, strikes squarely, and flows effortlessly through her transitions. She is pure melody in motion.

Her concentrated energy is infectious, upping the caliber of my own performance. In tune with her, in tune with the drum, I strive to harness the power emanating from the group and work to send only the clearest and purest voice from my drum out to join the thunderous chorus.

We play with increased ferocity, accelerating our driving tempo to a fever pitch. Sweat pours off my forehead and slickens my grip. My muscles strain in the urgent meter, pushing harder through exhaustion like a marathon runner just short of the finish line. Somewhere a drumroll begins, and within seconds, everyone follows suit, synchronizing our drums in the volatile rumble. As if possessed, the rhythm continues to build both in speed and in volume, tumbling over itself like an avalanche. Just when I am sure my physical limitations will not allow me to strike any harder, the momentum plateaus and sustains, holding me captive at the peak of my exertion. My heart pounds and I look up, directly into Lily's waiting eyes. The intensity of her stare at once energizes me, and we remain locked in each other's gaze, pushing together through the crashing waves of sound.

At the moment just before our inevitable collapse, Tom raises his *bachi* high in the air, preparing to signal our final strike. Lily lowers her head and expands her chest like a bull about to charge. She looks out at me from under hooded brows. I am overwhelmed with desire for her and can tell my feelings are fully reciprocated.

"*San! Ni! Ichi!*" Tom bellows, counting down the impending finish. With one supported motion and a loud *kiai,* he strikes both *bachi* down heavily on his drum.

Silence.

The echo fills my ears, dissipating slowly, readjusting to the openness of nothing. My expression softens, as does Lily's. We gaze upon each other gently like lovers caressing in a postcoital embrace.

Seconds pass. A trickle of whispers encroaches upon the thickness of the surrounding quiet. I do not speak but instead rush the few steps between Lily and me. Her dark eyes draw me in, and her outstretched hand welcomes my arrival.

"I had forgotten how beautifully you move," she breathes, squeezing my palm.

"I had forgotten how much you move me," I reply softly.

Her lips widen in the kindest of smiles, and she pulls me close, wrapping her arms tight around my neck, nuzzling her head into my shoulder.

"Let's not end this," she entreats. "Come home with me."

Embarrassment and awkwardness long forgotten, I answer her with the softest of kisses. Her response is so natural, so tender; it's as if we've kissed a million times before.

"Hey lovebirds," interrupts Sam, hurtling us back to reality for the umpteenth time. "Get out of here, I'll pack up your drums."

"Are you sure?" I ask, praying she is. There is nothing I would love more than to go home with Lily right now and make up for a hell of a lot of lost time.

"For chrissake, go already," she asserts, feigning frustration.

So we do.

And it's everything it should have been all those years. This time her back arches not in arabesque but ecstasy. Curved arms, once empty shapes, now fill and refill with each other. I follow her with heated skin instead of longing glances, lifting, sliding, turning over her in a context finally ringing true. My heightened senses rush to experience what my eyes had coveted for so long. With neck arched and exposed, I struggle to bury myself deeper in the folds of her flesh, drinking her in, eagerly smothering myself with her taste and scent.

My forearms burn from hours of drumming. In desperation, I continue over and over to reach inside her, fervidly attempting to satisfy years of hunger and depravation. She returns kiss for kiss, sweat and saliva sizzling and melting into the tangled sheets beneath us.

The music is our breath, hot and heavy, the melody our mingled groans and gasps of pure, unencumbered pleasure. An echo of the *taiko* lingers in the strong rhythm of our heartbeats and pulses in the clenched muscles of our orgasms.

In the end it all comes down to this, years of dancing only distant foreplay for these few earth-shattering moments. Our bodies finally sing as one voice, and the sound is deafening.

By Any Other Name

Kristina Wright

There are times when living with someone can be a joy. Waking to the feeling of a warm body beside you, their scent on your pillow. Having a friendly face to hold your hand across the dinner table as you recount the adventures of the day. Sharing your toaster and your heart with someone who knows you better than you know yourself. Yeah, living with someone can be wonderful.

And then there are the days when you'd give anything to live alone, with no one to worry about except yourself and maybe a goldfish. As I stared at the red Honda parked in front of my townhouse, I contemplated the perks of fish ownership.

Rosalie was home.

I coasted my bike to a stop, reluctant to go inside. She had stormed out the night before, angry and silent, leaving me to guess what the hell I'd done wrong.

I'd been up most of the night, alternating between worrying about her and being mad because she knew I was worrying about her. I called her office in the morning, but the bitchy receptionist said she was out showing houses all day. By six P.M. I'd worked myself into a self-righteous frenzy. Rosalie could be a moody wench when she wanted to be, and I was in no mood to put up with it.

I was half tempted to turn my bike around and spend the night at the library. Let her worry for a change. Instead, I grabbed my books out of the basket attached to the front of my bike and headed toward the house. Rosalie said I looked like a schoolgirl with my long red braids and shiny yellow bike. I told her I *was* still a schoolgirl—a twenty-six-year-old perpetual student. I was finishing my degree in women's studies at Florida State and working at the library in the evenings. When Rosalie had a couple of glasses of wine in her, she'd leer and say she could teach me all I needed to know about women. She was right.

I opened the front door and breathed in her unique scent of organic lavender shampoo and baby powder. No matter how mad I was, the smell of her made my heart flip-flop in my chest. I heard the shower shut off. My first impulse was to confront her and ask her where the hell she'd been. I decided that was exactly what she expected me to do. So instead, I grabbed a bottle of juice out of the fridge and curled up in a chair with a biography of Margaret Mead. Let Rosalie come to me for a change.

She walked into the room buck naked, a white towel wrapped around her head turban-style. "I didn't hear you come in."

I have to say, Rosalie looks better naked than most women look clothed. I tried to ignore the way her breasts swayed as she leaned over to grab an apple from the bowl on the table next to me. Her nipples were tightly puckered and as rosy as her name. I looked her over, hungry for her body but still angry at her for walking out.

"I didn't think you cared," I said. Despite my best intentions, I couldn't help noticing she'd trimmed her thick, dark muff into a neat little triangle.

"What the hell is that supposed to mean?" She looked like Eve tempting me with her apple.

I turned back to my book. "You're the one who took off. You didn't even bother calling." I sounded like a petulant child, but damn, she'd hurt me. She'd never been gone all night before.

"I was angry," she said softly. She tossed the apple back in the bowl. "You made me feel like shit last night."

Last night I'd dragged Rosalie to my family reunion despite her protests. We'd been together for nearly a year, and I thought it was about time to inflict my family on her. Everybody knew I was partial to girls, and Mom had long since given up on finding the right boy for me, thank God. It was funny to watch soft-spoken Rosalie in the midst of my boisterous clan.

"What did I do?" I asked, genuinely baffled.

I thought the evening had gone quite well. Even Gran had been smitten with Rosalie, and that woman doesn't like anyone who isn't Irish, or at least Catholic. Rosalie had been quieter than usual, but I chalked it up to nerves. It wasn't until we got home that I realized she was giving me the silent treatment. When I finally asked what her problem was, she split.

"There were thirty people there and you never once introduced me as anything other than your friend," she said now.

I closed my book and put it aside, trying to avoid the accusation in her eyes. I'd had two relationships go really bad. She knew that. I thought it was a pretty big step just bringing her to my parents' house. One look into those stormy dark eyes told me differently.

"So? What do you want me to call you?" I asked, torn between frustration and anger. Rosalie was always pushing for more than I wanted to give.

She strode across the room and stood in front of me, fisting her hands on her hips. Water droplets clung to her heavy breasts and the soft curve of her stomach. "Hell, I don't care. Anything would be better than 'This is my friend, Rosalie.' "

I didn't like her simpering tone. I stood up and brushed past her. "You're being ridiculous."

"Wait a minute. We're not finished here." She grabbed my arm and pushed me back in the chair. I couldn't do anything but gape at her. Rosalie is as sweet and gentle as they come. She can be a hellion in bed, but we weren't in bed, and I was starting to get pissed off.

"Knock it off, Rose," I said, not at all liking the nasty little smirk she gave me. "I need a shower."

She knelt in front of me and spread my thighs with her hands. "What you need is to learn some manners."

Before I could speak, she slid her hand up my skirt and cupped my crotch. A wave of heat spread through my belly and I groaned. She had that effect on me. One touch and I was lost. Instantly I spread my legs wider to allow her access, all thoughts of anger fleeing my mind as moisture flooded my crotch.

"You're hot." She toyed with the elastic on my underwear. "Are you wet?"

I knew my cunt was already slick with my juices. "Why don't you find out?" I gasped when her finger burrowed under the leg of my panties.

"Yeah, wet." She finger-fucked me gently, her baby-soft finger gliding inside me. "I love how wet you get."

The material of my panties restricted her motions, but her finger felt good inside my fevered cunt. My clit throbbed against the thin fabric of my panties, aching to be touched. I leaned my head back against the chair and closed my eyes. Suddenly, the finger was gone and I felt empty.

"Don't stop," I said, hearing a hint of desperation in my voice. Then it dawned on me that was what she wanted. "Touch me, Rose."

She sat back on her knees, one delicate eyebrow arched. She looked like some exotic harem girl in her towel turban, kneeling before me in supplication. But we both knew who was in charge. "Touch me...what?"

"Please?"

She laughed, but I could tell by the hitch in her voice that she was getting turned on too. "No, you said, 'Touch me, Rose.' What else could you call me?"

I grinned at her little game. Did I mention she can be a devious wench? "Touch me, baby."

She nodded, the towel on her head wobbling. "Better."

She pushed my panties to the side and pushed her finger inside me again. I arched my hips off the chair and felt her go deeper. When I started rocking on her finger, she pulled it away again. I sighed in frustration.

"Take off your skirt," she said. "Just your skirt."

I eagerly complied, stripping off my skirt and spreading my legs once more. The crotch of my panties was already soaked through and clinging to the plump lips of my cunt. Rosalie leaned forward and inhaled my scent, not quite touching me.

"Mmm, you smell good," she said. "What do you want?"

"Touch me," I pleaded.

"Touch me…" she prompted.

I reached down and tugged the towel from her head, letting her long, damp hair cascade over my thighs. "Touch me, sweetheart."

She nuzzled me with her lips, nipping my clit through the wet cotton. I groaned and tangled my hands in her hair, but she pushed them away and put them over my breasts. I pinched my hard nipples through my T-shirt, aching to feel her mouth on them. When I raised my crotch closer to her face, she moved away.

"Are you ashamed of me, Anne?" She said it with a smile, but I could see the vulnerability in her expression.

Desire forgotten, I wrapped my arms and legs around her and pulled her close. "Of course not, baby. I love you."

"So the next time I meet your family, you'll introduce me properly?" She pulled away and teased my clit through the fabric once more.

I nodded, wanting her. Needing her. "I promise."

"Lift up." I raised my ass so she could tug my panties off. She slid them down my legs and tossed them over her shoulder. They landed on a lamp like a jaunty pink beret. "How will you introduce me?"

"I'll think of something," I said. "Now, stop teasing me. Please."

She blew air over my engorged cunt and I gasped. "What will you say?"

"Whatever you want."

Rosalie had the nerve to shake her finger at me. The same finger she'd been fucking me with. "No. You tell me. I want to hear it."

"Touch me, Rose," I begged. "Lick me."

"Introduce me."

"Fine." I groaned in agony. My cunt was on fire and she wanted to play mind games. "This is my girlfriend, Rosalie."

A frown crinkled her brow. "Hmm. Better. Is that the best you can do?"

I was spread wide in front of her, her mouth inches from my swollen clit. My juices dripped from my cunt and down my crack, tickling my ass. I was probably leaving a wet spot on the chair. I didn't give a damn. "My significant other."

Her fingertip found my opening. "Too cold. I'm tired of your feminist bullshit. What else?"

I squirmed and clenched my muscles, trying to suck her finger into me. I groaned when I felt her go a little deeper. "My roommate."

The finger retreated. "That's worse than 'friend.' "

I moaned, my brain searching frantically for something that would please her. "My lover."

Rosalie cooed and the finger slid all the way inside. "That's nice. Very brave." Her thumb made gentle circles around my asshole and I whimpered.

She fucked me like that for a bit, her finger bumping my cervix as she massaged the walls of my cunt. I pushed my hips up to meet her thrusts, and her thumb lodged against my asshole. After a while one finger wasn't enough, I was too wet. I wanted to feel more of her.

"Please, baby," I said, "give me more."

She withdrew her finger and hooked her hands under my thighs, pushing my legs up on the arms of the chair. I was spread as wide as I could go, the lips of my cunt stretched taut, exposing me to her gaze. She bent her head and I could feel her breath. So close. So damn close.

"C'mon, Rose, don't tease me." I mauled my tits in frustration, wanting her to touch me and yet secretly thrilled by her newfound dominance.

"I like 'lover,' " she said, sounding as prim and proper as any librarian I'd ever worked with. "But it's a little blunt. What else do you have?"

I shook my head. I couldn't think.

"Tell me, Anne." Her fingernail lightly scraped the side of my clit and I jumped. "Tell me and I'll suck you until you come."

Every muscle in my body quivered with need. I stared down into her flushed face, seeing passion and something more. Something so tender and honest, it brought tears to my eyes.

"My love," I whispered. "This is Rosalie, my love."

I was rewarded by her brilliant smile. I had only a moment to enjoy it before she tucked her hands under my ass and raised my soaked crotch to her mouth. I groaned and squirmed against her face as she plunged her tongue into me. She feasted on my cunt lips and then moved up to my swollen clit, sucking it between her lips. She slid one hand up my thigh and used two fingers to fuck me hard and fast. I could hear the wet, squishy sounds of my cunt as I screamed her name over and over.

I came so hard I got an instant, blinding headache. She gently nursed on my quivering clit as I floated back to earth. The pain in my head faded to a dull ache as I looked down at her. Her mouth glistened with my juices while her fingers still made lazy circles inside me. I squeezed those fingers and smiled wickedly.

"What?" she asked, licking her lips.

I pulled her up on my lap and kissed her, loving the taste of me on her mouth. Gathering her damp hair in my hand, I tilted her head back to look at her. "What would you have done if I'd called you 'the old ball-and-chain' ?"

She reached down and tweaked my still-sensitive clit with her thumb and forefinger. "Why don't you find out?"

I grinned and squirmed before pushing her off my lap and leading her toward the bedroom. I decided I didn't really want a goldfish after all.

Exit 22
Alaina Zipp

First thing in the morning Jesse turns to me. From the moment I see her eyes glimmer, I know I'm in for it. This is the seven-year-old who rode her skateboard on the highway, who wore her father's pants to school instead of a dress. I didn't know her then, but I saw that look the year she finally managed to keep my birthday present a surprise, and the day she came home with a cat that we had only vaguely planned.

"Hon-e-e-e," she drawls, peeling me from the covers to meet her sassy grin. "Guess what I figured out?" In one smooth motion, Jesse rolls on top and my hands sink into her butt pads. We share this skin joy and the luxury of a timeless day without obligations. As we roll our heat together, my mind stops working as flesh unfolds to want. We're breast to breast; our hands fill in the small spaces between skin. I slip a finger between Jesse's thighs and into her nest of curls. I slowly slide into her wet heat, making both of us catch our breath. Sensuous as full-bellied cats in the sun, we lazily shape the sexual energy. What a luxury it is after a few delicious gropes to then realize we have time to continue this later. As lust recedes from my mind, I recall Jesse's question. She remembers at the same time, repeating, "Guess what I realized?"

"That we need another dog," I toss out, the one we already own erupting against the bed. Tail bruises the wall, thrums a staccato beat testifying to the potential of a new day, perfect for doggie play.

"No," Jesse says sharply to our 100-pound baby. After Athena is subdued, Jesse's languid energy returns. She leans back on her elbow, rustles the covers, and turns slowly, focusing her energy on me.

"Since we don't have to pay for a new truck transmission, we could reorganize the house! I stayed up marking the Ikea furniture catalog, and for only a few hundred dollars we can redo it all!" Her energy ricochets within our small bedroom. After our wedding, my aunt called Jesse "born raring to go." It fits her. Now me, I'm OK with impulsive things; I just need time to plan them.

Jesse hands me the catalog, and triangle-tabbed pages of sofas and tables fly at me until I choke. Pushing breath slower than my heartbeat, I try to keep my energy circulating, not tying my intestines into knots. As Jesse points to the furniture and repeats that we can "redo everything," my anxiety takes hold. I squeak, "The whole house?"

"Next," she says, "we can get rid of the clutter."

These words strike fear in my heart: I know I'll be overcome soon with a need to bead necklaces, build furniture, and find an article in the three-year supply of magazines hoarded in my closet. I don't like the term "pack rat." I prefer to think of myself as a "preparer." At the thought of my supplies being eliminated, I scream silently, and Jesse abruptly switches directions.

"We can organize your closet and make it easier for you to reach your clothes!" she bursts out. As I didn't have much opportunity for pretty clothes in childhood, I now revel in finery. I rationalize that it's cheap, since I shop in thrift stores, but I would pay even more for the joy of glancing in a closet and being sensually bombarded by textures and colors. I would never give up the delights of the peacock dance that is a mainstay of clothes-shopping for both Jesse and me. I love how she loves shopping as much, if not more, than I do. I know this is not always the case with butch/femme couples and often count this a blessing.

Knowing I can get stubborn when cornered, Jesse adds, "But if you're really not up to it, we can go another time. It's just that this is one of the ways I get rid of stress—just jump in the car and take off."

I know she's chomping at the bit, but if I say no, we won't go.

I don't know if she hears my internal wheels screech as they slowly change direction. If only she knew how much power that sweet smile has to melt my reserve, my hesitations. Our years of work to stay a happily evolving couple influence me. I have fought rabidly against fears of vulnerability to stay with Jesse, as she has fought her own childhood demons. I've finally learned that my knee-jerk reactions are not always the best responses.

A sudden breeze through the window frees me, and I say, "OK." Surprised at this unexpectedly easy persuasion, Jesse gives me a quick, wet kiss. Her smile reaches her gills and she cries happily, "We're going to Ikea! We're going to Ikea!"

The last words of the song hit an empty room: To spontaneously drive three hours away, I need to prepare. Drinks and food of course are automatic, although the steering wheel still turns fluorescent orange from Cheet-ohs no matter how well we plan. My contact lens case, fluid, glasses, reading material, pen and paper for inspirational strikes, and jeans, in case the weather cools. Then, our traveling pack of CDs, a baseball cap, and sunglasses round out the second bag.

I want nothing to spoil this day, and spend a few precious moments gathering another necessity. Jesse smiles understandingly as I run out triumphantly with the map, a few white hairs still attached to it and a disgruntled cat in my wake. Forgetting the map risks the day turning to trouble: deciding together what the definition of *lost* is, who will ask directions, and who will remember them. I am the forager for trips; Jesse is the packer. We have this teamwork down to a science.

As we head for the freeway ramp, I sink into the speed. Jesse is at the wheel, so I try to forget the anxiety that gnaws at me when faced with changes in my home or life. The cats and I both react this way, but I don't pee on shoes when it happens.

We glide over one-lane bridges, past fields crayoned green, the radio's tunes weaving our happy road before us. Suddenly a ball of fire strikes me: Exit 22, Interstate 5 north, from Portland to Seattle. DIKE ACCESS ROAD. I love this sign. It fills my head with visions of women, butchy women, lined up behind the exit. Butchy women in button-down shirts, tucked T-shirts, and that special "dyke butt." I get on my knees weekly and thank the jeans of choice (Levi Strauss, men's) "because they just fit better." I see this pride of lion women waiting off the exit ramp, ready to handle whatever comes along. This daydream usually occupies me happily, but I'm still pulsing from this morning. My fingers remember Jesse's ass and thigh, and the spirit drives me into action.

I send my rust-colored skirt skyward, grinning at my own daring and want. Legs forming a wide V, I turn my hips to offer a present to my love. My smile mainlines to my crotch and I yell "Dike access road!" pointing to myself gleefully.

Jesse turns, startled, then her left dimple sets as she remembers coffee sex: hot, bubbling, so strong we smell it long after. I love slow, dreamy sex, but sometimes nothing but this will do: sex that could bring back the dead.

Her right hand snakes across the gear shaft to dance with my thighs. The truck veers suddenly, and we're taking the exit. Still she grins, that smile I've warmed myself by for seven years.

As usual when riding with Jesse, I know I'm in good hands and release to her plans. The cool wind licks my labia as her fingers gently peel back my purple panties, but there is no cooling this heat. Not now, not without something more. I know she'll deliver what I want.

Clouds and pale-blue sky flash through the sunroof on the way to memory. I float on fingers of feeling and drink the meaty smell of my loins. My body sings. Jesse's eyes are restless, searching for something. This is how she looks trying to ensure our safety in crowds, especially when we walk holding hands. Leaving her on guard, I spin into myself.

We enter a cavern of green leaves as the truck jolts to a stop. My love's grin glints even wider; those clear white teeth that love to bite my underskin. A quick tongue flick, her warm soft orbs against mine, and she murmurs, "Stay right here." I doubt I'd move from this seat if the truck caught on fire, though I confess to wriggling my hips on the raspy seat, itching the fire in my loins.

In a moment, my door opens and her arms carry me to the air's cradle. I breathe Zest, Preferred Stock, and lust in her neck. Jesse's nipple grazes my arms. "Your nipples are like diamonds" fell out of my mouth the first time she bared them to me.

Jesse lowers me, and the truck's hot metal burns through the sheer fabric on my ass. Her cool hands slide up my thighs, and we lift together onto the blanket she has laid for us. A hawk standing guard commands the silence of this woodside hotel.

Jesse's denim knees caress the outside of my thighs as she kneels above me, blocking light. Unbuttoning her white shirt, I glimpse her flesh and drink in this moment. I know what lies beneath. I help pull the tangled sports bra over her sweet face, meeting her luscious breasts, their brave pink eyes upon me.

Jesse's smile slowly lowers to me. Our nakedness is a jigsaw of cloth, cream, and covered cunts. Her pelvis pins me first, then I pull her waist and breasts down to meet me. Muffled through my dress, her heart beats and we move in ancient song. Hairs of the black plaid blanket tickle my butt cheeks, creep into the crack, and make me giggle. Her tongue darts in my mouth and I forget to laugh, swept back into the building wave. My bare right leg is on top as I roll her onto her back. We both know she's letting me; I'm not nearly as strong as she is. I glory in my view from above and carefully peel my red pubic hair back from snaring in her belt buckle.

Jesse is crooning now as I rip open her belt, zipper, and button.

Fumbling in my desire, it's clear to me that jeans can be another form of chastity belt. I kiss a denimed cunt as Jesse writhes and we peel off her blue-jean skin. It's a long ride to the bottom of those glorious legs.

Once Jesse is clear of denim and Jockeys, I ride her toe and share my hot liquid lust. As I climb back up the muscled leg, my dress and bra sail to the corner of the truck bed; green lace and rust-colored cloth mingle with bungee cords, shoes, and a half-chewed dog toy. I smile, thinking of the odd assortment. It's true, my clothes are pretty, but you couldn't ever call them snobs.

Suddenly my lips seize her nipple, and I warm my cold pinky at her mouth. Tongue-painting a leisurely line to meet her lips, I lose myself in their fullness. Face-to-face, my curls crush between and they tickle us both.

I pull back, her hands kneading my ass, and we stare into each other's eyes. We're together in some far-off place, apart from time and space. With a blink, we fly back to our homemade bed and work together to fulfill our need.

My hand slides across my own flesh, blends into hers; sweet, simple planes that seep into wet curves. Three fingers find their nook and suck in her space, disappearing as my lover's hips snake up to the sky. My thumb has its own plans: riding the ridge to that sweet button, a bird circling round its beloved prey.

Jesse's music changes and I follow her lead, faster and faster. Then, with a buck, we reach home and the world erupts in her broad smile and shakes. My tongue sneaks a quick drink of her sweet lips as my fingers linger; Jesse hovers, and I cajole her back into vibrating sound. This is the moment the walls crash down, eating infinity.

Wearing the sly smile I adore, Jesse raises her torso from mine and slides me to my side. My hips and thighs, nuzzled by the truck's blanketed ridges, remember my finger's recent home and make me shiver. I rise to meet the loving hand that traces my flesh.

Jesse's rosebud mouth sucks heat to my left nipple, and my vagina drips sweat as electricity builds. Her hot wetness greases my thigh as she rides it to my source: a delta of orange, red, and brown hairs: the coat of a calico tabby, but without claws. This sweet friction drives me higher and I scream, a call on the edge of forever.

The instant her tongue touches my flesh I am soaring, each lick bringing the tides again. The third time she joins me, and we erupt in our cry of love as we ride the wave together. I lose count but know we'll giggle and guess later. We settle into a thick silence, satiation and love curling around us.

The caw of a bird pulls us back to the mundane world, a truck's rattle finally registering in my overheated senses. "Shit," Jesse says, jumping for clothes,

"Where's my shirt?" I jump too, but with a bright grin: orgasms stored away as fuel for difficult times. For me, this excitement (if it doesn't go too far) is part of the fun.

I start to hook my bra and then give up and just slip my dress back on, wet thighs sliding against each other. Another benefit of a dress's easy access is easy dressing. On the other hand, it's hard enough getting off jeans; it's almost impossible to pull them up, especially when trying to keep your head below the bed horizon. Our natural lube, so generous, isn't helping matters.

"Lie down," I say, and Jesse listens. If she doesn't move, I can slide the denim up to meet her cunt while she puts her shirt and bra on. The truck rattle grows closer, and I know the quick flash of fear: We could be in danger. I know Jesse heard it first and that her first thoughts are of me. Almost twice as big as me, she'd fare better than I face-to-face, but I know if it comes to that, we'll fight together. Waiting to see the truck, I trace my rib break (souvenir of an intolerant bash at a bar) and I know I will not hide again.

Our sexual hum has lowered to a thick, agonized waiting. I try to picture us from the approaching vehicle's perspective: two faces, one framed in long red curls, mussed; another courting androgyny, peering over the truck side with wide eyes; the air screaming neon sex. Air wafts under my skirt, tickling me, reminding me of those glorious hot moments not long ago. I silently beg the powers that be: *Please don't let it all end in ugliness.*

As the truck creeps into view, I can make out four eyes, round and speechless. The driver, shaved gray hair topping blue eyes, wears a denim uniform accentuated with familiar valleys and peaks. Her companion, in bright purple clothes, a crystal twined on a leather thong, sits shotgun. Ripe with unreality, they watch us, the zoo's misbehaving monkeys getting it on in a cage. Then, silent knowing sets in: They salute us and roll on by. I realize they had their own plans for an encounter here. The tension snaps. Jesse and I lock eyes and laugh, another hurdle faced and shared. My vagina twitches, calling for more attention.

Later when we climb into the cab, the tires crunch toward the highway and I silently drop lace and silk out the window. My bra drapes itself on rocks offering itself to the protectors of this grove. I smile, luxuriate in my lover's smooth skin on mine, and can admit the truth. I know those women will return to their spot, and I want them to have something to remember us by.

Contributor Notes

Adelina Anthony is an interdisciplinary Chicana lesbian artist. Her writing has been published in *Texas Short Stories 2, Corazon del Norte: North Texas Latino Writing,* and on Nerve.com. She is the cofounder/artistic director of MACHA Theatre Co., Los Angeles's only professional theater dedicated to producing works by women and lesbians of color.

Sally Bellerose received a National Endowment for the Arts fellowship to write a novel, *The GirlsClub.* Her prose has been chosen as a finalist for the Thomas Wolfe Fiction Prize in 1998, the James Jones First Novel Fellowship in 1999, and the Bellwether Prize in 2000. She is currently working on a novel titled *Legs.*

Wendy Caster is the author of *The Lesbian Sex Book.* She has also published stories, opinion columns, reviews, interviews, articles, and crossword puzzles. She lives in New York City, where she works as a senior writer at a medical education agency.

Raphaela Crown has published erotica on CleanSheets.com and has had a short story published in *Best Women's Erotica 2002.* Other work has appeared in *The Paris Review, The New Republic, The Massachusetts Review, University of Pennsylvania Law Review,* and *Seventeen* magazine. A lawyer and teacher, she lives in Jerusalem.

Dawn Dougherty is a writer and performer from the Boston area and has published work in *Lesbian Short Fiction, Best Lesbian Erotica* (1999 and 2000), *Philogyny: Girls Who Kiss and Tell, Scarlet Letters,* and *Paramour.* She is currently one third of the Princesses of Porn, a high-femme erotic drag trio.

Jane Futcher is the author of *Crush, Promise Not to Tell, Dream Lover,* and *Marin: The Place, The People.* Her work has appeared in many anthologies, including *Dyke Life, A Loving Testimony, Lesbian Adventure Stories,* and *Hot Ticket.* She lives in Novato, California, with her partner, Erin Carney.

Sacchi Green has had work published in *Best Lesbian Erotica* (1999, 2000, and 2001), *Zaftig, Set in Stone, Best Women's Erotica* (2001 and 2002), *Best Transgender Erotica,* and *More Technosex.*

Myriam Gurba is a Chicana femme dyke born and raised in semi-rural California. She works as an editorial assistant for *On Our Backs.* Her nonfiction has appeared in *On Our Backs, Girlfriends,* and *Inside Pride 2001.*

Ilsa Jule lives in New York City, where she spends some of her time writing. She dedicates "Mrs. Sullivan Takes Off" to Elizabeth Grainger and Leah Devun.

Julie Lieber has published a short story in *Love Shook My Heart II* and is finishing her first novel.

Rosalind Christine Lloyd identifies as a "womyn of color, native New Yorker, and Harlem resident." Her work has appeared in *Pillow Talk II, Hot & Bothered II, The Best American Erotica 2001, Skin Deep, Set in Stone,* and *Faster Pussycats.* She is working on her first novel.

Dawn Milton is a curly-haired renegade cowgirl living in Denver, where she works as a freelance writer and nonprofit activist.

Gina Ranalli has contributed fiction to *Pillow Talk II, Dykes With Baggage,* and *Set in Stone.* She lives in Oregon.

Ruthann Robson is the award-winning author of the short story collections *Cecile, Eye of a Hurricane,* and *The Struggle for Happiness;* the novels *a/k/a* and *Another Mother;* and the nonfiction books *Legal Issues for Lesbians and Gay Men, Lesbian (Out)Law: Survival Under the Rule of Law,* and *Sappho Goes to Law School: Fragments in Lesbian Legal Theory.*

Lana Gail Taylor has published nine erotic short stories in *Playgirl.* Her work has also appeared in *Best Women's Erotica 2002.* A single mother, she lives in Denver.

Sheila Traviss has written for the Out There comedy series, written and performed with the Groundlings in Los Angeles, and has performed her one-woman play *Tribes* in Los Angeles and off-Broadway.

Yolanda Wallace has had work published in *Uniform Sex* and *Maka,* a Canadian anthology of writing by authors of African descent. She is a bank officer in addition to being a writer.

Leslie Kimiko Ward is a dance instructor and *taiko* enthusiast living in Seattle. Her first short story, "Pas de Deux," appeared in *Pillow Talk II.* Since then she has published short pieces in various anthologies and local literary magazines.

Kristina Wright has published everything from novel-length romantic suspense to greeting cards. Her short erotica has appeared in *Jane's 'Net Sex Guide, Best Women's Erotica 2000* and *Scarlet Letters,* and on Libida.com. She lives in Virginia.

Alaina Zipp is a redheaded femme living in Portland, Oregon, where she enjoys biking, reading, shopping, and running. She has published several poems in the *Journal of Poetry Therapy.*

About the Editor

MARY VAZQUEZ

Lesléa Newman has edited several anthologies, including *Pillow Talk: Lesbian Stories Between the Covers* (volumes I and II) and *The Femme Mystique*. A fiction writer and poet, she has published many volumes of her own work, including the short-story collections *Girls Will Be Girls, A Letter to Harvey Milk,* and *She Loves Me, She Loves Me Not;* the poetry collections *Still Life With Buddy, Signs of Love,* and *The Little Butch Book;* and the children's books *Heather Has Two Mommies, Too Far Away to Touch, Saturday Is Pattyday,* and *Felicia's Favorite Story.* Six of her books have been Lambda Literary Award finalists. She lives with the butch of her dreams in Massachusetts. Visit her Web site at www.lesleanewman.com to learn more about her work.